Also by Alfred Bester

NOVELS
Who He? (1953)
The Demolished Man (1953)
The Stars My Destination (1956)
Extro (1975)
Golem^{100} (1980)
The Deceivers (1981)
Tender Loving Rage (1991)

SHORT STORY COLLECTIONS
Starburst (1958)
The Dark Side of the Earth (1964)
The Light Fantastic (1976)
Star Light, Star Bright (1976)
Starlight: The Great Short Fiction
of Alfred Bester (1976)

THE STARS MY DESTINATION

Alfred Bester

Copyright © Alfred Bester 1956
All rights reserved

Special restored text of this edition Copyright © 1996 by the Estate of Alfred Bester
Introduction copyright © 1996 by Neil Gaiman
Special calligraphy and ideographs in Chapter 15 created by Jack Gaughan.

The right of Alfred Bester to be identified as the author
of this work has been asserted by him in accordance with
the Copyright, Designs and Patents Act 1988.

This edition first published in Great Britain in 1999 by
Millennium

An imprint of Orion Books Ltd
Orion House, 5 Upper St Martin's Lane, London WC2H 9EA

An Hachette Livre UK company

Reissued by Gollancz
An imprint of the Orion Publishing Group

13 15 17 19 20 18 16 14 12

A CIP catalogue record for this book is available
from the British Library

ISBN 978-1-85798-814-7

Printed in Great Britain by
Clays Ltd, St Ives plc

The Orion Publishing Group's policy is to use papers that
are natural, renewable and recyclable products and
made from wood grown in sustainable forests. The logging
and manufacturing processes are expected to conform to
the environmental regulations of the country of origin.

www.orionbooks.co.uk

To Truman M. Talley

OF TIME, AND GULLY FOYLE

by Neil Gaiman

You can tell when a Hollywood historical film was made by looking at the eye makeup of the leading ladies, and you can tell the date of an old science fiction novel by every word on the page. Nothing dates harder and faster and more strangely than the future.

This was not always true, but somewhere in the last thirty years (somewhere between the beginning of the death of what John Clute and Peter Nicholls termed, in their *Encyclopedia of Science Fiction*, "First SF" in 1957 when *Sputnik* brought space down to earth and 1984, the year that George Orwell ended and

VII

William Gibson started) we lurched into the futures we now try to inhabit, and all the old SF futures found themselves surplus to requirements, standing alone on the sidewalk, pensioned off and abandoned. Or were they?

SF is a difficult and transient literature at the best of times, ultimately problematic. It claims to treat of the future, all the what-ifs and if-this-goes-ons; but the what-ifs and if-this-goes-ons are always founded here and hard in today. Whatever today is.

To put it another way, nothing dates harder than historical fiction and science fiction. Sir Arthur Conan Doyle's historical fiction and his SF are of a piece—and both have dated in a way in which Sherlock Holmes, pinned to his time in the gaslit streets of Victorian London, has not.

Dated? Rather, they are of their time.

For there are always exceptions. There may, for instance, be nothing in Alfred Bester's *Tiger! Tiger!* (1956 U.K.; republished in the U.S. under the original 1956 *Galaxy* magazine title, *The Stars My Destination*, in 1957) that radically transgresses any of the speculative notions SF writers then shared about the possible shape of a future solar system. But Gully Foyle, the obsessive protagonist who dominates every page of the tale, has not dated a moment. In a fashion which inescapably reminds us of the great grotesques of other literary traditions, of dark figures from Poe or Gogol or Dickens, Gully Foyle *controls* the world around him, so that the awkwardnesses of the 1956 future do not so much fade into the background as obey his obsessive dance. If he were not so intransigent, so utterly bloody-minded, so unborn, Gully Foyle could have become an icon like Sherlock Holmes. But he is; and even though Bester based him on a quote—he is a reworking of the Byronesque magus Edmond Dantès whose revenge over his oppressors takes a thousand pages of Alexandre Dumas's *The Count of Monte Cristo* (1844) to accomplish—he cannot himself be quoted.

When I read this book—or one very similar; you can no more read the same book again than you can step into the same river—in the early 1970s, as a young teenager, I read it under the title

Tiger! Tiger! It's a title I prefer to the rather more upbeat *The Stars My Destination*. It is a title of warning, of admiration. God, we are reminded in Blake's poem, created the tiger too. The God who made the lamb also made the carnivores that prey upon it. And Gully Foyle, our hero, is a predator. We meet him and are informed that he is everyman, a nonentity; then Bester lights the touchpaper, and we stand back and watch him flare and burn and illuminate: almost illiterate, stupid, single-minded, amoral (not in the hip sense of being too cool for morality, but simply utterly, blindly selfish), he is a murderer—perhaps a multiple murderer— a rapist, a monster. A tiger.

(And because Bester began working on the book in England, naming his characters from an English telephone directory, Foyle shares a name with the largest, and most irritating book shop in London—and with Lemuel Gulliver, who voyaged among strange peoples. Dagenham, Yeovil, and Sheffield are all English cities.)

We are entering a second-stage world of introductions to SF. It is not long since everyone knew everybody. I for one never met Alfred Bester: I never travelled to America as a young man, and by the time he was due to come to England, to the 1987 Brighton Worldcon, his health did not permit it, and he died shortly after the convention.

I can offer no personal encomia to Bester the man—author of many fine short stories, two remarkable SF novels in the first round of his career (*The Demolished Man* and the book you now hold in your hand); author of three somewhat less notable SF books in later life. (Also a fascinating psychological thriller called *The Rat Race*, about the world of New York television in the 1950s.)

He began his career as a writer in the SF pulps, moved from there to comics, writing Superman, Green Lantern (he created the "Green Lantern Oath"), and many other characters; he moved from there to radio, writing for *Charlie Chan* and *The Shadow*. "The comic book days were over, but the splendid training I received in visualization, attack, dialogue, and economy stayed with me forever," he said in a memoir.

He was one of the only—perhaps the only—SF writers to be revered by the old timers ("First SF"), by the radical "New Wave" of the 1960s and early 1970s, and, in the 1980s, by the "cyberpunks." When he died in 1987, three years into the flowering of cyberpunk, it was apparent that the 1980s genre owed an enormous debt to Bester—and to this book in particular.

The Stars My Destination is, after all, the perfect cyberpunk novel: it contains such cheerfully protocyber elements as multinational corporate intrigue; a dangerous, mysterious, hyperscientific McGuffin (PyrE); an amoral hero; a supercool thiefwoman . . .

But what makes *The Stars My Destination* more interesting—and ten years on, less dated—than most cyberpunk, is watching Gully Foyle become a moral creature, during his sequence of transfigurations (keep all heroes going long enough, and they become gods). The tiger tattoos force him to learn control. His emotional state is no longer written in his face—it forces him to move beyond predation, beyond rage, back to the womb, as it were. (And what a sequence of wombs the book gives us: the coffin, the *Nomad*, the Goufre Martel, St. Pat's, and finally the *Nomad* again.) It gives us more than that. It gives us:

Birth.

Symmetry.

Hate.

A word of warning: the vintage of the book demands more work from the reader than she or he may be used to. Were it written now, its author would have shown us the rape, not implied it, just as we would have been permitted to watch the sex on the grass in the night after the Goufre Martel, before the sun came up, and she saw his face . . .

So assume it's 1956 again. You are about to meet Gully Foyle, and to learn how to jaunte. You are on the way to the future.

It was, or is, or will be, as Bester might have said, had someone not beaten him to it, the best of times. It will be the worst of times. . . .

THE STARS MY
DESTINATION

22-04-2009

1·······6·99
*·······6·99TL
*·······7·00CA
*·······0·01C4
        001112
17·48   00

PART 1

Tiger! Tiger! burning bright
In the forests of the night,
What immortal hand or eye
Could frame thy fearful symmetry?

BLAKE

PROLOGUE

This was a Golden Age, a time of high adventure, rich living, and hard dying . . . but nobody thought so. This was a future of fortune and theft, pillage and rapine, culture and vice . . . but nobody admitted it. This was an age of extremes, a fascinating century of freaks . . . but nobody loved it.

All the habitable worlds of the solar system were occupied. Three planets and eight satellites and eleven million million people swarmed in one of the most exciting ages ever known, yet minds still yearned for other times, as always. The solar system seethed with activity . . . fighting, feeding, and breeding, learning the new technologies that spewed forth almost before the old had been mastered, girding itself for the first exploration of the far stars in deep space; but—

"Where are the new frontiers?" the Romantics cried, unaware that the frontier of the mind had opened in a laboratory on Callisto at the turn of the twenty-fourth century. A researcher named Jaunte set fire to his bench and himself (accidentally) and let out a yell for help with particular reference to a fire extinguisher. Who so surprised as Jaunte and his colleagues when he found himself standing alongside said extinguisher, seventy feet removed from his lab bench.

They put Jaunte out and went into the whys and wherefores of his instantaneous seventy-foot journey. Teleportation . . . the transportation of oneself through space by an effort of the mind alone . . . had long been a theoretic concept, and there were a few hundred badly documented proofs that it had happened in the past. This was the first time that it had ever taken place before professional observers.

They investigated the Jaunte Effect savagely. This was something too earth-shaking to handle with kid gloves, and Jaunte was anxious to make his name immortal. He made his will and said farewell to his friends. Jaunte knew he was going to die because his fellow researchers were determined to kill him, if necessary. There was no doubt about that.

Twelve psychologists, parapsychologists, and neurometrists of varying specialization were called in as observers. The experimenters sealed Jaunte into an unbreakable crystal tank. They opened a water valve, feeding water into the tank, and let Jaunte watch them smash the valve handle. It was impossible to open the tank; it was impossible to stop the flow of water.

The theory was that if it had required the threat of death to goad Jaunte into teleporting himself in the first place, they'd damned well threaten him with death again. The tank filled quickly. The observers collected data with the tense precision of an eclipse camera crew. Jaunte began to drown. Then he was outside the tank, dripping and coughing explosively. He'd teleported again.

The experts examined and questioned him. They studied graphs and X-rays, neural patterns and body chemistry. They began to get an inkling of how Jaunte had teleported. On the technical grapevine (this had to be kept secret) they sent out a call for suicide volunteers. They were still in the primitive stage of teleportation; death was the only spur they knew.

They briefed the volunteers thoroughly. Jaunte lectured on what he had done and how he thought he had done it. Then they proceeded to murder the volunteers. They drowned them, hanged them, burned them; they invented new forms of slow and controlled death. There was never any doubt in any of the subjects that death was the object.

Eighty per cent of the volunteers died, and the agonies and remorse of their murderers would make a fascinating and horrible study, but that has no place in this history except to highlight the monstrosity of the times. Eighty per cent of the volunteers died, but 20 per cent jaunted. (The name became a word almost immediately.)

"Bring back the romantic age," the Romantics pleaded, "when men could risk their lives in high adventure."

The body of knowledge grew rapidly. By the first decade of the twenty-fifth century the principles of jaunting were established and the first school was opened by Charles Fort Jaunte himself, then fifty-seven, immortalized, and ashamed to admit that he had never dared jaunte again. But the primitive days were past; it was no longer necessary to threaten a man with death to make him teleport. They had learned how to teach man to recognize, discipline, and exploit yet another resource of his limitless mind.

How, exactly, did man teleport? One of the most unsatisfactory explanations was provided by Spencer Thompson, publicity representative of the Jaunte Schools, in a press interview.

THOMPSON: Jaunting is like seeing; it is a natural aptitude of almost every human organism, but it can only be developed by training and experience.

REPORTER: You mean we couldn't see without practice?

THOMPSON: Obviously you're either unmarried or have no children . . . preferably both.

(*Laughter*)

REPORTER: I don't understand.

THOMPSON: Anyone who's observed an infant learning to use its eyes, would.

REPORTER: But what *is* teleportation?

THOMPSON: The transportation of oneself from one locality to another by an effort of the mind alone.

REPORTER: You mean we can *think* ourselves from . . . say . . . New York to Chicago?

THOMPSON: Precisely.

REPORTER: Would we arrive naked?

THOMPSON: If you started naked.

(*Laughter*)

REPORTER: I mean, would our clothes teleport with us?

THOMPSON: When people teleport, they also teleport the clothes they wear and whatever they are strong enough to carry. I hate to disappoint you, but even ladies' clothes would arrive with them.

(*Laughter*)

REPORTER: But how do we do it?

THOMPSON: How do we think?

REPORTER: With our minds.

THOMPSON: And how does the mind think? What is the thinking process? Exactly how do we remember, imagine, deduce, create? Exactly how do the brain cells operate?

REPORTER: I don't know. Nobody knows.

THOMPSON: And nobody knows exactly how we teleport either, but we know we can do it—just as we know that we can think. Have you ever heard of Descartes? He said: *Cogito ergo sum*. I think, therefore I am. We say: *Cogito ergo jaunteo*. I think, therefore I jaunte.

∞

If it is thought that Thompson's explanation is exasperating, inspect this report of Sir John Kelvin to the Royal Society on the mechanism of jaunting:

> We have established that the teleportative ability is associated with the Nissl bodies, or Tigroid Substance in nerve cells. The Tigroid Substance is easiest demonstrated by Nissl's method using 3.75 g. of methylene blue and 1.75 g. of Venetian soap dissolved in 1,000 cc. of water.
>
> Where the Tigroid Substance does not appear, jaunting is impossible. Teleportation is a Tigroid Function.
>
> (*Applause*)

Any man was capable of jaunting provided he developed two faculties, visualization and concentration. He had to visualize, completely and precisely, the spot to which he desired to teleport himself; and he had to concentrate the latent energy of his mind into a single thrust to get him there. Above all, he had to have faith . . . the faith that Charles Fort Jaunte never recovered. He had to believe he would jaunte. The slightest doubt would block the mind-thrust necessary for teleportation.

The limitations with which every man is born necessarily limited the ability to jaunte. Some could visualize magnificently and set the co-ordinates of their destination with precision, but lacked the power to get there. Others had the power but could not, so to speak, see where they were jaunting. And space set a final limitation, for no man had ever jaunted further than a thousand miles. He could work his way in jaunting jumps over land and water from Nome to Mexico, but no jump could exceed a thousand miles.

By the 2420's, this form of employment application blank had become a commonplace:

> This space
> reserved for
> retina pattern
> identification

NAME (Capital letters): ....
                           Last   First   Middle

RESIDENCE (Legal): ....
                        Continent   Country   County

JAUNTE CLASS (Official Rating; Check One Only):
    M (1,000 miles): .... L (50 miles): ....
    D (500 miles): .... X (10 miles): ....
    C (100 miles): .... V (5 miles): ....

The old Bureau of Motor Vehicles took over the new job and regularly tested and classed jaunte applicants, and the old American Automobile Association changed its initials to AJA.

Despite all efforts, no man had ever jaunted across the voids of space, although many experts and fools had tried. Helmut Grant, for one, who spent a month memorizing the co-ordinates of a jaunte stage on the moon and visualized every mile of the two hundred and forty thousand-mile trajectory from Times Square to Kepler City. Grant jaunted and disappeared. They never found him. They never found Enzio Dandridge, a Los Angeles revivalist looking for Heaven; Jacob Maria Freundlich, a paraphysicist who should have known better than to jaunte into deep space searching for metadimensions; Shipwreck Cogan, a professional seeker after notoriety; and hundreds of others, lunatic-fringers, neurotics, escapists, and suicides. Space was closed to teleportation. Jaunting was restricted to the surfaces of the planets of the solar system.

But within three generations the entire solar system was on the jaunte. The transition was more spectacular than the change-over from horse and buggy to gasoline age five centuries before. On three planets and eight satellites, social, legal, and economic structures crashed while the new customs and laws demanded by universal jaunting mushroomed in their place.

There were land riots as the jaunting poor deserted slums to squat in plains and forests, raiding the livestock and wildlife. There was a revolution in home and office building: labyrinths and masking devices had to be introduced to prevent unlawful entry by jaunting. There were crashes and panics and strikes and famines as pre-jaunte industries failed.

Plagues and pandemics raged as jaunting vagrants carried disease and vermin into defenseless countries. Malaria, elephantiasis, and the breakbone fever came north to Greenland; rabies returned to England after an absence of three hundred years. The Japanese beetle, the citrus scale, the chestnut blight, and the elm borer spread to every corner of the world, and from one forgotten pesthole in Borneo, leprosy, long imagined extinct, reappeared.

Crime waves swept the planets and satellites as their under-worlds took to jaunting with the night around the clock, and there were brutalities as the police fought them without quarter. There came a hideous return to the worst prudery of Victorianism as society fought the sexual and moral dangers of jaunting with protocol and taboo. A cruel and vicious war broke out between the Inner Planets—Venus, Terra, and Mars—and the Outer Satellites . . . a war brought on by the economic and political pressures of teleportation.

Until the Jaunte Age dawned, the three Inner Planets (and the Moon) had lived in delicate economic balance with the seven inhabited Outer Satellites: Io, Europa, Ganymede, and Callisto of Jupiter; Rhea and Titan of Saturn; and Lassell of Neptune. The United Outer Satellites supplied raw materials for the Inner Planets' manufactories, and a market for their finished goods. Within a decade this balance was destroyed by jaunting.

The Outer Satellites, raw young worlds in the making, had

bought 70 per cent of the I.P. transportation production. Jaunting ended that. They had bought 90 per cent of the I.P. communications production. Jaunting ended that too. In consequence I.P. purchase of O.S. raw materials fell off.

With trade exchange destroyed it was inevitable that the economic war would degenerate into a shooting war. Inner Planets' cartels refused to ship manufacturing equipment to the Outer Satellites, attempting to protect themselves against competition. The O.S. confiscated the plants already in operation on their worlds, broke patent agreements, ignored royalty obligations . . . and the war was on.

It was an age of freaks, monsters, and grotesques. All the world was misshapen in marvelous and malevolent ways. The Classicists and Romantics who hated it were unaware of the potential greatness of the twenty-fifth century. They were blind to a cold fact of evolution . . . that progress stems from the clashing merger of antagonistic extremes, out of the marriage of pinnacle freaks. Classicists and Romantics alike were unaware that the Solar System was trembling on the verge of a human explosion that would transform man and make him the master of the universe.

It is against this seething background of the twenty-fifth century that the vengeful history of Gulliver Foyle begins.

CHAPTER ONE

He was one hundred and seventy days dying and not yet dead. He fought for survival with the passion of a beast in a trap. He was delirious and rotting, but occasionally his primitive mind emerged from the burning nightmare of survival into something resembling sanity. Then he lifted his mute face to Eternity and muttered: "What's a matter, me? Help, you goddamn gods! Help, is all."

Blasphemy came easily to him: it was half his speech, all his life. He had been raised in the gutter school of the twenty-fifth century and spoke nothing but the gutter tongue. Of all brutes in the world he was among the least valuable alive and most likely to survive. So he struggled and prayed in blasphemy; but occasionally his raveling mind leaped backward thirty years to his childhood and remembered a nursery jingle:

> Gully Foyle is my name
> And Terra is my nation.
> Deep space is my dwelling place
> And death's my destination.

He was Gulliver Foyle, Mechanic's Mate 3rd Class, thirty years old, big boned and rough . . . and one hundred and seventy days adrift in space. He was Gully Foyle, the oiler, wiper, bunkerman; too easy for trouble, too slow for fun, too empty for friendship, too lazy for love. The lethargic outlines of his character showed in the official Merchant Marine records:

FOYLE, GULLIVER ------ AS-128/127:006

EDUCATION:	NONE
SKILLS:	NONE
MERITS:	NONE
RECOMMENDATIONS:	NONE

(PERSONNEL COMMENTS)

A man of physical strength and intellectual potential stunted by lack of ambition. Energizes at minimum. The stereotype Common Man. Some unexpected shock might possibly awaken him, but Psych cannot find the key. Not recommended for promotion. Has reached a dead end.

He had reached a dead end. He had been content to drift from moment to moment of existence for thirty years like some heavily armored creature, sluggish and indifferent—Gully Foyle, the stereotype Common Man—but now he was adrift in space for one hundred and seventy days, and the key to his awakening was in the lock. Presently it would turn and open the door to holocaust.

∞

The spaceship *Nomad* drifted halfway between Mars and Jupiter. Whatever war catastrophe had wrecked it had taken a sleek steel rocket, one hundred yards long and one hundred feet broad, and mangled it into a skeleton on which was mounted the remains of cabins, holds, decks, and bulkheads. Great rents in the hull were blazes of light on the sunside and frosty blotches of stars on the darkside. The S.S. *Nomad* was a weightless emptiness of blinding sun and jet shadow, frozen and silent.

The wreck was filled with a floating conglomerate of frozen debris that hung within the destroyed vessel like an instantaneous photograph of an explosion. The minute gravitational attraction of the bits of rubble for each other was slowly drawing them into clusters which were periodically torn apart by the passage through them of the one survivor still alive on the wreck, Gulliver Foyle, AS-128/127:006.

He lived in the only airtight room left intact in the wreck, a tool locker off the main-deck corridor. The locker was four feet wide, four feet deep, and nine feet high. It was the size of a giant's coffin. Six hundred years before, it had been judged the most exquisite Oriental torture to imprison a man in a cage that size for a few weeks. Yet Foyle had existed in this lightless coffin for five months, twenty days, and four hours.

∞

"Who are you?"
   "Gully Foyle is my name."
   "Where are you from?"
   "Terra is my nation."

"Where are you now?"

"Deep space is my dwelling place."

"Where are you bound?"

"Death's my destination."

On the one hundred and seventy-first day of his fight for survival, Foyle answered these questions and awoke. His heart hammered and his throat burned. He groped in the dark for the air tank which shared his coffin with him and checked it. The tank was empty. Another would have to be moved in at once. So this day would commence with an extra skirmish with death which Foyle accepted with mute endurance.

He felt through the locker shelves and located a torn space-suit. It was the only one aboard *Nomad* and Foyle no longer remembered where or how he had found it. He had sealed the tear with emergency spray, but had no way of refilling or replacing the empty oxygen cartridges on the back. Foyle got into the suit. It would hold enough air from the locker to allow him five minutes in vacuum . . . no more.

Foyle opened the locker door and plunged out into the black frost of space. The air in the locker puffed out with him and its moisture congealed into a tiny snow cloud that drifted down the torn main-deck corridor. Foyle heaved at the exhausted air tank, floated it out of the locker and abandoned it. One minute was gone.

He turned and propelled himself through the floating debris toward the hatch to the ballast hold. He did not run: his gait was the unique locomotion of free-fall and weightlessness . . . thrusts with foot, elbow and hand against deck, wall and corner, a slow-motion darting through space like a bat flying under water. Foyle shot through the hatch into the darkside ballast hold. Two minutes were gone.

Like all spaceships, *Nomad* was ballasted and stiffened with the mass of her gas tanks laid down the length of her keel like a long lumber raft tapped at the sides by a labyrinth of pipe fittings. Foyle took a minute disconnecting an air tank. He had no way of knowing whether it was full or already exhausted; whether he would fight it back to his locker only to discover that it was empty and his life was ended. Once a week he endured this game of space roulette.

There was a roaring in his ears; the air in his spacesuit was rapidly going foul. He yanked the massy cylinder toward the ballast hatch, ducked to let it sail over his head, then thrust himself after it. He swung the tank through the hatch. Four minutes had elapsed and he was shaking and blacking out. He guided the tank down the main-deck corridor and bulled it into the tool locker.

He slammed the locker door, dogged it, found a hammer on a shelf and swung it thrice against the frozen tank to loosen the valve. Foyle twisted the handle grimly. With the last of his strength he unsealed the helmet of his spacesuit, lest he suffocate within the suit while the locker filled with air . . . if this tank contained air. He fainted, as he had fainted so often before, never knowing whether this was death.

∞

"Who are you?"
　　"Gully Foyle."
"Where are you from?"
　　"Terra."
"Where are you now?"
　　"Space."
"Where are you bound?"
He awoke. He was alive. He wasted no time on prayer or thanks but continued the business of survival. In the darkness he explored the locker shelves where he kept his rations. There were only a few packets left. Since he was already wearing the patched spacesuit he might just as well run the gantlet of vacuum again and replenish his supplies.

He flooded his spacesuit with air from the tank, resealed his helmet and sailed out into the frost and light again. He squirmed down the main-deck corridor and ascended the remains of a stairway to control deck, which was no more than a roofed corridor in space. Most of the walls were destroyed.

With the sun on his right and the stars on his left, Foyle shot aft toward the galley storeroom. Halfway down the corridor he passed a door frame still standing foursquare between deck and roof. The leaf still hung on its hinges, half-open, a door to nowhere. Behind it was all space and the steady stars.

As Foyle passed the door he had a quick view of himself reflected in the polished chrome of the leaf . . . Gully Foyle, a giant black creature, bearded, crusted with dried blood and filth, emaciated, with sick, patient eyes . . . and followed always by a stream of floating debris, the raffle disturbed by his motion and following him through space like the tail of a festering comet.

Foyle turned into the galley storeroom and began looting with the methodical speed of five months' habit. Most of the bottled goods were frozen solid and exploded. Much of the canned goods had lost their containers, for tin crumbles to dust in the absolute zero of space. Foyle gathered up ration packets, concentrates, and a chunk of ice from the burst water tank. He threw everything into a large copper cauldron, turned and darted out of the storeroom, carrying the cauldron.

At the door to nowhere Foyle glanced at himself again, reflected in the chrome leaf framed in the stars. Then he stopped his motion in bewilderment. He stared at the stars behind the door which had become familiar friends after five months. There was an intruder among them; a comet, it seemed, with an invisible head and a short, spurting tail. Then Foyle realized he was staring at a spaceship, stern rockets flaring as it accelerated on a sunward course which must pass him.

"No," he muttered. "No, man. No."

He was continually suffering from hallucinations. He turned to resume the journey back to his coffin. Then he looked again. It was still a spaceship, stern rockets flaring as it accelerated on a sunward course which must pass him. He discussed the illusion with Eternity.

"Six months already," he said in his gutter tongue. "Is it now? You listen a me, lousy gods. I talkin' a deal, is all. I look again, sweet prayer-men. If it's a ship, I'm yours. You own me. But if it's a gaff, man . . . if it's no ship . . . I unseal right now and blow my guts. We both ballast level, us. Now reach me the sign, yes or no, is all."

He looked for a third time. For the third time he saw a spaceship, stern rockets flaring as it accelerated on a sunward course which must pass him.

It was the sign. He believed. He was saved.

Foyle shoved off and went hurtling down control-deck corridor toward the bridge. But at the companionway stairs he restrained himself. He could not remain conscious for more than a few more moments without refilling his spacesuit. He gave the approaching spaceship one pleading look, then shot down to the tool locker and pumped his suit full.

He mounted to the control bridge. Through the starboard observation port he saw the spaceship, stern rockets still flaring, evidently making a major alteration in course, for it was bearing down on him very slowly.

On a panel marked FLARES, Foyle pressed the DISTRESS button. There was a three-second pause during which he suffered. Then white radiance blinded him as the distress signal went off in three triple bursts, nine prayers for help. Foyle pressed the button twice again, and twice more the flares flashed in space while the radioactives incorporated in their combustion set up a static howl that must register on any waveband of any receiver.

The stranger's jets cut off. He had been seen. He would be saved. He was reborn. He exulted.

Foyle darted back to his locker and replenished his spacesuit again. He began to weep. He started to gather his possessions—a faceless clock which he kept wound just to listen to the ticking, a lug wrench with a hand-shaped handle which he would hold in lonely moments, an egg slicer upon whose wires he would pluck primitive tunes. . . . He dropped them in his excitement, hunted for them in the dark, then began to laugh at himself.

He filled his spacesuit with air once more and capered back to the bridge. He punched a flare button labelled: RESCUE. From the hull of the *Nomad* shot a sunlet that burst and hung, flooding miles of space with harsh white light.

"Come on, baby you," Foyle crooned. "Hurry up, man. Come on, baby baby you."

Like a ghost torpedo, the stranger slid into the outermost rim of light, approaching slowly, looking him over. For a moment Foyle's heart constricted; the ship was behaving so cautiously that he feared she was an enemy vessel from the Outer Satellites. Then he saw the famous red and blue emblem on her side, the trademark of the mighty industrial clan of Presteign; Presteign of Terra, powerful, munificent, beneficent. And he knew this was a sister ship, for the *Nomad* was also Presteign-owned. He knew this was an angel from space hovering over him.

"Sweet sister," Foyle crooned. "Baby angel, fly away home with me."

The ship came abreast of Foyle, illuminated ports along its side glowing with friendly light, its name and registry number clearly visible in illuminated figures on the hull: *Vorga*-T:1339. The ship was alongside him in a moment, passing him in a second, disappearing in a third.

The sister had spurned him; the angel had abandoned him.

Foyle stopped dancing and crooning. He stared in dismay. He leaped to the flare panel and slapped buttons. Distress signals, landing, take-off, and quarantine flares burst from the hull of the *Nomad* in a madness of white, red and green light, pulsing, pleading ... and *Vorga*-T:1339 passed silently and implacably, stern jets flaring again as it accelerated on a sunward course.

So, in five seconds, he was born, he lived, and he died. After thirty years of existence and six months of torture, Gully Foyle, the stereotype Common Man, was no more. The key turned in the lock of his soul and the door was opened. What emerged expunged the Common Man forever.

"You pass me by," he said with slow mounting fury. "You leave me rot like a dog. You leave me die, *Vorga* ... *Vorga*-T:1339.

No. I get out of here, me. I follow you, *Vorga*. I find you, *Vorga*. I pay you back, me. I rot you. I kill you, *Vorga*. I kill you filthy."

The acid of fury ran through him, eating away the brute patience and sluggishness that had made a cipher of Gully Foyle, precipitating a chain of reactions that would make an infernal machine of Gully Foyle. He was dedicated.

"*Vorga*, I kill you filthy."

∞

He did what the cipher could not do; he rescued himself.

For two days he combed the wreckage in five-minute forays, and devised a harness for his shoulders. He attached an air tank to the harness and connected the tank to his spacesuit helmet with an improvised hose. He wriggled through space like an ant dragging a log, but he had the freedom of the *Nomad* for all time.

He thought.

In the control bridge he taught himself to use the few navigation instruments that were still unbroken, studying the standard manuals that littered the wrecked navigation room. In the ten years of his service in space he had never dreamed of attempting such a thing, despite the rewards of promotion and pay; but now he had *Vorga*-T:1339 to reward him.

He took sights. The *Nomad* was drifting in space on the ecliptic, three hundred million miles from the sun. Before him were spread the constellations Perseus, Andromeda, and Pisces. Hanging almost in the foreground was a dusty orange spot that was Jupiter, distinctly a planetary disc to the naked eye. With any luck he could make a course for Jupiter and rescue.

Jupiter was not, could never be habitable. Like all the outer planets beyond the asteroid orbits, it was a frozen mass of methane and ammonia; but its four largest satellites swarmed with cities and populations now at war with the Inner Planets. He would be a war prisoner, but he had to stay alive to settle accounts with *Vorga*-T:1339.

Foyle inspected the engine room of the *Nomad*. There was

Hi-Thrust fuel remaining in the tanks and one of the four tail jets was still in operative condition. Foyle found the engine room manuals and studied them. He repaired the connection between fuel tanks and the one jet chamber. The tanks were on the sunside of the wreck and warmed above freezing point. The Hi-Thrust was still liquid, but it would not flow. In free-fall there was no gravity to draw the fuel down the pipes.

Foyle studied a space manual and learned something about theoretical gravity. If he could put the *Nomad* into a spin, centrifugal force would impart enough gravitation to the ship to draw fuel down into the combustion chamber of the jet. If he could fire the combustion chamber, the unequal thrust of the one jet would impart a spin to the *Nomad*.

But he couldn't fire the jet without first having the spin; and he couldn't get the spin without first firing the jet.

He thought his way out of the deadlock; he was inspired by *Vorga*.

Foyle opened the drainage petcock in the combustion chamber of the jet and torturously filled the chamber with fuel by hand. He had primed the pump. Now, if he ignited the fuel, it would fire long enough to impart the spin and start gravity. Then the flow from the tanks would commence and the rocketing would continue.

He tried matches.

Matches will not burn in the vacuum of space.

He tried flint and steel.

Sparks will not glow in the absolute zero of space.

He thought of red-hot filaments.

He had no electric power of any description aboard the *Nomad* to make a filament red hot.

He found texts and read. Although he was blacking out frequently and close to complete collapse, he thought and planned. He was inspired to greatness by *Vorga*.

Foyle brought ice from the frozen galley tanks, melted it with his own body heat, and added water to the jet combustion chamber. The fuel and the water were nonmiscible, they did not mix. The water floated in a thin layer over the fuel.

From the chemical stores Foyle brought a silvery bit of wire, pure sodium metal. He poked the wire through the open petcock. The sodium ignited when it touched the water and flared with high heat. The heat touched off the Hi-Thrust which burst in a needle flame from the petcock. Foyle closed the petcock with a wrench. The ignition held in the chamber and the lone aft jet slammed out flame with a soundless vibration that shook the ship.

The off-center thrust of the jet twisted the *Nomad* into a slow spin. The torque imparted a slight gravity. Weight returned. The floating debris that cluttered the hull fell to decks, walls and ceilings; and the gravity kept the fuel feeding from tanks to combustion chamber.

Foyle wasted no time on cheers. He left the engine room and struggled forward in desperate haste for a final, fatal observation from the control bridge. This would tell him whether the *Nomad* was committed to a wild plunge out into the no-return of deep space, or a course for Jupiter and rescue.

The slight gravity made his air tank almost impossible to drag. The sudden forward surge of acceleration shook loose masses of debris which flew backward through the *Nomad*. As Foyle struggled up the companionway stairs to the control deck, the rubble from the bridge came hurtling back down the corridor and smashed into him. He was caught up in this tumbleweed in space, rolled back the length of the empty corridor, and brought up against the galley bulkhead with an impact that shattered his last hold on consciousness. He lay pinned in the center of half a ton of wreckage, helpless, barely alive, but still raging for vengeance.

"Who are you?"

"Where are you from?"

"Where are you now?"

"Where are you bound?"

CHAPTER
TWO

etween Mars and Jupiter is spread the broad belt of the
asteroids. Of the thousands, known and unknown, most
unique to the Freak Century was the Sargasso Asteroid, a
tiny planet manufactured of natural rock and wreckage salvaged
by its inhabitants in the course of two hundred years.

They were savages, the only savages of the twenty-fifth century; descendants of a research team of scientists that had been

lost and marooned in the asteroid belt two centuries before when their ship had failed. By the time their descendants were rediscovered they had built up a world and a culture of their own, and preferred to remain in space, salvaging and spoiling, and practicing a barbaric travesty of the scientific method they remembered from their forebears. They called themselves The Scientific People. The world promptly forgot them.

S.S. *Nomad* looped through space, neither on a course for Jupiter nor the far stars, but drifting across the asteroid belt in the slow spiral of a dying animalcule. It passed within a mile of the Sargasso Asteroid, and it was immediately captured by The Scientific People to be incorporated into their little planet. They found Foyle.

He awoke once while he was being carried in triumph on a litter through the natural and artificial passages within the scavenger asteroid. They were constructed of meteor metal, stone, and hull plates. Some of the plates still bore names long forgotten in the history of space travel: INDUS QUEEN, TERRA; SYRTIS RAMBLER, MARS; THREE RING CIRCUS, SATURN. The passages led to great halls, storerooms, apartments, and homes, all built of salvaged ships cemented into the asteroid.

In rapid succession Foyle was borne through an ancient Ganymede scow, a Lassell ice borer, a captain's barge, a Callisto heavy cruiser, a twenty-second-century fuel transport with glass tanks still filled with smoky rocket fuel. Two centuries of salvage were gathered in this hive: armories of weapons, libraries of books, museums of costumes, warehouses of machinery, tools, rations, drink, chemicals, synthetics, and surrogates.

A crowd around the litter was howling triumphantly. "Quant Suff!" they shouted. A woman's chorus began an excited bleating:

Ammonium bromide ....gr. 1½
Potassium bromide ....gr. 3
Sodium bromide ....gr. 2
Citric acid ....quant. suff.

"Quant Suff!" The Scientific People roared. "Quant Suff!"
Foyle fainted.

He awoke again. He had been taken out of his spacesuit. He was in the greenhouse of the asteroid where plants were grown for fresh oxygen. The hundred-yard hull of an old ore carrier formed the room, and one wall had been entirely fitted with salvaged windows . . . round ports, square ports, diamond, hexagonal . . . every shape and age of port had been introduced until the vast wall was a crazy quilt of glass and light.

The distant sun blazed through; the air was hot and moist. Foyle gazed around dimly. A devil face peered at him. Cheeks, chin, nose, and eyelids were hideously tattooed like an ancient Maori mask. Across the brow was tattooed JÓSEPH. The "O" in JÓSEPH had a tiny arrow thrust up from the right shoulder, turning it into the symbol of Mars, used by scientists to designate male sex.

"We are The Scientific People," Jóseph said. "I am Jóseph; these are my brethren."

He gestured. Foyle gazed at the grinning crowd surrounding his litter. All faces were tattooed into devil masks; all brows had names blazoned across them.

"How long did you drift?" Jóseph asked.

"*Vorga*," Foyle mumbled.

"You are the first to arrive alive in fifty years. You are a puissant man. Very. Arrival of the fittest is the doctrine of Holy Darwin. Most scientific."

"Quant Suff!" the crowd bellowed.

Jóseph seized Foyle's elbow in the manner of a physician taking a pulse. His devil mouth counted solemnly up to ninety-eight.

"Your pulse. Ninety-eight-point-six," Jóseph said, producing a thermometer and shaking it reverently. "Most scientific."

"Quant Suff!" came the chorus.

Jóseph proffered an Erlenmeyer flask. It was labeled: *Lung, Cat, c.s., hematoxylin & eosin.* "Vitamin?" Jóseph inquired.

When Foyle did not respond, Jóseph removed a large pill from the flask, placed it in the bowl of a pipe, and lit it. He puffed once and then gestured. Three girls appeared before Foyle. Their faces were hideously tattooed. Across each brow was a name: JƠAN and MƠIRA and PƠLLY. The "O" of each name had a tiny cross at the base.

"Choose," Jóseph said. "The Scientific People practice Natural Selection. Be scientific in your choice. Be genetic."

As Foyle fainted again, his arm slid off the litter and glanced against Mọira.

"Quant Suff!"

∞

He was in a circular hall with a domed roof. The hall was filled with rusting antique apparatus: a centrifuge, an operating table, a wrecked fluoroscope, autoclaves, cases of corroded surgical instruments.

They strapped Foyle down on the operating table while he raved and rambled. They fed him. They shaved and bathed him. Two men began turning the ancient centrifuge by hand. It emitted a rhythmic clanking like the pounding of a war drum. Those assembled began tramping and chanting.

They turned on the ancient autoclave. It boiled and geysered, filling the hall with howling steam. They turned on the old fluoroscope. It was short-circuited and spat sizzling bolts of lightning across the steaming hall.

A ten foot figure loomed up to the table. It was Jóseph on stilts. He wore a surgical cap, a surgical mask, and a surgeon's gown that hung from his shoulders to the floor. The gown was heavily embroidered with red and black thread illustrating anatomical sections of the body. Jóseph was a lurid tapestry out of a surgical text.

"I pronounce you Nomad!" Jóseph intoned.

The uproar became deafening. Jóseph tilted a rusty can over Foyle's body. There was the reek of ether.

Foyle lost his tatters of consciousness and darkness enveloped him. Out of the darkness *Vorga*-T:1339 surged again and again, accelerating on a sunward course that burst through Foyle's blood and brains until he could not stop screaming silently for vengeance.

∞

He was dimly aware of washings and feedings and trampings and chantings. At last he awoke to a lucid interval. There was silence. He was in a bed. The girl, Moira, was in bed with him.

"Who you?" Foyle croaked.

"Your wife, Nomad."

"What?"

"Your wife. You chose me, Nomad. We are gametes."

"What?"

"Scientifically mated," Moira said proudly. She pulled up the sleeve of her nightgown and showed him her arm. It was disfigured by four ugly slashes. "I have been inoculated with something old, something new, something borrowed, and something blue."

Foyle struggled out of the bed.

"Where we now?"

"In our home."

"What home?"

"Yours. You are one of us, Nomad. You must marry every month and beget many children. That will be scientific. But I am the first."

Foyle ignored her and explored. He was in the main cabin of a small rocket launch of the early 2300's . . . once a private yacht. The main cabin had been converted into a bedroom.

He lurched to the ports and looked out. The launch was sealed into the mass of the asteroid, connected by passages to the main body. He went aft. Two smaller cabins were filled with growing plants for oxygen. The engine room had been converted into a kitchen. There was Hi-Thrust in the fuel tanks, but it fed the burners of a small stove atop the rocket chambers. Foyle went forward. The control cabin was now a parlor, but the controls were still operative.

He thought.

He went aft to the kitchen and dismantled the stove. He reconnected the fuel tanks to the original jet combustion chambers. Moira followed him curiously.

"What are you doing, Nomad?"

"Got to get out of here, girl," Foyle mumbled. "Got business with a ship called *Vorga*. You dig me, girl? Going to ram out in this boat, is all."

Moira backed away in alarm. Foyle saw the look in her eyes and leaped for her. He was so crippled that she avoided him easily. She opened her mouth and let out a piercing scream. At that moment a mighty clangor filled the launch; it was Jóseph and his devil-faced Scientific People outside, banging on the metal hull, going through the ritual of a scientific charivari for the newlyweds.

Moira screamed and dodged while Foyle pursued her patiently. He trapped her in a corner, ripped her nightgown off and bound and gagged her with it. Moira made enough noise to split the asteroid open, but the scientific charivari was louder.

Foyle finished his rough patching of the engine room; he was almost an expert by now. He picked up the writhing girl and took her to the main hatch.

"Leaving," he shouted in Moira's ear. "Takeoff. Blast right out of asteroid. Hell of a smash, girl. Maybe all die, you. Everything busted wide open. Guesses for grabs what happens. No more air. No more asteroid. Go tell'm. Warn'm. Go, girl."

He opened the hatch, shoved Moira out, slammed the hatch and dogged it. The charivari stopped abruptly.

At the controls Foyle pressed ignition. The automatic take-off siren began a howl that had not sounded in decades. The jet chambers ignited with dull concussions. Foyle waited for the temperature to reach firing heat. While he waited he suffered. The launch was cemented into the asteroid. It was surrounded by stone and iron. Its rear jets were flush on the hull of another ship packed into the mass. He didn't know what would happen when his jets began their thrust, but he was driven to gamble by *Vorga*.

He fired the jets. There was a hollow explosion as Hi-Thrust flamed out of the stern of the ship. The launch shuddered, yawed, heated. A squeal of metal began. Then the launch grated forward. Metal, stone, and glass split asunder and the ship burst out of the asteroid into space.

∞

The Inner Planets navy picked him up ninety thousand miles outside Mars's orbit. After seven months of shooting war, the I.P. patrols were alert but reckless. When the launch failed to answer and give recognition countersigns, it should have been shattered with a blast and questions could have been asked of the wreckage later. But the launch was small and the cruiser crew was hot for prize money. They closed and grappled.

They found Foyle inside, crawling like a headless worm through a junk heap of spaceship and home furnishings. He was bleeding again, ripe with stinking gangrene, and one side of his head was pulpy. They brought him into the sick bay aboard the cruiser and carefully curtained his tank. Foyle was no sight even for the tough stomachs of lower deck navy men.

They patched his carcass in the amniotic tank while they completed their tour of duty. On the jet back to Terra, Foyle recovered consciousness and bubbled words beginning with V. He knew he was saved. He knew that only time stood between him and vengeance. The sick bay orderly heard him exulting in his tank and parted the curtains. Foyle's filmed eyes looked up. The orderly could not restrain his curiosity.

"You hear me, man?" he whispered.

Foyle grunted. The orderly bent lower.

"What happened? Who in hell done that to you?"

"What?" Foyle croaked.

"Don't you know?"

"What? What's a matter, you?"

"Wait a minute, is all."

The orderly disappeared as he jaunted to a supply cabin, and reappeared alongside the tank five seconds later. Foyle struggled up out of the fluid. His eyes blazed.

"It's coming back, man. Some of it. Jaunte. I couldn't jaunte on the *Nomad*, me."

"What?"

"I was off my head."

"Man, you didn't have no head left, you."

"I couldn't jaunte. I forgot how, is all. I forgot everything, me. Still don't remember much. I—"

He recoiled in terror as the orderly thrust the picture of a hideous tattooed face before him. It was a Maori mask. Cheeks, chin, nose, and eyelids were decorated with stripes and swirls. Across the brow was blazoned NÓMAD. Foyle stared, then cried out in agony. The picture was a mirror. The face was his own.

CHAPTER THREE

Bravo, Mr. Harris! Well done! L-E-S, gentlemen. Never forget. Location. Elevation. Situation. That's the only way to remember your jaunte co-ordinates. *Etre entre le marteau et l'enclume. French. English translation will not follow.* Don't jaunte yet, Mr. Peters. Wait your turn. Be patient, you'll all be C class by and by. Has anyone seen Mr. Foyle? He's missing. *Oh, look at that heavenly brown thrasher. Listen to him. Mozart on the wing.* Oh dear,

I'm thinking all over the place . . . or have I been speaking, gentlemen?"

"Half and half, m'am."

"It does seem unfair. One-way telepathy is a nuisance. I do apologize for shrapneling you with my thoughts."

"We like it, m'am. You think pretty."

"*How sweet of you, Mr. Gorgas.* All right, class; all back to school and we start again. Has Mr. Foyle jaunted already? I never can keep track of him."

Robin Wednesbury was conducting her re-education class in jaunting on its tour through New York City, and it was as exciting a business for the cerebral cases as it was for the children in her primer class. She treated the adults like children and they rather enjoyed it. For the past month they had been memorizing jaunte stages at street intersections, chanting: "L-E-S, m'am. Location. Elevation. Situation."

She was a tall, lovely Negro girl, brilliant and cultivated, but handicapped by the fact that she was a telesend, a one-way telepath. She could broadcast her thoughts to the world, but could receive nothing. This was a disadvantage that barred her from more glamorous careers, yet suited her for teaching. Despite her volatile temperament, Robin Wednesbury was a thorough and methodical jaunte instructor.

The men were brought down from General War Hospital to the jaunte school, which occupied an entire building in the Hudson Bridge at 42nd Street. They started from the school and marched in a sedate crocodile to the vast Times Square jaunte stage, which they earnestly memorized. Then they all jaunted to the school and back to Times Square. The crocodile reformed and they marched up to Columbus Circle and memorized its coordinates. Then all jaunted back to school via Times Square and returned by the same route to Columbus Circle. Once more the crocodile formed and off they went to Grand Army Plaza to repeat the memorizing and the jaunting.

Robin was re-educating the patients (all head injuries who had lost the power to jaunte) to the express stops, so to speak, of the public jaunte stages. Later they would memorize the local stops at street intersections. As their horizons expanded (and their powers returned) they would memorize jaunte stages in widening circles, limited as much by income as ability; for one thing was certain: you had to actually see a place to memorize it, which meant you first had to pay for the transportation to get you there. Even 3-D photographs would not do the trick. The Grand Tour had taken on a new significance for the rich.

"Location. Elevation. Situation," Robin Wednesbury lectured, and the class jaunted by express stages from Washington Heights to the Hudson Bridge and back again in primer jumps of a quarter mile each, following their lovely Negro teacher earnestly.

The little technical sergeant with the platinum skull suddenly spoke in the gutter tongue: "But there ain't no elevation, m'am. We're on the ground, us."

"*Isn't, Sgt. Logan. 'Isn't any' would be better.* I beg your pardon. Teaching becomes a habit and I'm having trouble controlling my thinking today. The war news is so bad. We'll get to Elevation when we start memorizing the stages on top of skyscrapers, Sgt. Logan."

The man with the rebuilt skull digested that, then asked: "We hear you when you think, is a matter you?"

"Exactly."

"But you don't hear us?"

"Never. I'm a one-way telepath."

"We all hear you, or just I, is all?"

"That depends, Sgt. Logan. When I'm concentrating, just the one I'm thinking at; when I'm at loose ends, anybody and everybody . . . poor souls. Excuse me." Robin turned and called: "Don't hesitate before jaunting, Chief Harris. That starts doubting, and doubting ends jaunting. Just step up and bang off."

"I worry sometimes, m'am," a chief petty officer with a tightly bandaged head answered. He was obviously stalling at the edge of the jaunte stage.

"Worry? About what?"

"Maybe there's gonna be somebody standing where I arrive. Then there'll be a hell of a real bang, m'am. Excuse me."

"Now I've explained that a hundred times. Experts have gauged every jaunte stage in the world to accommodate peak traffic. That's why private jaunte stages are small, and the Times Square stage is two hundred yards wide. It's all been worked out mathematically and there isn't one chance in ten million of a simultaneous arrival. That's less than your chance of being killed in a jet accident."

The bandaged C.P.O. nodded dubiously and stepped up on the raised stage. It was of white concrete, round, and decorated on its face with vivid black and white patterns as an aid to memory. In the center was an illuminated plaque which gave its name and jaunte co-ordinates of latitude, longitude, and elevation.

At the moment when the bandaged man was gathering courage for his primer jaunte, the stage began to flicker with a sudden flurry of arrivals and departures. Figures appeared momentarily as they jaunted in, hesitated while they checked their surroundings and set new co-ordinates, and then disappeared as they jaunted off. At each disappearance there was a faint "Pop" as displaced air rushed into the space formerly occupied by a body.

"Wait, class," Robin called. "There's a rush on. Everybody off the stage, please."

Laborers in heavy work clothes, still spattered with snow, were on their way south to their homes after a shift in the north woods. Fifty white clad dairy clerks were headed west toward St. Louis. They followed the morning from the Eastern Time Zone to the Pacific Zone. And from eastern Greenland, where it was already noon, a horde of white-collar office workers was pouring into New York for their lunch hour.

The rush was over in a few moments. "All right, class," Robin called. "We'll continue. Oh dear, where *is* Mr. Foyle? He always seems to be missing."

"With a face like he's got, him, you can't blame him for hiding it, m'am. Up in the cerebral ward we call him Boogey."

"He does look dreadful, doesn't he, Sgt. Logan. Can't they get those marks off?"

"They're trying, Miss Robin, but they don't know how yet. It's called 'tattooing' and it's sort of forgotten, is all."

"Then how did Mr. Foyle acquire his face?"

"Nobody knows, Miss Robin. He's up in cerebral because he's lost his mind, him. Can't remember nothing. Me personal, if I had a face like that I wouldn't want to remember nothing too."

"It's a pity. He looks frightful. Sgt. Logan, d'you suppose I've let a thought about Mr. Foyle slip and hurt his feelings?"

The little man with the platinum skull considered. "No, m'am. You wouldn't hurt nobody's feelings, you. And Foyle ain't got none to hurt, him. He's just a big, dumb ox, is all."

"I have to be so careful, Sgt. Logan. You see, no one likes to know what another person really thinks about him. We imagine that we do, but we don't. *This telesending of mine makes me loathed. And lonesome. I—Please don't listen to me. I'm having trouble controlling my thinking.* Ah! There you are, Mr. Foyle. Where in the world have you been wandering?"

Foyle had jaunted in on the stage and stepped off quietly, his hideous face averted. "Been practicing, me," he mumbled.

Robin repressed the shudder of revulsion in her and went to him sympathetically. She took his arm. "You really should be with us more. We're all friends and having a lovely time. Join in."

Foyle refused to meet her glance. As he pulled his arm away from her sullenly, Robin suddenly realized that his sleeve was soaking wet. His entire hospital uniform was drenched.

"Wet? He's been in the rain somewhere. But I've seen the morning weather reports. No rain east of St. Louis. Then he must have jaunted further than that. But he's not supposed to be able. He's supposed to have lost all memory and ability to jaunte. He's malingering."

Foyle leapt at her. "Shut up, you!" The savagery of his face was terrifying.

"Then you are malingering."

"How much do you know?"

"That you're a fool. Stop making a scene."

"Did they hear you?"

"I don't know. Let go of me." Robin turned away from Foyle. "All right, class. We're finished for the day. All back to school for the hospital bus. You jaunte first, Sgt. Logan. Remember: L-E-S. Location. Elevation. Situation . . ."

"What do you want?" Foyle growled. "A pay-off, you?"

"Be quiet. Stop making a scene. Now don't hesitate, Chief Harris. Step up and jaunte off."

"I want to talk to you."

"Certainly not. Wait your turn, Mr. Peters. Don't be in such a hurry."

"You going to report me in the hospital?"

"Naturally."

"I want to talk to you."

"No."

"They gone now, all. We got time. I'll meet you in your apartment."

"My apartment?" Robin was genuinely frightened.

"In Green Bay, Wisconsin."

"This is absurd. I've got nothing to discuss with this—"

"You got plenty, Miss Robin. You got a family to discuss."

Foyle grinned at the terror she radiated. "Meet you in your apartment," he repeated.

"You can't possibly know where it is," she faltered.

"Just told you, didn't I?"

"Y-You couldn't possibly jaunte that far. You—"

"No?" The mask grinned. "You just told me I was mal— that word. You told the truth, you. We got half an hour. Meet you there."

Robin Wednesbury's apartment was in a massive building set alone on the shore of Green Bay. The apartment house looked as though a magician had removed it from a city residential area and abandoned it amidst the Wisconsin pines. Buildings like this were a commonplace in the jaunting world. With self-contained heat and light plants, and jaunting to solve the transportation problem, single and multiple dwellings were built in desert, forest, and wilderness.

The apartment itself was a four-room flat, heavily insulated to protect neighbors from Robin's telesending. It was crammed with books, music, paintings, and prints . . . all evidence of the cultured and lonely life of this unfortunate wrong-way telepath.

Robin jaunted into the living room of the apartment a few seconds after Foyle, who was waiting for her with ferocious impatience.

"So now you know for sure," he began without preamble. He seized her arm in a painful grip. "But you ain't gonna tell nobody in the hospital about me, Miss Robin. Nobody."

"Let go of me!" Robin lashed him across the face. *"Beast! Savage! Don't you dare touch me!"*

Foyle released her and stepped back. The impact of her revulsion made him turn away angrily to conceal his face.

"So you've been malingering. You knew how to jaunte. You've been jaunting all the while you've been pretending to learn in the primer class . . . taking big jumps around the country; around the world, for all I know."

"Yeah. I got from Times Square to Columbus Circle by way of . . . most anywhere, Miss Robin."

"And that's why you're always missing. But why? Why? What are you up to?"

An expression of possessed cunning appeared on the hideous face. "I'm holed up in General Hospital, me. It's my base of operations, see? I'm settling something, Miss Robin. I got a debt to pay off, me. I had to find out where a certain ship is. Now I got to pay her back. Now I rot you, *Vorga*. I kill you, *Vorga*. I kill you filthy!"

He stopped shouting and glared at her in wild triumph. Robin backed away in alarm.

"For God's sake, what are you talking about?"

"*Vorga. Vorga*-T:1339. Ever hear of her, Miss Robin? I found out where she is from Bo'ness & Uig's ship registry. Bo'ness & Uig are out in SanFran. I went there, me, the time when you was learning us the crosstown jaunte stages. Went out to SanFran, me. Found *Vorga*, me. She's in Vancouver shipyards. She's owned by Presteign of Presteign. Heard of him, Miss Robin? Presteign's the biggest man on Terra, is all. But he won't stop me. I'll kill *Vorga* filthy. And you won't stop me neither, Miss Robin."

Foyle thrust his face close to hers. "Because I cover myself, Miss Robin. I cover every weak spot down the line. I got something on everybody who could stop me before I kill *Vorga* . . . including you, Miss Robin."

"No."

"Yeah. I found out where you live. They know up at the hospital. I come here and looked around. I read your diary, Miss Robin. You got a family on Callisto, mother and two sisters."

"For God's sake!"

"So that makes you alien-belligerent. When the war started you and all the rest was given one month to get out of the Inner Planets and go home. Any which didn't became spies by law." Foyle opened his hand. "I got you right here, girl." He clenched his hand.

"My mother and sisters have been trying to leave Callisto for a year and a half. We belong here. We—"

"Got you right here," Foyle repeated. "You know what they do to spies? They cut information out of them. They cut you apart, Miss Robin. They take you apart, piece by piece—"

Robin screamed. Foyle nodded happily and took her shaking shoulders in his hands. "I got you, is all, girl. You can't even run from me because all I got to do is tip Intelligence and where are you? There ain't nothing nobody can do to stop me; not the hospital or even Mr. Holy Mighty Presteign of Presteign."

"Get out, you filthy, hideous . . . thing. Get out!"

"You don't like my face, Miss Robin? There ain't nothing you can do about that either."

Suddenly he picked her up and carried her to a deep couch. He threw her down on the couch.

"Nothing," he repeated.

∞

Devoted to the principle of conspicuous waste, on which all society is based, Presteign of Presteign had fitted his Victorian mansion in Central Park with elevators, house phones, dumb-waiters and all the other labor-saving devices which jaunting had made obsolete. The servants in that giant gingerbread castle walked dutifully from room to room, opening and closing doors, and climbing stairs.

Presteign of Presteign arose, dressed with the aid of his valet and barber, descended to the morning room with the aid of an elevator, and breakfasted, assisted by a butler, footman, and waitresses. He left the morning room and entered his study. In an age when communication systems were virtually extinct—when it was far easier to jaunte directly to a man's office for a discussion than to telephone or telegraph—Presteign still maintained an antique telephone switchboard with an operator in his study.

"Get me Dagenham" he said.

The operator struggled and at last put a call through to Dagenham Couriers, Inc. This was a hundred million credit organization of bonded jaunters guaranteed to perform any public or confidential service for any principal. Their fee was ₵r 1 per mile. Dagenham guaranteed to get a courier around the world in eighty minutes.

Eighty seconds after Presteign's call was put through, a Dagenham courier appeared on the private jaunte stage outside Presteign's home, was identified and admitted through the jaunte-proof labyrinth behind the entrance. Like every member of the Dagenham staff, he was an M class jaunter, capable of teleporting a thousand miles a jump indefinitely, and familiar with thousands of jaunte co-ordinates. He was a senior specialist in chicanery and cajolery, trained to the incisive efficiency and boldness that characterized Dagenham Couriers and reflected the ruthlessness of its founder.

"Presteign?" he said, wasting no time on protocol.

"I want to hire Dagenham."

"Ready, Presteign."

"Not you. I want Saul Dagenham himself."

"Mr. Dagenham no longer gives personal service for less than Ɋr 100,000."

"The amount will be five times that."

"Fee or percentage?"

"Both. Quarter of a million fee, and a quarter of a million guaranteed against 10 per cent of the total amount at risk."

"Agreed. The matter?"

"PyrE."

"Spell it, please."

"The name means nothing to you?"

"No."

"Good. It will to Dagenham. PyrE. Capital P-y-r Capital E. Pronounced 'pyre' as in funeral pyre. Tell Dagenham we've located the PyrE. He's engaged to get it . . . at all costs . . . through a man named Foyle. Gulliver Foyle."

The courier produced a tiny silver pearl, a memo-bead, repeated Presteign's instructions into it, and left without another word. Presteign turned to his telephone operator. "Get me Regis Sheffield," he directed.

Ten minutes after the call went through to Regis Sheffield's law office, a young law clerk appeared on Presteign's private jaunte stage, was vetted and admitted through the maze. He was a bright young man with a scrubbed face and the expression of a delighted rabbit.

"Excuse the delay, Presteign," he said. "We got your call in Chicago and I'm still only a D class five hundred miler. Took me a while getting here."

"Is your chief trying a case in Chicago?"

"Chicago, New York, *and* Washington. He's been on the jaunte from court to court all morning. We fill in for him when he's in another court."

"I want to retain him."

"Honored, Presteign, but Mr. Sheffield's pretty busy."

"Not too busy for PyrE."

"Sorry, sir; I don't quite—"

"No, you don't, but Sheffield will. Just tell him: PyrE as in funeral pyre, and the amount of his fee."

"Which is?"

"Quarter of a million retainer and a quarter of a million guaranteed against 10 per cent of the total amount at risk."

"And what performance is required of Mr. Sheffield?"

"To prepare every known legal device for kidnaping a man and holding him against the army, the navy, and the police."

"Quite. And the man?"

"Gulliver Foyle."

The law clerk muttered quick notes into a memo-bead, thrust the bead into his ear, listened, nodded and departed. Presteign left the study and ascended the plush stairs to his daughter's suite to pay his morning respects.

In the homes of the wealthy, the rooms of the female members were blind, without windows or doors, open only to the jaunting of intimate members of the family. Thus was morality maintained and chastity defended. But since Olivia Presteign was herself blind to normal sight, she could not jaunte. Consequently her suite was entered through doors closely guarded by ancient retainers in the Presteign clan livery.

Olivia Presteign was a glorious albino. Her hair was white silk, her skin was white satin, her nails, her lips, and her eyes were coral. She was beautiful and blind in a wonderful way, for she could see in the infrared only, from 7,500 angstroms to one millimeter wavelengths. She saw heat waves, magnetic fields, radio waves, radar, sonar, and electromagnetic fields.

She was holding her Grand Levee in the drawing room of the suite. She sat in a brocaded wing chair, sipping tea, guarded by her duenna, holding court, chatting with a dozen men and women standing about the room. She looked like an exquisite statue of marble and coral, her blind eyes flashing as she saw and yet did not see.

She saw the drawing room as a pulsating flow of heat emanations ranging from hot highlights to cool shadows. She saw the dazzling magnetic patterns of clocks, phones, lights, and locks. She saw and recognized people by the characteristic heat patterns radiated by their faces and bodies. She saw, around each head, an aura of the faint electromagnetic brain pattern and, sparkling through the heat radiation of each body, the everchanging tone of muscle and nerve.

Presteign did not care for the artists, musicians, and fops Olivia kept about her, but he was pleased to see a scattering of society notables this morning. There was a Sears-Roebuck, a Gillette, young Sidney Kodak who would one day be Kodak of Kodak, a Houbigant, Buick of Buick, and R. H. Macy XVI, head of the powerful Saks-Gimbel clan.

Presteign paid his respects to his daughter and left the house. He set off for his clan headquarters at 99 Wall Street in a coach and four driven by a coachman assisted by a groom, both wearing the Presteign trademark of red, black, and blue. That black "P" on a field of scarlet and cobalt was one of the most ancient and distinguished trademarks in the social register, rivaling the "57" of the Heinz clan and the "RR" of the Rolls-Royce dynasty in antiquity.

The head of the Presteign clan was a familiar sight to New York jaunters. Iron gray, handsome, powerful, impeccably dressed and mannered in the old-fashioned style, Presteign of Presteign was the epitome of the socially elect, for he was so exalted in station that he employed coachmen, grooms, hostlers, stableboys, and horses to perform a function for him which ordinary mortals performed by jaunting.

As men climbed the social ladder, they displayed their position by their refusal to jaunte. The newly adopted into a great commercial clan rode an expensive bicycle. A rising clansman drove a small sports car. The captain of a sept was transported in a chauffeur-driven antique from the old days, a vintage Bentley or Cadillac or a towering Lagonda. An heir presumptive in direct line of succession to the clan chieftainship staffed a yacht or a plane. Presteign of Presteign, head of the clan Presteign, owned carriages, cars, yachts, planes, and trains. His position in society was so lofty that he had not jaunted in forty years. Secretly he scorned the bustling new-rich like the Dagenhams and Sheffields who still jaunted and were unashamed.

Presteign entered the crenelated keep at 99 Wall Street that was Castle Presteign. It was staffed and guarded by his famous Jaunte-Watch, all in clan livery. Presteign walked with the stately gait of a chieftain as they piped him to his office. Indeed he was grander than a chieftain, as an importunate government official awaiting audience discovered to his dismay. That unfortunate man leaped forward from the waiting crowd of petitioners as Presteign passed.

"Mr. Presteign," he began. "I'm from the Internal Revenue Department, I must see you this morn—" Presteign cut him short with an icy stare.

"There are thousands of Presteigns," he pronounced. "All are addressed as Mister. But I am Presteign of Presteign, head of house and sept, first of the family, chieftain of the clan. I am addressed as Presteign. Not 'Mister' Presteign. Presteign."

He turned and entered his office where his staff greeted him with a muted chorus: "Good morning, Presteign."

Presteign nodded, smiled his basilisk smile and seated himself behind the enthroned desk while the Jaunte-Watch skirled their pipes and ruffled their drums. Presteign signaled for the audience to begin. The Household Equerry stepped forward with a scroll. Presteign disdained memo-beads and all mechanical business devices.

"Report on Clan Presteign enterprises," the Equerry began. "Common Stock: High—201½, Low—201¼. Average quotations New York, Paris, Ceylon, Tokyo—"

Presteign waved his hand irritably. The Equerry retired to be replaced by Black Rod.

"Another Mr. Presto to be invested, Presteign."

Presteign restrained his impatience and went through the tedious ceremony of swearing in the 497th Mr. Presto in the hierarchy of Presteign Prestos who managed the shops in the Presteign retail division. Until recently the man had had a face and body of his own. Now, after years of cautious testing and careful indoctrination, he had been elected to join the Prestos.

After six months of surgery and psycho-conditioning, he was identical with the other 496 Mr. Prestos and to the idealized portrait of Mr. Presto which hung behind Presteign's dais . . . a kindly, honest man resembling Abraham Lincoln, a man who instantly inspired affection and trust. Around the world purchasers entered an identical Presteign store and were greeted by an identical manager, Mr. Presto. He was rivaled, but not surpassed, by the Kodak clan's Mr. Kwik and Montgomery Ward's Uncle Monty.

When the ceremony was completed, Presteign arose abruptly to indicate that the public investiture was ended. The office was cleared of all but the high officials. Presteign paced, obviously repressing his seething impatience. He never swore, but his restraint was more terrifying than profanity.

"Foyle," he said in a suffocated voice. "A common sailor. Dirt. Dregs. Gutter scum. But that man stands between me and—"

"If you please, Presteign," Black Rod interrupted timidly. "It's eleven o'clock Eastern time; eight o'clock Pacific time."

"What?"

"If you please, Presteign, may I remind you that there is a launching ceremony at nine, Pacific time? You are to preside at the Vancouver shipyards."

"Launching?"

"Our new freighter, the Presteign *Princess*. It will take some time to establish three dimensional broadcast contact with the shipyard so we had better—"

"I will attend in person."

"In person!" Black Rod faltered. "But we cannot possibly fly to Vancouver in an hour, Presteign. We—"

"I will jaunte," Presteign of Presteign snapped. Such was his agitation.

His appalled staff made hasty preparations. Messengers jaunted ahead to warn the Presteign offices across the country, and the private jaunte stages were cleared. Presteign was ushered to the stage within his New York office. It was a circular platform in a black-hung room without windows—a masking and conceal-ment necessary to prevent unauthorized persons from discover-ing and memorizing co-ordinates. For the same reason, all homes and offices had one-way windows and confusion labyrinths be-hind their doors.

To jaunte it was necessary (among other things) for a man to know exactly where he was and where he was going, or there was little hope of arriving anywhere alive. It was as impossible to jaunte from an undetermined starting point as it was to arrive at an unknown destination. Like shooting a pistol, one had to know where to aim and which end of the gun to hold. But a glance through a window or door might be enough to enable a man to memorize the L-E-S co-ordinates of a place.

Presteign stepped on the stage, visualized the co-ordinates of his destination in the Philadelphia office, seeing the picture clearly and the position accurately. He relaxed and energized one concentrated thrust of will and belief toward the target. He jaunted. There was a dizzy moment in which his eyes blurred. The New York stage faded out of focus; the Philadelphia stage blurred into focus. There was a sensation of falling down, and then up. He arrived. Black Rod and others of his staff arrived a re-spectful moment later.

So, in jaunts of one and two hundred miles each, Presteign crossed the continent, and arrived outside the Vancouver ship-ping yards at exactly nine o'clock in the morning, Pacific time. He had left New York at 11 A.M. He had gained two hours of daylight. This, too, was a commonplace in a jaunting world.

The square mile of unfenced concrete (what fence could bar a jaunter?) looked like a white table covered with black pennies neatly arranged in concentric circles. But on closer approach, the pennies enlarged into the hundred-foot mouths of black pits dug deep into the bowels of the earth. Each circular mouth was rimmed with concrete buildings, offices, check rooms, canteens, changing rooms.

These were the take-off and landing pits, the drydock and

construction pits of the shipyards. Spaceships, like sailing vessels, were never designed to support their own weight unaided against the drag of gravity. Normal terran gravity would crack the spine of a spaceship like an eggshell. The ships were built in deep pits, standing vertically in a network of catwalks and construction grids, braced and supported by anti-gravity screens. They took off from similar pits, riding the anti-grav beams upward like motes mounting the vertical shaft of a searchlight until at last they reached the Roche Limit and could thrust with their own jets. Landing spacecraft cut drive jets and rode the same beams downward into the pits.

As the Presteign entourage entered the Vancouver yards they could see which of the pits were in use. From some the noses and hulls of spaceships extruded, raised a quarterway or halfway above ground by the anti-grav screens as workmen in the pits below brought their aft sections to particular operational levels. Three Presteign V-class transports, *Vega*, *Vestal*, and *Vorga*, stood partially raised near the center of the yards, undergoing flaking and replating, as the heat-lightning flicker of torches around *Vorga* indicated.

At the concrete building marked: ENTRY, the Presteign entourage stopped before a sign that read:

YOU ARE ENDANGERING YOUR LIFE IF YOU ENTER THESE PREMISES UNLAWFULLY. *YOU HAVE BEEN WARNED!*

Visitor badges were distributed to the party, and even Presteign of Presteign received a badge. He dutifully pinned it on for he well knew what the result of entry without such a protective badge would be. The entourage continued, winding its way through pits until it arrived at 0-3, where the pit mouth was decorated with bunting in the Presteign colors and a small grandstand had been erected.

Presteign was welcomed and, in turn, greeted his various officials. The Presteign band struck up the clan song, bright and brassy, but one of the instruments appeared to have gone insane.

It struck a brazen note that blared louder and louder until it engulfed the entire band and the surprised exclamations. Only then did Presteign realize that it was not an instrument sounding, but the shipyard alarm.

An intruder was in the yard, someone not wearing an identification or visitor's badge. The radar field of the protection system was tripped and the alarm sounded. Through the raucous bellow of the alarm, Presteign could hear a multitude of "pops" as the yard guards jaunted from the grandstand and took positions around the square mile of concrete field. His own Jaunte-Watch closed in around him, looking wary and alert.

A voice began blaring on the P.A., co-ordinating defense. "UNKNOWN IN YARD. UNKNOWN IN YARD AT E FOR EDWARD NINE. E FOR EDWARD NINE MOVING WEST ON FOOT."

"Someone must have broken in," Black Rod shouted.

"I'm aware of that," Presteign answered calmly.

"He must be a stranger if he's not jaunting in here."

"I'm aware of that also."

"UNKNOWN APPROACHING D FOR DAVID FIVE. D FOR DAVID FIVE. STILL ON FOOT. D FOR DAVID FIVE ALERT."

"What in God's name is he up to?" Black Rod exclaimed.

"You are aware of my rule, sir," Presteign said coldly. "No associate of the Presteign clan may take the name of the Divinity in vain. You forget yourself."

"UNKNOWN NOW APPROACHING C FOR CHARLEY FIVE. NOW APPROACHING C FOR CHARLEY FIVE."

Black Rod touched Presteign's arm. "He's coming this way, Presteign. Will you take cover, please?"

"I will not."

"Presteign, there have been assassination attempts before. Three of them. If—"

"How do I get to the top of this stand?"

"Presteign!"

"Help me up."

Aided by Black Rod, still protesting hysterically, Presteign climbed to the top of the grandstand to watch the power of the

Presteign clan in action against danger. Below he could see workmen in white jumpers swarming out of the pits to watch the excitement. Guards were appearing as they jaunted from distant sectors toward the focal point of the action.

"UNKNOWN MOVING SOUTH TOWARD B FOR BAKER THREE. B FOR BAKER THREE."

Presteign watched the B-3 pit. A figure appeared, dashing swiftly toward the pit, veering, dodging, bulling forward. It was a giant man in hospital blues with a wild thatch of black hair and a distorted face that appeared, in the distance, to be painted in livid colors. His clothes were flickering like heat lightning as the protective induction field of the defense system seared him.

"B FOR BAKER THREE ALERT. B FOR BAKER THREE CLOSE IN."

There were shouts and a distant rattle of shots, the pneumatic whine of scope guns. Half a dozen workmen in white leaped for the intruder. He scattered them like ninepins and drove on and on toward B-3 where the nose of *Vorga* showed. He was a lightning bolt driving through workmen and guards, pivoting, bludgeoning, boring forward implacably.

Suddenly he stopped, reached inside his flaming jacket and withdrew a black cannister. With the convulsive gesture of an animal writhing in death throes, he bit the end of the cannister and hurled it, straight and true on a high arc toward *Vorga*. The next instant he was struck down.

"EXPLOSIVE. TAKE COVER. EXPLOSIVE. TAKE COVER. EXPLOSIVE. TAKE COVER!"

"Presteign!" Black Rod squawked.

Presteign shook him off and watched the cannister curve up and then down toward the nose of *Vorga*, spinning and glinting in the cold sunlight. At the edge of the pit it was caught by the antigrav beam and flicked upwards as by a giant invisible thumbnail. Up and up and up it whirled, one hundred, five hundred, a thousand feet. Then there was a blinding flash, and an instant later a titanic clap of thunder that smote ears and jarred teeth and bone.

Presteign picked himself up and descended the grandstand to

the launching podium. He placed his finger on the launching button of the Presteign *Princess*.

"Bring me that man, if he's still alive," he said to Black Rod. He pressed the button. "I christen thee . . . the Presteign *Power*," he called in triumph.

CHAPTER
FOUR

The star chamber in Castle Presteign was an oval room with ivory panels picked out with gold, high mirrors, and stained glass windows. It contained a gold organ with robot organist by Tiffany, a gold-tooled library with android librarian on library ladder, a Louis Quinze desk with android secretary before a manual memo-bead recorder, an American bar with robot bartender. Presteign would have preferred human servants, but androids and robots kept secrets.

"Be seated, Captain Yeovil," he said courteously. "This is Mr. Regis Sheffield, representing me in this matter. That young man is Mr. Sheffield's assistant."

"Bunny's my portable law library," Sheffield grunted.

Presteign touched a control. The still life in the star chamber came alive. The organist played, the librarian sorted books, the secretary typed, the bartender shook drinks. It was spectacular; and the impact, carefully calculated by industrial psychometrists, established control for Presteign and put visitors at a disadvantage.

"You spoke of a man named Foyle, Captain Yeovil?" Presteign prompted.

Captain Peter Y'ang-Yeovil of Central Intelligence was a lineal descendant of the learned Mencius and belonged to the Intelligence Tong of the Inner Planets Armed Forces. For two hundred years the IPAF had entrusted its intelligence work to the Chinese who, with a five thousand-year history of cultivated subtlety behind them, had achieved wonders. Captain Y'ang-Yeovil was a member of the dreaded Society of Paper Men, an adept of the Tientsin Image Makers, a Master of Superstition, and fluent in the Secret Speech. He did not look Chinese.

Y'ang-Yeovil hesitated, fully aware of the psychological pressures operating against him. He examined Presteign's ascetic, basilisk face; Sheffield's blunt, aggressive expression; and the eager young man named Bunny whose rabbit features had an unmistakable Oriental cast. It was necessary for Yeovil to re-establish control or effect a compromise.

He opened with a flanking movement. "Are we related anywhere within fifteen degrees of consanguinity?" he asked Bunny in the Mandarin dialect. "I am of the house of the learned Meng-Tse whom the barbarians call Mencius."

"Then we are hereditary enemies," Bunny answered in faltering Mandarin. "For the formidable ancestor of my line was deposed as governor of Shan-tung in 342 B.C. by the earth pig Meng-Tse."

"With all courtesy I shave your ill-formed eyebrows," Y'ang-Yeovil said.

"Most respectfully I singe your snaggle teeth." Bunny laughed.

"Come, sirs," Presteign protested.

"We are reaffirming a three-thousand-year blood feud," Y'ang-Yeovil explained to Presteign, who looked sufficiently unsettled by the conversation and the laughter which he did not understand. He tried a direct thrust. "When will you be finished with Foyle?" he asked.

"What Foyle?" Sheffield cut in.

"What Foyle have you got?"

"There are thirteen of that name associated with the clan Presteign."

"An interesting number. Did you know I was a Master of Superstition? Some day I must show you the Mirror-And-Listen Mystery. I refer to the Foyle involved in a reported attempt on Mr. Presteign's life this morning."

"Presteign," Presteign corrected. "I am not 'Mister.' I am Presteign of Presteign."

"Three attempts have been made on Presteign's life," Sheffield said. "You'll have to be more specific."

"Three this morning? Presteign must have been busy." Y'ang-Yeovil sighed. Sheffield was proving himself a resolute opponent. The Intelligence man tried another diversion. "I do wish our Mr. Presto had been more specific."

"*Your* Mr. Presto!" Presteign exclaimed.

"Oh yes. Didn't you know one of your five hundred Prestos was an agent of ours? That's odd. We took it for granted you'd find out and went ahead with a confusion operation."

Presteign looked appalled. Y'ang-Yeovil crossed his legs and continued to chat breezily. "That's the basic weakness in routine intelligence procedure; you start finessing before finesse is required."

"He's bluffing," Presteign burst out. "None of our Prestos could possibly have any knowledge of Gulliver Foyle."

"Thank you." Y'ang-Yeovil smiled. "That's the Foyle I want. When can you let us have him?"

Sheffield scowled at Presteign and then turned on Y'ang-Yeovil. "Who's 'us'?" he demanded.

"Central Intelligence."

"Why do you want him?"

"Do you make love to a woman before or after you take your clothes off?"

"That's a damned impertinent question to ask."

"And so was yours. When can you let us have Foyle?"

"When you show cause."

"To whom?"

"To me." Sheffield hammered a heavy forefinger against his palm. "This is a civilian matter concerning civilians. Unless war material, war personnel, or the strategy and tactics of a war-in-being are involved, civilian jurisdiction shall always prevail."

"303 Terran Appeals 191," murmured Bunny.

"The *Nomad* was carrying war material."

"The *Nomad* was transporting platinum bullion to Mars Bank," Presteign snapped. "If money is a—"

"*I* am leading this discussion," Sheffield interrupted. He swung around on Y'ang-Yeovil. "Name the war material."

This blunt challenge knocked Y'ang-Yeovil off balance. He knew that the crux of the *Nomad* situation was the presence on board the ship of 20 pounds of PyrE, the total world supply, which was probably irreplaceable now that its discoverer had disappeared. He knew that Sheffield knew that they both knew this. He had assumed that Sheffield would prefer to keep PyrE unnamed. And yet, here was the challenge to name the unnamable.

He attempted to meet bluntness with bluntness. "All right, gentlemen, I'll name it now. The *Nomad* was transporting twenty pounds of a substance called PyrE."

Presteign started; Sheffield silenced him. "What's PyrE?"

"According to our reports—"

"From Presteign's Mr. Presto?"

"Oh, that was bluff," Y'ang-Yeovil laughed, and momentarily regained control. "According to Intelligence, PyrE was developed for Presteign by a man who subsequently disappeared. PyrE is a Misch Metal, a pyrophore. That's all we know for a fact. But we've had vague reports about it . . . Unbelievable reports from reputable agents. If a fraction of our inferences are correct, PyrE could make the difference between a victory and a defeat."

"Nonsense. No war material has ever made that much difference."

"No? I cite the fission bomb of 1945. I cite the Null-G antigravity installations of 2022. Talley's All-Field Radar Trip Screen of 2194. Material can often make the difference, especially when there's the chance of the enemy getting it first."

"There's no such chance now."

"Thank you for admitting the importance of PyrE."

"I admit nothing; I deny everything."

"Central Intelligence is prepared to offer an exchange. A man for a man. The inventor of PyrE for Gully Foyle."

"You've got him?" Sheffield demanded. "Then why badger us for Foyle?"

"Because we've got a corpse!" Y'ang-Yeovil flared. "The Outer Satellites command had him on Lassell for six months trying to carve information out of him. We pulled him out with a raid at a cost of 79 per cent casualties. We rescued a corpse. We still don't know if the Outer Satellites were having a cynical laugh at our expense letting us recapture a body. We still don't know how much they ripped out of him."

Presteign sat bolt upright at this. His merciless fingers tapped slowly and sharply.

"Damn it," Y'ang-Yeovil stormed. "Can't you recognize a crisis, Sheffield? We're on a tightrope. What the devil are you doing backing Presteign in this shabby deal? You're the leader of the Liberal party . . . Terra's archpatriot. You're Presteign's political archenemy. Sell him out, you fool, before he sells us all out."

"Captain Yeovil," Presteign broke in with icy venom. "These expressions cannot be countenanced."

"We want and need PyrE," Y'ang-Yeovil continued. "We'll have to investigate that twenty pounds of PyrE, rediscover the synthesis, learn to apply it to the war effort . . . and all this before the O.S. beats us to the punch, if they haven't already. But Presteign refuses to co-operate. Why? Because he's opposed to the party in power. He wants no military victories for the Liberals. He'd rather we lost the war for the sake of politics because rich men like Presteign never lose. Come to your senses, Sheffield. You've been retained by a traitor. What in God's name are you trying to do?"

Before Sheffield could answer, there was a discreet tap on the door of the Star Chamber and Saul Dagenham was ushered in. Time was when Dagenham was one of the Inner Planets' research wizards, a physicist with inspired intuition, total recall, and a sixth-order computer for a brain. But there was an accident at Tycho Sands, and the fission blast that should have killed him did not. Instead it turned him dangerously radioactive; it turned him "hot"; it transformed him into a twenty-fifth century "Typhoid Mary."

He was paid ₡r 25,000 a year by the Inner Planets government to take precautions which they trusted him to carry out. He avoided physical contact with any person for more than five minutes per day. He could not occupy any room other than his own for more than thirty minutes a day. Commanded and paid by the IP to isolate himself, Dagenham had abandoned research and built the colossus of Dagenham Couriers, Inc.

When Y'ang-Yeovil saw the short blond cadaver with leaden skin and death's-head smile enter the Star Chamber, he knew he was assured of defeat in this encounter. He was no match for the three men together. He arose at once.

"I'm getting an Admiralty order for Foyle," he said. "As far as Intelligence is concerned, all negotiations are ended. From now on it's war."

"Captain Yeovil is leaving," Presteign called to the Jaunte-Watch officer who had guided Dagenham in. "Please see him out through the maze."

Y'ang-Yeovil waited until the officer stepped alongside him and bowed. Then, as the man courteously motioned to the door, Y'ang-Yeovil looked directly at Presteign, smiled ironically, and disappeared with a faint Pop!

"Presteign!" Bunny exclaimed. "He jaunted. This room isn't blind to him. He—"

"Evidently," Presteign said icily. "Inform the Master of the Household," he instructed the amazed Watch officer. "The co-ordinates of the Star Chamber are no longer secret. They must be changed within twenty-four hours. And now, Mr. Dagenham . . ."

"One minute," Dagenham said. "There's that Admiralty order."

Without apology or explanation he disappeared too. Presteign raised his eyebrows. "Another party to the Star Chamber secret," he murmured. "But at least he had the tact to conceal his knowledge until the secret was out."

Dagenham reappeared. "No point wasting time going through the motions of the maze," he said. "I've given orders in Washington. They'll hold Yeovil up; two hours guaranteed, three hours probably, four hours possible."

"How will they hold him up?" Bunny asked.

Dagenham gave him his deadly smile. "Standard FFCC Operation of Dagenham Couriers. Fun, fantasy, confusion, catastrophe. . . . We'll need all four hours. Damn! I've disrupted your dolls, Presteign." The robots were suddenly capering in lunatic fashion as Dagenham's hard radiation penetrated their electronic systems. "No matter, I'll be on my way."

"Foyle?" Presteign asked.

"Nothing yet." Dagenham grinned his death's-head smile. "He's really unique. I've tried all the standard drugs and routines on him . . . Nothing. Outside, he's just an ordinary spaceman . . . if you forget the tattoo on his face . . . but inside he's got steel guts. Something's got hold of him and he won't give."

"What's got hold of him?" Sheffield asked.

"I hope to find out."

"How?"

"Don't ask; you'd be an accessory. Have you got a ship ready, Presteign?"

Presteign nodded.

"I'm not guaranteeing there'll be any *Nomad* for us to find, but we'll have to get a jump on the navy if there is. Law ready, Sheffield?"

"Ready. I'm hoping we won't have to use it."

"I'm hoping too; but again, I'm not guaranteeing. All right. Stand by for instructions. I'm on my way to crack Foyle."

"Where have you got him?"

Dagenham shook his head. "This room isn't secure." He disappeared.

He jaunted Cincinnati-New Orleans-Monterey to Mexico City, where he appeared in the Psychiatry Wing of the giant hospital of the Combined Terran Universities. Wing was hardly an adequate name for this section which occupied an entire city in the metropolis which was the hospital. Dagenham jaunted up to the 43rd floor of the Therapy Division and looked into the isolated tank where Foyle floated, unconscious. He glanced at the distinguished bearded gentlemen in attendance.

"Hello, Fritz."

"Hello, Saul."

"Hell of a thing, the Head of Psychiatry minding a patient for me."

"I think we owe you favors, Saul."

"You still brooding about Tycho Sands, Fritz? I'm not. Am I lousing your wing with radiation?"

"I've had everything shielded."

"Ready for the dirty work?"

"I wish I knew what you were after."

"Information."

"And you have to turn my therapy department into an inquisition to get it?"

"That was the idea."

"Why not use ordinary drugs?"

"Tried them already. No good. He's not an ordinary man."

"You know this is illegal."

"I know. Changed your mind? Want to back out? I can duplicate your equipment for a quarter of a million."

"No, Saul. We'll always owe you favors."

"Then let's go. Nightmare Theater first."

They trundled the tank down a corridor and into a hundred feet square padded room. It was one of therapy's by-passed experiments. Nightmare Theater had been an early attempt to shock schizophrenics back into the objective world by rendering the phantasy world into which they were withdrawing uninhabitable. But the shattering and laceration of patients' emotions had proved to be too cruel and dubious a treatment.

For Dagenham's sake, the head of Psychiatry had dusted off the 3D visual projectors and reconnected all sensory projectors. They decanted Foyle from his tank, gave him a reviving shot and left him in the middle of the floor. They removed the tank, turned off the lights and entered the concealed control booth. There, they turned on the projectors.

Every child in the world imagines that its phantasy world is unique to itself. Psychiatry knows that the joys and terrors of private phantasies are a common heritage shared by all mankind. Fears, guilts, terrors, and shames could be interchanged, from one man to the next, and none would notice the difference. The therapy department at Combined Hospital had recorded thousands of emotional tapes and boiled them down to one all-inclusive all-terrifying performance in Nightmare Theater.

Foyle awoke, panting and sweating, and never knew that he had awakened. He was in the clutch of the serpent-haired bloody-eyed Eumenides. He was pursued, entrapped, precipitated from heights, burned, flayed, bowstringed, vermin-covered, devoured. He screamed. He ran. The radar Hobble-Field in the Theater clogged his steps and turned them into the ghastly slow motion of dream-running. And through the cacophony of grinding, shrieking, moaning, pursuing that assailed his ears, muttered the thread of a persistent voice.

"Where is *Nomad* where is *Nomad* where is *Nomad* where is *Nomad* where is *Nomad?*"

"*Vorga*," Foyle croaked. "*Vorga.*"

He had been inoculated by his own fixation. His own nightmare had rendered him immune.

"Where is *Nomad*? where have you left *Nomad*? what happened to *Nomad*? where is *Nomad*?"

"*Vorga*," Foyle shouted. "*Vorga. Vorga. Vorga.*"

In the control booth, Dagenham swore. The head of psychiatry, monitoring the projectors, glanced at the clock. "One minute and forty-five seconds, Saul. He can't stand much more."

"He's got to break. Give him the final effect."

They buried Foyle alive, slowly, inexorably, hideously. He was carried down into black depths and enclosed in stinking slime that cut off light and air. He slowly suffocated while a distant voice boomed: "WHERE IS *NOMAD*? WHERE HAVE YOU LEFT *NOMAD*? YOU CAN ESCAPE IF YOU FIND *NOMAD*. WHERE IS *NOMAD*?"

But Foyle was back aboard *Nomad* in his lightless, airless coffin, floating comfortably between deck and roof. He curled into a tight fetal ball and prepared to sleep. He was content. He would escape. He would find *Vorga*.

"Impervious bastard!" Dagenham swore. "Has anyone ever resisted Nightmare Theater before, Fritz?"

"Not many. You're right. That's an uncommon man, Saul."

"He's got to be ripped open. All right, to hell with any more of this. We'll try the Megal Mood next. Are the actors ready?"

"All ready."

"Then let's go."

There are six directions in which delusions of grandeur can run. The Megal (short for Megalomania) Mood was therapy's dramatic diagnosis technique for establishing and plotting the particular course of megalomania.

Foyle awoke in a luxurious four-poster bed. He was in a bedroom hung with brocade, papered in velvet. He glanced around curiously. Soft sunlight filtered through latticed windows. Across the room a valet was quietly laying out clothes.

"Hey . . ." Foyle grunted.

The valet turned. "Good morning, Mr. Fourmyle," he murmured.

"What?"

"It's a lovely morning, sir. I've laid out the brown twill and the cordovan pumps, sir."

"What's a matter, you?"

"I've—" The valet gazed at Foyle curiously. "Is anything wrong, Mr. Fourmyle?"

"What you call me, man?"

"By your name, sir."

"My name is . . . Fourmyle?" Foyle struggled up in the bed. "No, it's not. It's Foyle. Gully Foyle, that's my name, me."

The valet bit his lip. "One moment, sir . . ." He stepped outside and called. Then he murmured. A lovely girl in white came running into the bedroom and sat down on the edge of the bed. She took Foyle's hands and gazed into his eyes. Her face was distressed.

"Darling, darling, darling," she whispered. "You aren't going to start all that again, are you? The doctor swore you were over it."

"Start what again?"

"All that Gulliver Foyle nonsense about your being a common sailor and—"

"I am Gully Foyle. That's my name, Gully Foyle."

"Sweetheart, you're not. That's just a delusion you've had for weeks. You've been overworking and drinking too much."

"Been Gully Foyle all my life, me."

"Yes, I know darling. That's the way it's seemed to you. But you're not. You're Geoffrey Fourmyle. *The* Geoffrey Fourmyle. You're— Oh, what's the sense telling you? Get dressed, my love. You've got to come downstairs. Your office has been frantic."

Foyle permitted the valet to dress him and went downstairs in a daze. The lovely girl, who evidently adored him, conducted him through a giant studio littered with drawing tables, easels, and half-finished canvases. She took him into a vast hall filled with desks, filing cabinets, stock tickers, clerks, secretaries, office personnel. They entered a lofty laboratory cluttered with glass and chrome. Burners flickered and hissed; bright colored liquids bubbled and churned; there was a pleasant odor of interesting chemicals and odd experiments.

"What's all this?" Foyle asked.

The girl seated Foyle in a plush armchair alongside a giant desk littered with interesting papers scribbled with fascinating symbols. On some Foyle saw the name: Geoffrey Fourmyle, scrawled in an imposing, authoritative signature.

"There's some crazy kind of mistake, is all," Foyle began.

The girl silenced him. "Here's Doctor Regan. He'll explain."

An impressive gentleman with a crisp, comforting manner, came to Foyle, touched his pulse, inspected his eyes, and nodded in satisfaction.

"Good," he said. "Excellent. You are close to complete recovery, Mr. Fourmyle. Now you will listen to me for a moment, eh?"

Foyle nodded.

"You remember nothing of the past. You have only a false memory. You were overworked. You are an important man and there were too many demands on you. You started to drink heavily a month ago— No, no, denial is useless. You drank. You lost yourself."

"I—"

"You became convinced you were not the famous Jeff Fourmyle. An infantile attempt to escape responsibility. You imagined you were a common spaceman named Foyle. Gulliver Foyle, yes? With an odd number . . ."

"Gully Foyle. AS:128/127:006. But that's me. That's—"

"It is not you. *This* is you." Dr. Regan waved at the interesting offices they could see through the transparent glass wall.

"You can only recapture the true memory if you discharge the old. All this glorious reality is yours, if we can help you discard the dream of the spaceman." Dr. Regan leaned forward, his polished spectacles glittering hypnotically. "Reconstruct this false memory of yours in detail, and I will tear it down. Where do you imagine you left the spaceship *Nomad?* How did you escape? Where do you imagine the *Nomad* is now?"

Foyle wavered before the romantic glamour of the scene which seemed to be just within his grasp.

"It seems to me I left *Nomad* out in—" He stopped short.

A devil-face peered at him from the highlights reflected in Dr. Regan's spectacles . . . a hideous tiger mask with NÓMAD blazoned across the distorted brow. Foyle stood up.

"Liars!" he growled. "It's real, me. This here is phoney. What happened to me is real. I'm real, me."

Saul Dagenham walked into the laboratory. "All right," he called. "Strike. It's a washout."

The bustling scene in laboratory, office, and studio ended. The actors quietly disappeared without another glance at Foyle. Dagenham gave Foyle his deadly smile. "Tough, aren't you? You're really unique. My name is Saul Dagenham. We've got five minutes for a talk. Come into the garden."

The Sedative Garden atop the Therapy Building was a triumph of therapeutic planning. Every perspective, every color, every contour had been designed to placate hostility, soothe resistance, melt anger, evaporate hysteria, absorb melancholia and depression.

"Sit down," Dagenham said, pointing to a bench alongside a pool in which crystal waters tinkled. "Don't try to jaunte—you're drugged. I'll have to walk around a bit. Can't come too close to you. I'm 'hot.' D'you know what that means?"

Foyle shook his head sullenly. Dagenham cupped both hands around the flaming blossom of an orchid and held them there for a moment. "Watch that flower," he said. "You'll see."

He paced up a path and turned suddenly. "You're right, of course. Everything that happened to you is real. . . . Only what did happen?"

"Go to hell," Foyle growled.

"You know, Foyle, I admire you."

"Go to hell."

"In your own primitive way you've got ingenuity and guts. You're Cro-Magnon, Foyle. I've been checking on you. That bomb you threw in the Presteign shipyards was lovely, and you nearly wrecked General Hospital getting the money and material together." Dagenham counted fingers. "You looted lockers, stole from the blind ward, stole drugs from the pharmacy, stole apparatus from the lab stockrooms."

"Go to hell, you."

"But what have you got against Presteign? Why'd you try to blow up his shipyard? They tell me you broke in and went tearing through the pits like a wild man. What were you trying to do, Foyle?"

"Go to hell."

Dagenham smiled. "If we're going to chat," he said. "You'll have to hold up your end. Your conversation's getting monotonous. What happened to *Nomad?*"

"I don't know about *Nomad*, nothing."

"The ship was last reported over seven months ago. Then . . . *spurlos versenkt*. Are you the sole survivor? And what have you been doing all this time? Having your face decorated?"

"I don't know about *Nomad*, nothing."

"No, no, Foyle, that won't do. You show up with *Nomad* tattooed across your face. Fresh tattooed. Intelligence checks and finds you were aboard *Nomad* when she sailed. Foyle, Gulliver: AS:128/127:006, Mechanic's Mate, 3rd Class. As if all this isn't enough to throw Intelligence into a tizzy, you come back in a private launch that's been missing fifty years. Man, you're cooking in the reactor. Intelligence wants the answers to all these questions. And you ought to know how Central Intelligence butchers its answers out of people."

Foyle started. Dagenham nodded as he saw his point sink home. "Which is why I think you'll listen to reason. We want information, Foyle. I tried to trick it out of you; admitted. I failed because you're too tough; admitted. Now I'm offering an honest deal. We'll protect you if you'll co-operate. If you don't, you'll spend five years in an Intelligence lab having information chopped out of you."

It was not the prospect of the butchery that frightened Foyle, but the thought of the loss of freedom. A man had to be free to avenge himself, to raise money and find *Vorga* again, to rip and tear and gut *Vorga*.

"What kind of deal?" he asked.

"Tell us what happened to *Nomad* and where you left her."

"Why, man?"

"Why? Because of the salvage, man."

"There ain't nothing to salvage. She's a wreck, is all."

"Even a wreck's salvagable."

"You mean you'd jet out a million miles to pick up pieces? Don't joker me, man."

"All right," Dagenham said in exasperation. "There's the cargo."

"She was split wide open. No cargo left."

"It was a cargo you don't know about," Dagenham said confidentially. "*Nomad* was transporting platinum bullion to Mars Bank. Every so often, banks have to adjust accounts. Normally, enough trade goes on between planets so that accounts can be balanced on paper. The war's disrupted normal trade, and Mars Bank found that Presteign owed them twenty odd million credits without any way of getting the money short of actual delivery. Presteign was delivering the money in bar platinum aboard the *Nomad*. It was locked in the purser's safe."

"Twenty million," Foyle whispered.

"Give or take a few thousand. The ship was insured, but that just means that the underwriters, Bo'ness and Uig, get the salvage rights and they're even tougher than Presteign. However, there'll be a reward for you. Say . . . twenty thousand credits."

"Twenty million," Foyle whispered again.

"We're assuming that an O.S. raider caught up with *Nomad* somewhere on course and let her have it. They couldn't have boarded and looted or you wouldn't have been left alive. This means that the purser's safe is still—Are you listening, Foyle?"

But Foyle was not listening. He was seeing twenty million . . . not twenty thousand . . . twenty million in platinum bullion as a broad highway to *Vorga*. No more petty thefts from lockers and labs; twenty million for the taking and the razing of *Vorga*.

"Foyle!"

Foyle awoke. He looked at Dagenham. "I don't know about *Nomad*, nothing," he said.

"What the hell's got into you now? Why're you dummying up again?"

"I don't know about *Nomad*, nothing."

"I'm offering a fair reward. A spaceman can go on a hell of a tear with twenty thousand credits . . . a one-year tear. What more do you want?"

"I don't know about *Nomad*, nothing."

"It's us or Intelligence, Foyle."

"You ain't so anxious for them to get me, or you wouldn't be flipping through all this. But it ain't no use, anyway. I don't know about *Nomad*, nothing."

"You son of a ———" Dagenham tried to repress his anger. He had revealed just a little too much to this cunning, primitive creature. "You're right," he said. "We're not anxious for Intelligence to get you. But we've made our own preparations." His voice hardened. "You think you can dummy up and stand us off. You think you can leave us to whistle for *Nomad*. You've even got an idea that you can beat us to the salvage."

"No," Foyle said.

"Now listen to this. We've got a lawyer waiting in New York. He's got a criminal prosecution for piracy pending against you; piracy in space, murder, and looting. We're going to throw the book at you. Presteign will get a conviction in twenty-four hours. If you've got a criminal record of any kind, that means a lobotomy. They'll open up the top of your skull and burn out half your brain to stop you from ever jaunting again."

Dagenham stopped and looked hard at Foyle. When Foyle shook his head, Dagenham continued.

"If you haven't got a record, they'll hand you ten years of what is laughingly known as medical treatment. We don't punish criminals in our enlightened age, we cure 'em; and the cure is worse than punishment. They'll stash you in a black hole in one of the cave hospitals. You'll be kept in permanent darkness and solitary confinement so you can't jaunte out. They'll go through the motions of giving you shots and therapy, but you'll be rotting in the dark. You'll stay there and rot until you decide to talk. We'll keep you there forever. So make up your mind."

"I don't know nothing about *Nomad*. Nothing!" Foyle said.

"All right," Dagenham spat. Suddenly he pointed to the orchid blossom he had enclosed with his hands. It was blighted and rotting. "That's what's going to happen to you."

CHAPTER
FIVE

South of Saint-Girons near the Spanish-French border is the deepest abyss in France, the Gouffre Martel. Its caverns twist for miles under the Pyrenees. It is the most formidable cavern hospital on Terra. No patient has ever jaunted out of its pitch darkness. No patient has ever succeeded in getting his bearings and learning the jaunte co-ordinates of the black hospital depths.

Short of prefrontal lobotomy, there are only three ways to

stop a man from jaunting: a blow on the head producing concussion, sedation which prevents concentration, and concealment of jaunte co-ordinates. Of the three, the jaunting age considered concealment the most practical.

The cells that line the winding passages of Gouffre Martel are cut out of living rock. They are never illuminated. The passages are never illuminated. Infrared lamps flood the darkness. It is black light visible only to guards and attendants wearing snooper goggles with specially treated lenses. For the patients there is only the black silence of Gouffre Martel broken by the distant rush of underground waters.

For Foyle there was only the silence, the rushing, and the hospital routine. At eight o'clock (or it may have been any hour in this timeless abyss) he was awakened by a bell. He arose and received his morning meal, slotted into the cell by pneumatic tube. It had to be eaten at once, for the china surrogate of cups and plates was timed to dissolve in fifteen minutes. At eight-thirty the cell door opened and Foyle and hundreds of others shuffled blindly through the twisting corridors to Sanitation.

Here, still in darkness, they were processed like beef in a slaughter house: cleansed, shaved, irradiated, disinfected, dosed, and inoculated. Their paper uniforms were removed and sent back to the shops to be pulped. New uniforms were issued. Then they shuffled back to their cells which had been automatically scrubbed out while they were in Sanitation. In his cell, Foyle listened to interminable therapeutic talks, lectures, moral and ethical guidance for the rest of the morning. Then there was silence again, and nothing but the rush of distant water and the quiet steps of goggled guards in the corridors.

In the afternoon came occupational therapy. The TV screen in each cell illuminated and the patient thrust his hands into the shadow frame of the screen. He saw three-dimensionally and he felt the broadcast objects and tools. He cut hospital uniforms, sewed them, manufactured kitchen utensils, and prepared foods. Although actually he touched nothing, his motions were

transmitted to the shops where the work was accomplished by re-
mote control. After one short hour of this relief came the darkness and silence again.

But every so often . . . once or twice a week (or perhaps once
or twice a year) came the muffled thud of a distant explosion. The
concussions were startling enough to distract Foyle from the furnace of vengeance that he stoked all through the silences. He
whispered questions to the invisible figures around him in Sanitation.

"What's them explosions?"

"Explosions?"

"Blow-ups. Hear 'em a long way off, me."

"Them's Blue Jauntes."

"What?"

"Blue Jauntes. Every sometime a guy gets fed up with old
Jeffrey. Can't take it no more, him. Jauntes into the wild blue
yonder."

"Jesus."

"Yep. Don't know where they are, them. Don't know where
they're going. Blue Jaunte into the dark . . . and we hear 'em ex-
ploding in the mountains. Boom! Blue Jaunte."

He was appalled, but he could understand. The darkness, the
silence, the monotony destroyed sense and brought on desperation. The loneliness was intolerable. The patients buried in Gouffre Martel prison hospital looked forward eagerly to the morning
Sanitation period for a chance to whisper a word and hear a
word. But these fragments were not enough, and desperation
came. Then there would be another distant explosion.

Sometimes the suffering men would turn on each other and
then a savage fight would break out in Sanitation. These were instantly broken up by the goggled guards, and the morning lecture
would switch on the Moral Fiber record preaching the Virtue of
Patience.

Foyle learned the records by heart, every word, every click
and crack in the tapes. He learned to loathe the voices of the lec-

turers: the Understanding Baritone, the Cheerful Tenor, the Man-to-Man Bass. He learned to deafen himself to the therapeutic monotony and perform his occupational therapy mechanically, but he was without resources to withstand the endless solitary hours. Fury was not enough.

He lost count of the days, of meals, of sermons. He no longer whispered in Sanitation. His mind came adrift and he began to wander. He imagined he was back aboard *Nomad*, reliving his fight for survival. Then he lost even this feeble grasp on illusion and began to sink deeper and deeper into the pit of catatonia: of womb silence, womb darkness, and womb sleep.

There were fleeting dreams. An angel hummed to him once. Another time she sang quietly. Thrice he heard her speak: "Oh God . . ." and "God damn!" and "Oh . . ." in a heart-rending descending note.

He sank into his abyss, listening to her.

"There is a way out," his angel murmured in his ear, sweetly, comforting. Her voice was soft and warm, yet it burned with anger. It was the voice of a furious angel. "There is a way out."

It whispered in his ear from nowhere, and suddenly, with the logic of desperation, it came to him that there was a way out of Gouffre Martel. He had been a fool not to see it before.

"Yes," he croaked. "There's a way out."

There was a soft gasp, then a soft question: "Who's there?"

"Me, is all," Foyle said. "You know me."

"Where are you?"

"Here. Where I always been, me."

"But there's no one. I'm alone."

"Got to thank you for helping me."

"Hearing voices is bad," the furious angel murmured. "The first step off the deep end. I've got to stop."

"You showed me the way out. Blue Jaunte."

"Blue Jaunte! My God, this must be real. You're talking the gutter lingo. You must be real. Who are you?"

"Gully Foyle."

"But you're not in my cell. You're not even near. Men are in the north quadrant of Gouffre Martel. Women are in the south. I'm South-900. Where are you?"

"North-111."

"You're a quarter of a mile away. How can we— Of course! It's the Whisper Line. I always thought that was a legend, but it's true. It's working now."

"Here I go, me," Foyle whispered. "Blue Jaunte."

"Foyle, listen to me. Forget the Blue Jaunte. Don't throw this away. It's a miracle."

"What's a miracle?"

"There's an acoustical freak in Gouffre Martel . . . they happen in underground caves . . . a freak of echoes, passages, and whispering galleries. Old-timers call it the Whisper Line. I never believed them. No one ever did, but it's true. We're talking to each other over the Whisper Line. No one can hear us but us. We can talk, Foyle. We can plan. Maybe we can escape."

∞

Her name was Jisbella McQueen. She was hot-tempered, independent, intelligent, and she was serving five years of cure in Gouffre Martel for larceny. Jisbella gave Foyle a cheerfully furious account of her revolt against society.

"You don't know what jaunting's done to women, Gully. It's locked us up, sent us back to the seraglio."

"What's seraglio, girl?"

"A harem. A place where women are kept on ice. After a thousand years of civilization (it says here) we're still property. Jaunting's such a danger to our virtue, our value, our mint condition, that we're locked up like gold plate in a safe. There's nothing for us to do . . . nothing respectable. No jobs. No careers. There's no getting out, Gully, unless you bust out and smash all the rules."

"Did you have to, Jiz?"

"I had to be independent, Gully. I had to live my own life, and that's the only way society would let me. So I ran away from home and turned crook." And Jiz went on to describe the lurid details of her revolt: the Temper Racket, the Cataract Racket, the Honeymoon and Obituary Robs, the Badger Jaunte, and the Glim-Drop.

Foyle told her about *Nomad* and *Vorga*, his hatred and his plans. He did not tell Jisbella about his face or the twenty millions in platinum bullion waiting out in the asteroids.

"What happened to *Nomad?*" Jisbella asked. "Was it like that man, Dagenham, said? Was she blasted by an O.S. raider?"

"I don't know, me. Can't remember, girl."

"The blast probably wiped out your memory. Shock. And being marooned for six months didn't help. Did you notice anything worth salvaging from *Nomad?*"

"No."

"Did Dagenham mention anything?"

"No," Foyle lied.

"Then he must have another reason for hounding you into Gouffre Martel. There must be something else he wants from *Nomad*."

"Yeah, Jiz."

"But you were a fool trying to blow up *Vorga* like that. You're like a wild beast trying to punish the trap that injured it. Steel isn't alive. It doesn't think. You can't punish *Vorga*."

"Don't know what you mean, girl. *Vorga* passed me by."

"You punish the brain, Gully. The brain that sets the trap. Find out who was aboard *Vorga*. Find out who gave the order to pass you by. Punish him."

"Yeah. How?"

"Learn to think, Gully. The head that could figure out how to get *Nomad* under way and how to put a bomb together ought to be able to figure that out. But no more bombs; brains instead. Locate a member of *Vorga*'s crew. He'll tell you who was aboard. Track them down. Find out who gave the order. Then punish him. But it'll take time, Gully . . . time and money; more than you've got."

"I got a whole life, me."

They murmured for hours across the Whisper Line, their voices sounding small yet close to the ear. There was only one particular spot in each cell where the other could be heard, which was why so much time had passed before they discovered the miracle. But now they made up for lost time. And Jisbella educated Foyle.

"If we ever break out of Gouffre Martel, Gully, it'll have to be together, and I'm not trusting myself to an illiterate partner."

"Who's illiterate?"

"You are," Jisbella answered firmly. "I have to talk gutter a you half the time, me."

"I can read and write."

"And that's about all . . . which means that outside of brute strength you'll be useless."

"Talk sense, you," he said angrily.

"I am talking sense, me. What's the use of the strongest chisel in the world if it doesn't have an edge? We've got to sharpen your wits, Gully. Got to educate you, man, is all."

He submitted. He realized she was right. He would need training not only for the bust-out but for the search for *Vorga* as well. Jisbella was the daughter of an architect and had received an education. This she drilled into Foyle, leavened with the cynical experience of five years in the underworld. Occasionally he rebelled against the hard work, and then there would be whispered quarrels, but in the end he would apologize and submit again. And sometimes Jisbella would tire of teaching, and then they would ramble on, sharing dreams in the dark.

"I think we're falling in love, Gully."

"I think so too, Jiz."

"I'm an old hag, Gully. A hundred and five years old. What are you like?"

"Awful."

"How awful?"

"My face."

"You make yourself sound romantic. Is it one of those exciting scars that make a man attractive?"

"No. You'll see when we meet, us. That's wrong, isn't it, Jiz? Just plain: 'When we meet.' Period."

"Good boy."

"We will meet some day, won't we, Jiz?"

"Soon, I hope, Gully." Jisbella's faraway voice became crisp and businesslike. "But we've got to stop hoping and get down to work. We've got to plan and prepare."

From the underworld, Jisbella had inherited a mass of information about Gouffre Martel. No one had ever jaunted out of the cavern hospitals, but for decades the underworld had been collecting and collating information about them. It was from this data that Jisbella had formed her quick recognition of the Whisper Line that joined them. It was on the basis of this information that she began to discuss escape.

"We can pull it off, Gully. Never doubt that for a minute. There must be dozens of loopholes in their security system."

"No one's ever found them before."

"No one's ever worked with a partner before. We'll pool our information and we'll make it."

He no longer shambled to Sanitation and back. He felt the corridor walls, noted doors, noted their texture, counted, listened, deduced, and reported. He made a note of every separate step in the Sanitation pens and reported them to Jiz. The questions he whispered to the men around him in the shower and scrub rooms had purpose. Together, Foyle and Jisbella built up a picture of the routine of Gouffre Martel and its security system.

One morning, on the return from Sanitation, he was stopped as he was about to step back into his cell.

"Stay in line, Foyle."

"This is North-111. I know where to get off by now."

"Keep moving."

"But—" He was terrified. "You're changing me?"

"Visitor to see you."

He was marched up to the end of the north corridor where it met the three other main corridors that formed the huge cross of the hospital. In the center of the cross were the administration offices, maintenance workshops, clinics, and plants. Foyle was thrust into a room, as dark as his cell. The door was shut behind him. He become aware of a faint shimmering outline in the blackness. It was no more than the ghost of an image with a blurred body and a death's head. Two black discs on the skull face were either eye sockets or infrared goggles.

"Good morning," said Saul Dagenham.

"You?" Foyle exclaimed.

"Me. I've got five minutes. Sit down. Chair behind you."

Foyle felt for the chair and sat down slowly.

"Enjoying yourself?" Dagenham inquired.

"What do you want, Dagenham?"

"There's been a change," Dagenham said dryly. "Last time we talked your dialogue consisted entirely of 'Go to hell.'"

"Go to hell, Dagenham, if it'll make you feel any better."

"Your repartee's improved; your speech, too. You've changed," Dagenham said. "Changed a damned sight too much and a damned sight too fast. I don't like it. What's happened to you?"

"I've been going to night school."

"You've had ten months in this night school."

"Ten months!" Foyle echoed in amazement. "That long?"

"Ten months without sight and without sound. Ten months in solitary. You ought to be broke."

"Oh, I'm broke, all right."

"You ought to be whining. I was right. You're unusual. At this rate it's going to take too long. We can't wait. I'd like to make a new offer."

"Make it."

"Ten per cent of *Nomad*'s bullion. Two million."

"Two million!" Foyle exclaimed. "Why didn't you offer that in the first place?"

"Because I didn't know your caliber. Is it a deal?"

"Almost. Not yet."

"What else?"

"I get out of Gouffre Martel."

"Naturally."

"And someone else, too."

"It can be arranged." Dagenham's voice sharpened. "Anything else?"

"I get access to Presteign's files."

"Out of the question. Are you insane? Be reasonable."

"His shipping files."

"What for?"

"A list of personnel aboard one of his ships."

"Oh." Dagenham's eagerness revived. "That, I can arrange. Anything else?"

"No."

"Then it's a deal." Dagenham was delighted. The ghostly blur of light arose from its chair. "We'll have you out in six hours. We'll start arrangements for your friend at once. It's a pity we wasted this time, but no one can figure you, Foyle."

"Why didn't you send in a telepath to work me over?"

"A telepath? Be reasonable, Foyle. There aren't ten full telepaths in all the Inner Planets. Their time is earmarked for the next ten years. We couldn't persuade one to interrupt his schedule for love or money."

"I apologize, Dagenham. I thought you didn't know your business."

"You very nearly hurt my feelings."

"Now I know you're just lying."

"You're flattering me."

"You could have hired a telepath. For a cut in twenty million you could have hired one easy."

"The government would never—"

"They don't all work for the government. No. You've got something too hot to let a telepath get near."

The blur of light leaped across the room and seized Foyle. "How much do you know, Foyle? What are you covering? Who are you working for?" Dagenham's hands shook. "Christ! What a fool I've been. Of course you're unusual. You're no common spaceman. I asked you: who are you working for?"

Foyle tore Dagenham's hands away from him. "No one," he said. "No one, except myself."

"No one, eh? Including your friend in Gouffre Martel you're so eager to rescue? By God, you almost swindled me, Foyle. Tell Captain Y'ang-Yeovil I congratulate him. He's got a better staff than I thought."

"I never heard of any Y'ang-Yeovil."

"You and your colleague are going to rot here. It's no deal. You'll fester here. I'll have you moved to the worst cell in the hospital. I'll sink you to the bottom of Gouffre Martel. I'll— Guard, here! G—"

Foyle grasped Dagenham's throat, dragged him down to the floor and hammered his head on the flagstones. Dagenham squirmed once and then was still. Foyle ripped the goggles off his face and put them on. Sight returned in soft red and rose lights and shadows.

He was in a small reception room with a table and two chairs. Foyle stripped Dagenham's jacket off and put it on with two quick jerks that split the shoulders. Dagenham's cocked highwayman's hat lay on the table. Foyle clapped it over his head and pulled the brim down before his face.

On opposite walls were two doors. Foyle opened one a crack. It led out to the north corridor. He closed it, leaped across the room and tried the other. It opened onto a jaunte-proof maze. Foyle slipped through the door and entered the maze. Without a guide to lead him through the labyrinth, he was immediately lost. He began to run around the twists and turns and found himself back at the reception room. Dagenham was struggling to his knees.

Foyle turned back into the maze again. He ran. He came to a closed door and thrust it open. It revealed a large workshop illuminated by normal light. Two technicians working at a machine bench looked up in surprise.

Foyle snatched up a sledge hammer, leaped on them like a

caveman, and felled them. Behind him he heard Dagenham shouting in the distance. He looked around wildly, dreading the discovery that he was trapped in a cul-de-sac. The workshop was L-shaped. Foyle tore around the corner, burst through the entrance of another jaunte-proof maze and was lost again. The Gouffre Martel alarm system began clattering. Foyle battered at the walls of the labyrinth with the sledge, shattered the thin plastic masking, and found himself in the infrared-lit south corridor of the women's quadrant.

Two women guards came up the corridor, running hard. Foyle swung the sledge and dropped them. He was near the head of the corridor. Before him stretched a long perspective of cell doors, each bearing a glowing red number. Overhead the corridor was lit by glowing red globes. Foyle stood on tiptoe and clubbed the globe above him. He hammered through the socket and smashed the current cable. The entire corridor went dark . . . even to goggles.

"Evens us up; all in the dark now," Foyle gasped and tore down the corridor feeling the wall as he ran and counting cell doors. Jisbella had given him an accurate word picture of the South Quadrant. He was counting his way toward South-900. He blundered into a figure, another guard. Foyle hacked at her once with his sledge. She shrieked and fell. The women patients began shrieking. Foyle lost count, ran on, stopped.

"Jiz!" he bellowed.

He heard her voice. He encountered another guard, disposed of her, ran, located Jisbella's cell.

"Gully, for God's sake . . ." Her voice was muffled.

"Get back, girl. Back." He hammered thrice against the door with his sledge and it burst inward. He staggered in and fell against a figure.

"Jiz?" he gasped. "Excuse me . . . Was passing by. Thought I'd drop in."

"Gully, in the name of—"

"Yeah. Hell of a way to meet, eh? Come on. Out, girl. Out!" He dragged her out of the cell. "We can't try a break through the offices. They don't like me back there. Which way to your Sanitation pens?"

"Gully, you're crazy."

"Whole quadrant's dark. I smashed the power cable. We've got half a chance. Go, girl. Go."

He gave her a powerful thrust and she led him down the passages to the automatic stalls of the women's Sanitation pens. While mechanical hands removed their uniforms, soaped, soaked, sprayed and disinfected them, Foyle felt for the glass pane of the medical observation window. He found it, swung the sledge and smashed it.

"Get in, Jiz."

He hurled her through the window and followed. They were both stripped, greasy with soap, slashed and bleeding. Foyle slipped and crashed through the blackness searching for the door through which the medical officers entered.

"Can't find the door, Jiz. Door from the clinic. I—"

"Shh!"

"But—"

"Be quiet, Gully."

A soapy hand found his mouth and clamped over it. She gripped his shoulder so hard that her fingernails pierced his skin. Through the bedlam in the caverns sounded the clatter of steps close at hand. Guards were running blindly through the Sanitation stalls. The infrared lights had not yet been repaired.

"They may not notice the window," Jisbella hissed. "Be quiet."

They crouched on the floor. Steps trampled through the pens in bewildering succession. Then they were gone.

"All clear, now," Jisbella whispered. "But they'll have searchlights any minute. Come on, Gully. Out."

"But the door to the clinic, Jiz. I thought—"

"There is no door. They use spiral stairs and they pull them up. They've thought of this escape too. We'll have to try the laundry lift. God knows what good it'll do us. Oh Gully, you fool! You utter fool!"

They climbed through the observation window back into the pens. They searched through the darkness for the lifts by which soiled uniforms were removed and fresh uniforms issued. And in the darkness the automatic hands again soaped, sprayed and disinfected them. They could find nothing.

The caterwauling of a siren suddenly echoed through the caverns, silencing all other sound. There came a hush as suffocating as the darkness.

"They're using the G-phone to track us, Gully."

"The what?"

"Geophone. It can trace a whisper through half a mile of solid rock. That's why they've sirened for silence."

"The laundry lift?"

"Can't find it."

"Then come on."

"Where?"

"We're running."

"Where?"

"I don't know, but I'm not getting caught flat-footed. Come on. The exercise'll do you good."

Again he thrust Jisbella before him and they ran, gasping and stumbling, through the blackness, down into the deepest reaches of South Quadrant. Jisbella fell twice, blundering against turns in the passages. Foyle took the lead and ran, holding the twenty-pound sledge in his hand, the handle extended before him as an antenna. Then they crashed into a blank wall and realized they had reached the dead end of the corridor. They were boxed, trapped.

"What now?"

"Don't know. Looks like the dead end of my ideas, too. We can't go back for sure. I clobbered Dagenham in the offices. Hate that man. Looks like a poison label. You got a flash, girl?"

"Oh Gully . . . Gully . . ." Jisbella sobbed.

"Was counting on you for ideas. 'No more bombs,' you said. Wish I had one now. Could— Wait a minute." He touched the oozing wall against which they were leaning. He felt the checkerboard indentations of mortar seams. "Bulletin from G. Foyle. This isn't a natural cave wall. It's made. Brick and stone. Feel."

Jisbella felt the wall. "So?"

"Means this passage don't end here. Goes on. They blocked it off. Out of the way."

He shoved Jisbella up the passage, ground his hands into the floor to grit his soapy palms, and began swinging the sledge against the wall. He swung in steady rhythm, grunting and gasping. The steel sledge struck the wall with the blunt concussion of stones struck under water.

"They're coming," Jiz said. "I hear them."

The blunt blows took on a crumbling, crushing overtone. There was a whisper, then a steady pebble-fall of loose mortar. Foyle redoubled his efforts. Suddenly there was a crash and a gush of icy air blew in their faces.

"Through," Foyle muttered.

He attacked the edges of the hole pierced through the wall with ferocity. Bricks, stones, and old mortar flew. Foyle stopped and called Jisbella.

"Try it."

He dropped the sledge, seized her, and held her up to the chest-high opening. She cried out in pain as she tried to wriggle past the sharp edges. Foyle pressed her relentlessly until she got her shoulders and then her hips through. He let go of her legs and heard her fall on the other side.

Foyle pulled himself up and tore himself through the jagged breach in the wall. He felt Jisbella's hands trying to break his fall as he crashed down in a mass of loose brick and mortar. They were both through into the icy blackness of the unoccupied caverns of Gouffre Martel . . . miles of unexplored grottos and caves.

"By God, we'll make it yet," Foyle mumbled.

"I don't know if there's a way out, Gully." Jisbella was shaking with cold. "Maybe this is all cul-de-sac, walled off from the hospital."

"There has to be a way out."

"I don't know if we can find it."

"We've got to find it. Let's go, girl."

They blundered forward in the darkness. Foyle tore the useless set of goggles from his eyes. They crashed against ledges, corners, low ceilings; they fell down slopes and steep steps. They climbed over a razor-back ridge to a level plain and their feet shot from under them. Both fell heavily to a glassy floor. Foyle felt and touched it with his tongue.

"Ice," he muttered. "Good sign. We're in an ice cavern, Jiz. Underground glacier."

They arose shakily, straddling their legs and worked their way across the ice that had been forming in the Gouffre Martel abyss for millenia. They climbed into a forest of stone saplings that were stalagmites and stalactites thrusting up from the jagged floor and down from the ceilings. The vibrations of every step loosened the huge stalactites, ponderous stone spears that thundered down from overhead. At the edge of the forest, Foyle stopped, reached out and tugged. There was a clear metallic ring. He took Jisbella's hand and placed the long tapering cone of a stalagmite in it.

"Cane," he grunted. "Use it like a blind man."

He broke off another and they went tapping, feeling, stumbling through the darkness. There was no sound but the gallop of panic . . . their gasping breath and racing hearts, the taps of their stone canes, the multitudinous drip of water, the distant rushing of the underground river beneath Gouffre Martel.

"Not that way, girl," Foyle nudged her shoulder. "More to the left."

"Have you the faintest notion where we're headed, Gully?"

"Down, Jiz. Follow any slope that leads down."

"You've got an idea?"

"Yeah. Surprise, surprise! Brains instead of bombs."

"Brains instead of—" Jisbella shrieked with hysterical laughter. "You exploded into South Quadrant w-with a sledge hammer and th-that's your idea of b-brains instead of b-b-b—" She brayed and hooted beyond all control until Foyle grasped her and shook her.

"Shut up, Jiz. If they're tracking us by G-phone they could hear you from Mars."

"S-sorry, Gully. Sorry. I . . ." She took a breath. "Why down?"

"The river, the one we hear all the time. It must be near. It probably melts off the glacier back there."

"The river?"

"The only sure way out. It must break out of the mountain somewhere. We'll swim."

"Gully, you're insane!"

"What's a matter, you? You can't swim?"

"I can swim, but—"

"Then we've got to try. Got to, Jiz. Come on."

The rush of the river grew louder as their strength began to fail. Jisbella pulled to a halt at last, gasping.

"Gully, I've got to rest."

"Too cold. Keep moving."

"I can't."

"Keep moving." He felt for her arm.

"Get your hands off me," she cried furiously. In an instant she was all spitfire. He released her in amazement.

"What's the matter with you? Keep your head, Jiz. I'm depending on you."

"For what? I told you we had to plan . . . work out an escape . . . and now you've trapped us into this."

"I was trapped myself. Dagenham was going to change my cell. No more Whisper Line for us. I had to, Jiz . . . and we're out, aren't we?"

"Out where? Lost in Gouffre Martel. Looking for a damned river to drown in. You're a fool, Gully, and I'm an idiot for letting you trap me into this. Damn you! Damn you! You pull everything down to your imbecile level and you've pulled me down too. Run. Fight. Punch. That's all you know. Beat. Break. Blast. Destroy— Gully!"

Jisbella screamed. There was a clatter of loose stone in the darkness, and her scream faded down and away to a heavy splash.

Foyle heard the thrash of her body in water. He leaped forward, shouted: "Jiz!" and staggered over the edge of a precipice.

He fell and struck the water flat with a stunning impact. The icy river enclosed him, and he could not tell where the surface was. He struggled, suffocated, felt the swift current drag him against the chill slime of rocks, and then was borne bubbling to the surface. He coughed and shouted. He heard Jisbella answer, her voice faint and muffled by the roaring torrent. He swam with the current, trying to overtake her.

He shouted and heard her answering voice growing fainter and fainter. The roaring grew louder, and abruptly he was shot down the hissing sheet of a waterfall. He plunged to the bottom of a deep pool and struggled once more to the surface. The whirling current entangled him with a cold body bracing itself against a smooth rock wall.

"Jiz!"

"Gully! Thank God!"

They clung together for a moment while the water tore at them.

"Gully . . ." Jisbella coughed. "It goes through here."

"The river?"

"Yes."

He squirmed past her, bracing himself against the wall, and felt the mouth of an underwater tunnel. The current was sucking them into it.

"Hold on," Foyle gasped. He explored to the left and the right. The walls of the pool were smooth, without handhold.

"We can't climb out. Have to go through."

"There's no air, Gully. No surface."

"Couldn't be forever. We'll hold our breath."

"It could be longer than we can hold our breath."

"Have to gamble."

"I can't do it."

"You must. No other way. Pump your lungs. Hold on to me."

They supported each other in the water, gasping for breath,

filling their lungs. Foyle nudged Jisbella toward the underwater tunnel. "You go first. I'll be right behind. . . . Help you if you get into trouble."

"Trouble!" Jisbella cried in a shaking voice. She submerged and permitted the current to suck her into the tunnel mouth. Foyle followed. The fierce waters drew them down, down, down, caroming from side to side of a tunnel that had been worn glass-smooth. Foyle swam close behind Jisbella, feeling her thrashing legs beat his head and shoulders.

They shot through the tunnel until their lungs burst and their blind eyes started. Then there was a roaring again and a surface, and they could breathe. The glassy tunnel sides were replaced by jagged rocks. Foyle caught Jisbella's leg and seized a stone projection at the side of the river.

"Got to climb out here," he shouted.

"What?"

"Got to climb out. You hear that roaring up ahead? Cataracts. Rapids. Be torn to pieces. Out, Jiz."

She was too weak to climb out of the water. He thrust her body up onto the rocks and followed. They lay on the dripping stones, too exhausted to speak. At last Foyle got wearily to his feet.

"Have to keep on," he said. "Follow the river. Ready?"

She could not answer; she could not protest. He pulled her up and they went stumbling through the darkness, trying to follow the bank of the torrent. The boulders they traversed were gigantic, standing like dolmens, heaped, jumbled, scattered into a labyrinth. They staggered and twisted through them and lost the river. They could hear it in the darkness; they could not get back to it. They could get nowhere.

"Lost . . ." Foyle grunted in disgust. "We're lost again. Really lost this time. What are we going to do?"

Jisbella began to cry. She made helpless yet furious sounds. Foyle lurched to a stop and sat down, drawing her down with him.

"Maybe you're right, girl," he said wearily. "Maybe I am a

damned fool. I got us trapped into this no-jaunte jam, and we're licked."

She didn't answer.

"So much for brainwork. Hell of an education you gave me." He hesitated. "You think we ought to try backtracking to the hospital?"

"We'll never make it."

"Guess not. Was just practicing m'brain. Should we start a racket? Make a noise so they can track us by G-phone?"

"They'd never hear us . . . Never find us in time."

"We could make enough noise. You could knock me around a little. Be a pleasure for both of us."

"Shut up."

"What a mess!" He sagged back, cushioning his head on a tuft of soft grass. "At least I had a chance aboard *Nomad*. There was food and I could see where I was trying to go. I could—" He broke off and sat bolt upright. "Jiz!"

"Don't talk so much."

He felt the ground under him and clawed up sods of earth and tufts of grass. He thrust them into her face.

"Smell this," he laughed. "Taste it. It's grass, Jiz. Earth and grass. We must be out of Gouffre Martel."

"What?"

"It's night outside. Pitch-black. Overcast. We came out of the caves and never knew it. We're out, Jiz! We made it."

They leaped to their feet, peering, listening, sniffing. The night was impenetrable, but they heard the soft sigh of night winds, and the sweet scent of green growing things came to their nostrils. Far in the distance a dog barked.

"My God, Gully," Jisbella whispered incredulously. "You're right. We're out of Gouffre Martel. All we have to do is wait for dawn."

She laughed. She flung her arms about him and kissed him, and he returned the embrace. They babbled excitedly. They sank down on the soft grass again, weary, but unable to rest, eager, impatient, all life before them.

"Hello, Gully, darling Gully. Hello Gully, after all this time."

"Hello, Jiz."

"I told you we'd meet some day . . . some day soon. I told you, darling. And this is the day."

"The night."

"The night, so it is. But no more murmuring in the night along the Whisper Line. No more night for us, Gully, dear."

Suddenly they became aware that they were nude, lying close, no longer separated. Jisbella fell silent but did not move. He clasped her, almost angrily, and enveloped her with a desire that was no less than hers.

When dawn came, he saw that she was lovely: long and lean with smoky red hair and a generous mouth.

But when dawn came, she saw his face.

CHAPTER SIX

Harley Baker, M.D., had a small general practice in Montana-Oregon which was legitimate and barely paid for the diesel oil he consumed each weekend participating in the rallies for vintage tractors which were the vogue in Sahara. His real income was earned in his Freak Factory in Trenton to which Baker jaunted every Monday, Wednesday, and Friday night. There, for enormous fees and no questions asked, Baker created monstrosities for the entertainment business and refashioned skin, muscle, and bone for the underworld.

Looking like a male midwife, Baker sat on the cool veranda of his Spokane mansion listening to Jiz McQueen finish the story of her escape.

"Once we hit the open country outside Gouffre Martel it was easy. We found a shooting lodge, broke in, and got some clothes. There were guns there too . . . lovely old steel things for killing with explosives. We took them and sold them to some locals. Then we bought rides to the nearest jaunte stage we had memorized."

"Which?"

"Biarritz."

"Traveled by night, eh?"

"Naturally."

"Do anything about Foyle's face?"

"We tried makeup but that didn't work. The damned tattooing showed through. Then I bought a dark skin-surrogate and sprayed it on."

"Did that do it?"

"No," Jiz said angrily. "You have to keep your face quiet or else the surrogate cracks and peels. Foyle couldn't control himself. He never can. It was hell."

"Where is he now?"

"Sam Quatt's got him in tow."

"I thought Sam retired from the rackets."

"He did," Jisbella said grimly, "but he owes me a favor. He's minding Foyle. They're circulating on the jaunte to stay ahead of the cops."

"Interesting," Baker murmured. "Haven't seen a tattoo case in all my life. Thought it was a dead art. I'd like to add him to my collection. You know I collect curios, Jiz?"

"Everybody knows that zoo of yours in Trenton, Baker. It's ghastly."

"I picked up a genuine fraternal cyst last month," Baker began enthusiastically.

"I don't want to hear about it," Jiz snapped. "And I don't want Foyle in your zoo. Can you get the muck off his face? Clean it up? He says they were stymied at General Hospital."

"They haven't had my experience, dear. Hmm. I seem to remember reading something once . . . somewhere . . . Now where did I—? Wait a minute." Baker stood up and disappeared with a faint pop. Jisbella paced the veranda furiously until he reappeared twenty minutes later with a tattered book in his hands and a triumphant expression on his face.

"Got it," Baker said. "Saw it in the Caltech stacks three years ago. You may admire my memory."

"To hell with your memory. What about his face?"

"It can be done." Baker flipped the fragile pages and meditated. "Yes, it can be done. Indigotin disulphonic acid. I may have to synthesize the acid but . . ." Baker closed the text and nodded emphatically. "I can do it. Only it seems a pity to tamper with that face if it's as unique as you describe."

"Will you get off your hobby," Jisbella exclaimed in exasperation. "We're hot, understand? The first that ever broke out of Gouffre Martel. The cops won't rest until they've got us back. This is extra-special for them."

"But—"

"How long d'you think we can stay out of Gouffre Martel with Foyle running around with that tattooed face?"

"What are you so angry about?"

"I'm not angry. I'm explaining."

"He'd be happy in the zoo," Baker said persuasively. "And he'd be under cover there. I'd put him in the room next to the cyclops girl—"

"The zoo is out. That's definite."

"All right, dear. But why are you worried about Foyle being recaptured? It won't have anything to do with you."

"Why should you worry about me worrying? I'm asking you to do a job. I'm paying for the job."

"It'll be expensive, dear, and I'm fond of you. I'm trying to save you money."

"No you're not."

"Then I'm curious."

"Then let's say I'm grateful. He helped me; now I'm helping him."

Baker smiled cynically. "Then let's help him by giving him a brand new face."

"No."

"I thought so. You want his face cleaned up because you're interested in his face."

"Damn you, Baker, will you do the job or not?"

"It'll cost five thousand."

"Break that down."

"A thousand to synthesize the acid. Three thousand for the surgery. And one thousand for—"

"Your curiosity?"

"No, dear." Baker smiled again. "A thousand for the anesthetist."

"Why anesthesia?"

Baker reopened the ancient text. "It looks like a painful operation. You know how they tattoo? They take a needle, dip it in dye, and hammer it into the skin. To bleach that dye out I'll have to go over his face with a needle, pore by pore, and hammer in the indigotin disulphonic. It'll hurt."

Jisbella's eyes flashed. "Can you do it without the dope?"

"I can, dear, but Foyle—"

"To hell with Foyle. I'm paying four thousand. No dope, Baker. Let Foyle suffer."

"Jiz! You don't know what you're letting him in for."

"I know. Let him suffer." She laughed so furiously that she startled Baker. "Let his face make him suffer too."

∞

Baker's Freak Factory occupied a round brick three-story building that had once been the roundhouse in a suburban railway yard before jaunting ended the need for suburban railroads. The ancient ivy-covered roundhouse was alongside the Trenton rocket pits, and the rear windows looked out on the mouths of the pits thrusting their anti-grav beams upward, and Baker's patients could amuse themselves watching the spaceships riding silently up and down the beams, their portholes blazing, recognition signals blinking, their hulls rippling with St. Elmo's fire as the atmosphere carried off the electrostatic charges built up in outer space.

The basement floor of the factory contained Baker's zoo of anatomical curiosities, natural freaks and monsters bought, hired, kidnapped, abducted. Baker, like the rest of his world, was passionately devoted to these creatures and spent long hours with them, drinking in the spectacle of their distortions the way other men saturated themselves with the beauty of art. The middle floor of the roundhouse contained bedrooms for post-operative patients, laboratories, staff rooms, and kitchens. The top floor contained the operating theaters.

In one of the latter, a small room usually used for retinal experiments, Baker was at work on Foyle's face. Under a harsh battery of lamps, he bent over the operating table working meticulously with a small steel hammer and a platinum needle. Baker was following the pattern of the old tattooing on Foyle's face, searching out each minute scar in the skin, and driving the needle into it. Foyle's head was gripped in a clamp, but his body was unstrapped. His muscles writhed at each tap of the hammer, but he never moved his body. He gripped the sides of the operating table.

"Control," he said through his teeth. "You wanted me to learn control, Jiz. I'm practicing." He winced.

"Don't move," Baker ordered.

"I'm playing it for laughs."

"You're doing all right, son," Sam Quatt said, looking sick. He glanced sidelong at Jisbella's furious face. "What do you say, Jiz?"

"He's learning."

Baker continued dipping and hammering the needle.

"Listen, Sam," Foyle mumbled, barely audible. "Jiz told me you own a private ship. Crime pays, huh?"

"Yeah. Crime pays. I got a little four-man job. Twin-jet. Kind they call a Saturn Weekender."

"Why Saturn Weekender?"

"Because a weekend on Saturn would last ninety days. She can carry food and fuel for three months."

"Just right for me," Foyle muttered. He writhed and controlled himself. "Sam, I want to rent your ship."

"What for?"

"Something hot."

"Legitimate?"

"No."

"Then it's not for me, son. I've lost my nerve. Jaunting the circuit with you, one step ahead of the cops, showed me that. I've retired for keeps. All I want is peace."

"I'll pay fifty thousand. Don't you want fifty thousand? You could spend Sundays counting it."

The needle hammered remorselessly. Foyle's body was twitching at each impact.

"I already got fifty thousand. I got ten times that in cash in a bank in Vienna." Quatt reached into his pocket and took out a ring of glittering radioactive keys. "Here's the key for the bank. This is the key to my place in Joburg. Twenty rooms; twenty acres. This here's the key to my Weekender in Montauk. You ain't temptin' me, son. I quit while I was ahead. I'm jaunting back to Joburg and live happy for the rest of my life."

"Let me have the Weekender. You can sit safe in Joburg and collect."

"Collect when?"

"When I get back."

"You want my ship on trust and a promise to pay?"

"A guarantee."

Quatt snorted. "What guarantee?"

"It's a salvage job in the asteroids. Ship named *Nomad*."

"What's on the *Nomad*? What makes the salvage pay off?"

"I don't know."

"You're lying."

"I don't know," Foyle mumbled stubbornly. "But there has to be something valuable. Ask Jiz."

"Listen," Quatt said, "I'm going to teach you something. We do business legitimate, see? We don't slash and scalp. We don't hold out. I know what's on your mind. You got something juicy but you don't want to cut anybody else in on it. That's why you're begging for favors . . ."

Foyle writhed under the needle, but, still gripped in the vise of his possession, was forced to repeat: "I don't know, Sam. Ask Jiz."

"If you've got an honest deal, make an honest proposition," Quatt said angrily. "Don't come prowling around like a damned tattooed tiger figuring how to pounce. We're the only friends you got. Don't try to slash and scalp—"

Quatt was interrupted by a cry torn from Foyle's lips.

"Don't move," Baker said in an abstracted voice. "When you twitch your face I can't control the needle." He looked hard and long at Jisbella. Her lips trembled. Suddenly she opened her purse and took out two Ꝗr 500 banknotes. She dropped them alongside the beaker of acid.

"We'll wait outside," she said.

She fainted in the hall. Quatt dragged her to a chair, and found a nurse who revived her with aromatic ammonia. She began to cry so violently that Quatt was frightened. He dismissed the nurse and hovered until the sobbing subsided.

"What the hell has been going on?" he demanded. "What was that money supposed to mean?"

"It was blood money."

"For what?"

"I don't want to talk about it."

"Are you all right?"

"No."

"Anything I can do?"

"No."

There was a long pause. Then Jisbella asked in a weary voice: "Are you going to make that deal with Gully?"

"Me? No. It sounds like a thousand-to-one shot."

"There has to be something valuable on the *Nomad*. Otherwise Dagenham wouldn't have hounded Gully."

"I'm still not interested. What about you?"

"Me? Not interested either. I don't want any part of Gully Foyle again."

After another pause, Quatt asked: "Can I go home now?"

"You've had a rough time, haven't you, Sam?"

"I think I died about a thousand times nurse-maidin' that tiger around the circuit."

"I'm sorry, Sam."

"I had it coming to me after what I did to you when you were copped in Memphis."

"Running out on me was only natural, Sam."

"We always do what's natural, only sometimes we shouldn't do it."

"I know, Sam. I know."

"And you spend the rest of your life trying to make up for it. I figure I'm lucky, Jiz. I was able to square it tonight. Can I go home now?"

"Back to Joburg and the happy life?"

"Uh-huh."

"Don't leave me alone, yet, Sam. I'm ashamed of myself."

"What for?"

"Cruelty to dumb animals."

"What's that supposed to mean?"

"Never mind. Hang around a little. Tell me about the happy life. What's so happy about it?"

"Well," Quatt said reflectively. "It's having everything you wanted when you were a kid. If you can have everything at fifty that you wanted when you were fifteen, you're happy. Now when I was fifteen . . ." And Quatt went on and on describing the symbols, ambitions, and frustrations of his boyhood which he was now satisfying until Baker came out of the operating theater.

"Finished?" Jisbella asked eagerly.

"Finished. After I put him under I was able to work faster. They're bandaging his face now. He'll be out in a few minutes."

"Weak?"

"Naturally."

"How long before the bandages come off?"

"Six or seven days."

"His face'll be clean?"

"I thought you weren't interested in his face, dear. It ought to be clean. I don't think I missed a spot of pigment. You may admire my skill, Jisbella . . . also my sagacity. I'm going to back Foyle's salvage trip."

"What?" Quatt laughed. "You taking a thousand-to-one gamble, Baker? I thought you were smart."

"I am. The pain was too much for him and he talked under the anesthesia. There's twenty million in platinum bullion aboard the *Nomad*."

"Twenty million!" Sam Quatt's face darkened and he turned on Jisbella. But she was furious too.

"Don't look at me, Sam. I didn't know. He held out on me too. Swore he never knew why Dagenham was hounding him."

"It was Dagenham who told him," Baker said. "He let that slip too."

"I'll kill him," Jisbella said. "I'll tear him apart with my own two hands and you won't find anything inside his carcass but black rot. He'll be a curio for your zoo, Baker; I wish to God I'd let you have him!"

The door of the operating theater opened and two orderlies wheeled out a trolley on which Foyle lay, twitching slightly. His entire head was one white globe of bandage.

"Is he conscious?" Quatt asked Baker.

"I'll handle this," Jisbella burst out. "I'll talk to the son of a— Foyle!"

Foyle answered faintly through the mask of bandage. As Jisbella drew a furious breath for her onslaught, one wall of the hospital disappeared and there was a clap of thunder that knocked them off their feet. The entire building rocked from repeated explosions, and through the gaps in the walls uniformed men began jaunting in from the streets outside, like rooks swooping into the gut of a battlefield.

"Raid!" Baker shouted. "Raid!"

"Christ Jesus!" Quatt shook.

The uniformed men were swarming all over the building, shouting: "Foyle! Foyle! Foyle! Foyle!" Baker disappeared with a pop. The attendants jaunted too, deserting the trolley on which Foyle waved his arms and legs feebly, making faint sounds.

"It's a goddamn raid!" Quatt shook Jisbella. "Go, girl! Go!"

"We can't leave Foyle!" Jisbella cried.

"Wake up, girl! Go!"

"We can't run out on him."

Jisbella seized the trolley and ran it down the corridor. Quatt pounded alongside her. The roaring in the hospital grew louder: "Foyle! Foyle! Foyle!"

"Leave him, for God's sake!" Quatt urged. "Let them have him."

"No."

"It's a lobo for us, girl, if they get us."

"We can't run out on him."

They skidded around a corner into a shrieking mob of postoperative patients, bird men with fluttering wings, mermaids dragging themselves along the floor like seals, hermaphrodites, giants, pygmies, two-headed twins, centaurs, and a mewling sphinx. They clawed at Jisbella and Quatt in terror.

"Get him off the trolley," Jisbella yelled.

Quatt yanked Foyle off the trolley. Foyle came to his feet and sagged. Jisbella took his arm, and between them Sam and Jiz hauled him through a door into a ward filled with Baker's temporal freaks . . . subjects with accelerated time sense, darting about the ward with the lightning rapidity of humming birds and emitting piercing batlike squeals.

"Jaunte him out, Sam."

"After the way he tried to cross and scalp us?"

"We can't run out on him, Sam. You ought to know that by now. Jaunte him out. Caister's place!"

Jisbella helped Quatt haul Foyle to his shoulder. The temporal freaks seemed to fill the ward with shrieking streaks. The ward doors burst open. A dozen bolts from pneumatic guns whined through the ward, dropping the temporal patients in their gyrations. Quatt was slammed back against a wall, dropping Foyle. A black and blue bruise appeared on his temple.

"Get to hell out of here," Quatt roared. "I'm done."

"Sam!"

"I'm done. Can't jaunte. Go, girl!"

Trying to shake off the concussion that prevented him from jaunting, Quatt straightened and charged forward, meeting the uniformed men who poured into the ward. Jisbella took Foyle's arm and dragged him out the back of the ward, through a pantry, a clinic, a laundry supply, and down flights of ancient stairs that buckled and threw up clouds of termite dust.

They came into a victual cellar. Baker's zoo had broken out of their cells in the chaos and were raiding the cellar like bees glutting themselves with honey in an attacked hive. A Cyclops girl was cramming her mouth with handfuls of butter scooped from a tub. Her single eye above the bridge of her nose leered at them.

Jisbella dragged Foyle through the victual cellar, found a bolted wooden door and kicked it open. They stumbled down a flight of crumbling steps and found themselves in what had once been a coal cellar. The concussions and roarings overhead sounded deeper and hollow. A chute slot on one side of the cellar was barred with an iron door held by iron clamps. Jisbella placed Foyle's hands on the clamps. Together they opened them and climbed out of the cellar through the coal chute.

They were outside the Freak Factory, huddled against the rear wall. Before them were the Trenton rocket pits, and as they gasped for breath, Jiz saw a freighter come sliding down an anti-grav beam into a waiting pit. Its portholes blazed and its recognition signals blinked like a lurid neon sign, illuminating the back wall of the hospital.

A figure leaped from the roof of the hospital. It was Sam Quatt, attempting a desperate flight. He sailed out into space, arms and legs flailing, trying to reach the up-thrusting anti-grav beam of the nearest pit which might catch him in mid-flight and cushion his fall. His aim was perfect. Seventy feet above ground he dropped squarely into the shaft of the beam. It was not in operation. He fell and was smashed on the edge of the pit.

Jisbella sobbed. Still automatically retaining her grip on Foyle's arm, she ran across the seamed concrete to Sam Quatt's body. There she let go of Foyle and touched Quatt's head tenderly. Her fingers were stained with blood. Foyle tore at the bandage before his eyes, working eye holes through the gauze. He muttered to himself, listening to Jisbella weep and hearing the shouts behind him from Baker's factory. His hands fumbled at Quatt's body, then he arose and tried to pull Jisbella up.

"Got to go," he croaked. "Got to get out. They've seen us."

Jisbella never moved. Foyle mustered all his strength and pulled her upright.

"Times Square," he muttered. "Jaunte, Jiz!"

Uniformed figures appeared around them. Foyle shook Jisbella's arm and jaunted to Times Square where masses of jaunters on the gigantic stage stared in amazement at the huge man with the white bandaged globe for a head. The stage was the size of two football fields. Foyle stared around dimly through the bandages. There was no sign of Jisbella but she might be anywhere. He lifted his voice to a shout.

"Montauk, Jiz! Montauk! The Folly Stage!"

Foyle jaunted with a last thrust of energy and a prayer. An icy nor'easter was blowing in from Block Island and sweeping brittle ice crystals across the stage on the site of a medieval ruin known as Fisher's folly. There was another figure on the stage. Foyle tottered to it through the wind and the snow. It was Jisbella, looking frozen and lost.

"Thank God," Foyle muttered. "Thank God. Where does Sam keep his Weekender?" He shook Jisbella's elbow. "Where does Sam keep his Weekender?"

"Sam's dead."

"Where does he keep that Saturn Weekender?"

"He's retired, Sam is. He's not scared any more."

"Where's the ship, Jiz?"

"In the yards down at the lighthouse."

"Come on."

"Where?"

"To Sam's ship." Foyle thrust his big hand before Jisbella's eyes; a bunch of radiant keys lay in his palm. "I took his keys. Come on."

"He gave them to you?"

"I took them off his body."

"Ghoul!" She began to laugh. "Liar . . . Lecher . . . Tiger . . . Ghoul. The walking cancer . . . Gully Foyle."

Nevertheless she followed him through the snowstorm to Montauk Light.

∞

To three acrobats wearing powdered wigs, four flamboyant women carrying pythons, a child with golden curls and a cynical mouth, a professional duellist in medieval armor, and a man wearing a hollow glass leg in which goldfish swam, Saul Dagenham said: "All right, the operation's finished. Call the rest off and tell them to report back to Courier headquarters."

The side show jaunted and disappeared. Regis Sheffield rubbed his eyes and asked: "What was that lunacy supposed to be, Dagenham?"

"Disturbs your legal mind, eh? That was part of the cast of our FFCC operation. Fun, fantasy, confusion, and catastrophe." Dagenham turned to Presteign and smiled his death's-head smile. "I'll return your fee if you like, Presteign."

"You're not quitting?"

"No, I'm enjoying myself. I'll work for nothing. I've never tangled with a man of Foyle's caliber before. He's unique."

"How?" Sheffield demanded.

"I arranged for him to escape from Gouffre Martel. He escaped, all right, but not my way. I tried to keep him out of police hands with confusion and catastrophe. He ducked the police, but not my way . . . his own way. I tried to keep him out of Central Intelligence's hands with fun and fantasy. He stayed clear . . . again his own way. I tried to detour him into a ship so he could make his try for *Nomad*. He wouldn't detour, but he got his ship. He's on his way out now."

"You're following?"

"Naturally." Dagenham hesitated. "But what was he doing in Baker's factory?"

"Plastic surgery?" Sheffield suggested. "A new face?"

"Not possible. Baker's good, but he can't do a plastic that quick. It was minor surgery. Foyle was on his feet with his head bandaged."

"The tattoo," Presteign said.

Dagenham nodded and the smile left his lips. "That's what's worrying me. You realize, Presteign, that if Baker removed the tattooing we'll never recognize Foyle?"

"My dear Dagenham, his face won't be changed."

"We've never seen his face . . . only the mask."

"I haven't met the man at all," Sheffield said. "What's the mask like?"

"Like a tiger. I was with Foyle for two long sessions. I ought to know his face by heart, but I don't. All I know is the tattooing."

"Ridiculous," Sheffield said bluntly.

"No. Foyle has to be seen to be believed. However, it doesn't matter. He'll lead us out to *Nomad*. He'll lead us to your bullion and PyrE, Presteign. I'm almost sorry it's all over. Or nearly. As I said, I've been enjoying myself. He really is unique."

CHAPTER
SEVEN

The Saturn Weekender was built like a pleasure yacht; it was ample for four, spacious for two, but not spacious enough for Foyle and Jiz McQueen. Foyle slept in the main cabin; Jiz kept to herself in the stateroom.

On the seventh day out, Jisbella spoke to Foyle for the second time: "Let's get those bandages off, Ghoul."

Foyle left the galley where he was sullenly heating coffee, and kicked back to the bathroom. He floated in after Jisbella and wedged himself into the alcove before the washbasin mirror. Jisbella braced herself on the basin, opened an ether capsule and began soaking and stripping the bandage off with hard, hating hands. The strips of gauze peeled slowly. Foyle was in agony of suspense.

"D'you think Baker did the job?" he asked.

No answer.

"Could he have missed anywhere?"

The stripping continued.

"It stopped hurting two days ago."

No answer.

"For God's sake, Jiz! Is it still war between us?"

Jisbella's hands stopped. She looked at Foyle's bandaged face with hatred. "What do you think?"

"I asked you."

"The answer is yes."

"Why?"

"You'll never understand."

"Make me understand."

"Shut up."

"If it's war, why'd you come with me?"

"To get what's coming to Sam and me."

"Money?"

"Shut up."

"You didn't have to. You could have trusted me."

"Trusted you? You?" Jisbella laughed without mirth and recommenced the peeling. Foyle struck her hands away.

"I'll do it myself."

She lashed him across his bandaged face. "You'll do what I tell you. Be still, Ghoul!"

She continued unwinding the bandage. A strip came away revealing Foyle's eyes. They stared at Jisbella, dark and brooding. The eyelids were clean; the bridge of the nose was clean. A strip came away from Foyle's chin. It was blue-black. Foyle, watching intently in the mirror, gasped.

"He missed the chin!" he exclaimed. "Baker goofed—"

"Shut up," Jiz answered shortly. "That's beard."

The innermost strips came away quickly, revealing cheeks, mouth, and brow. The brow was clean. The cheeks under the eyes were clean. The rest was covered with blue-black seven day beard.

"Shave," Jiz commanded.

Foyle ran water, soaked his face, rubbed in shave ointment, and washed the beard off. Then he leaned close to the mirror and inspected himself, unaware that Jisbella's head was close to his as she too stared into the mirror. Not a mark of tattooing remained. Both sighed.

"It's clean," Foyle said. "Clean. He did the job." Suddenly he leaned further forward and inspected himself more closely. His face looked new to him, as new as it looked to Jisbella. "I'm changed. I don't remember looking like this. Did he do surgery on me too?"

"No," Jisbella said. "What's inside you changed it. That's the ghoul you're seeing, along with the liar and the cheat."

"For God's sake! Lay off. Let me alone!"

"Ghoul," Jisbella repeated, staring at Foyle's face with glowing eyes. "Liar. Cheat."

He took her shoulders and shoved her out into the companionway. She went sailing down into the main lounge, caught a guide bar and spun herself around. "Ghoul!" she cried. "Liar! Cheat! Ghoul! Lecher! Beast!"

Foyle pursued her, seized her again and shook her violently. Her red hair burst out of the clip that gathered it at the nape of her neck and floated out like a mermaid's tresses. The burning expression on her face transformed Foyle's anger into passion. He enveloped her and buried his new face in her breast.

"Lecher," Jiz murmured. "Animal . . ."

"Oh, Jiz . . ."

"The light," Jisbella whispered. Foyle reached out blindly toward the wall switches and pressed buttons, and the Saturn Weekender drove on toward the asteroids with darkened portholes.

∞

They floated together in the cabin, drowsing, murmuring, touching tenderly for hours.

"Poor Gully," Jisbella whispered. "Poor darling Gully . . ."

"Not poor," he said. "Rich . . . soon."

"Yes, rich and empty. You've got nothing inside you, Gully dear . . . Nothing but hatred and revenge."

"It's enough."

"Enough for now. But later?"

"Later? That depends."

"It depends on your inside, Gully; what you get hold of."

"No. My future depends on what I get rid of."

"Gully . . . why did you hold out on me in Gouffre Martel? Why didn't you tell me you knew there was a fortune aboard *Nomad?*"

"I couldn't."

"Didn't you trust me?"

"It wasn't that. I couldn't help myself. That's what's inside me . . . what I have to get rid of."

"Control again, eh Gully? You're driven."

"Yes, I'm driven. I can't learn control, Jiz. I want to, but I can't."

"Do you try?"

"I do. God knows, I do. But then something happens, and . . ."

"And then you pounce like a tiger. 'Remorseless, lecherous, treacherous, kindless villain . . .'"

"What's that?"

"Something a man named Shakespeare wrote. It describes you, Gully . . . when you're out of control."

"If I could carry you in my pocket, Jiz . . . to warn me . . . stick a pin in me . . ."

"Nobody can do it for you, Gully. You have to learn yourself."

He digested that for a long moment. Then he spoke hesitantly: "Jiz . . . about the money . . . ?"

"To hell with the money."

"Can I hold you to that?"

"Oh, Gully."

"Not that I . . . that I'm trying to hold out on you. If it wasn't for *Vorga*, I'd give you all you wanted. All! I'll give you every cent left over when I'm finished. But I'm scared, Jiz. *Vorga* is tough . . . what with Presteign and Dagenham and that lawyer, Sheffield. I've got to hold on to every cent, Jiz. I'm afraid if I let you take one credit, that could make the difference between *Vorga* and I."

"Me."

"Me." He waited. "Well?"

"You're all possessed," she said wearily. "Not just a part of you, but all of you."

"No."

"Yes, Gully. All of you. It's just your skin making love to me. The rest is feeding on *Vorga*."

At that moment the radar alarm in the forward control cabin burst upon them, unwelcome and warning.

"Destination zero," Foyle muttered, no longer relaxed, once more possessed. He shot forward into the control cabin.

∞

Foyle overran the asteroid with the sudden fury of a Vandal raid. He came blasting out of space, braked with a spume of flame from the forward jets, and kicked the Weekender into a tight spin around the junkheap. They whirled around, passing the blackened ports, the big hatch from which Jóseph and his Scientific People emerged to collect the drifting debris of space, the new crater Foyle had torn out of the side of the asteroid in his first plunge back to Terra. They whipped past the giant patchwork windows of the asteroid greenhouse and saw hundreds of faces peering out at them, tiny white dots mottled with tattooing.

"So I didn't murder them," Foyle grunted. "They've pulled

back into the asteroid . . . Probably living deep inside while they get the rest repaired."

"Will you help them, Gully?"

"Why?"

"You did the damage."

"To hell with them. I've got my own problems. But it's a relief. They won't be bothering us."

He circled the asteroid once more and brought the Weekender down in the mouth of the new crater.

"We'll work from here," he said. "Get into a suit, Jiz. Let's go! Let's go!"

He drove her, mad with impatience; he drove himself. They corked up in their spacesuits, left the Weekender, and went sprawling through the debris in the crater into the bleak bowels of the asteroid. It was like squirming through the crawling tunnels of giant worm-holes. Foyle switched on his micro-wave suit set and spoke to Jiz.

"Be easy to get lost in here. Stay with me. Stay close."

"Where are we going, Gully?"

"After *Nomad*. I remember they were cementing her into the asteroid when I left. Don't remember where. Have to find her."

The passages were airless, and their progress was soundless, but the vibrations carried through metal and rock. They paused once for breath alongside the pitted hull of an ancient warship. As they leaned against it they felt the vibrations of signals from within, a rhythmic knocking.

Foyle smiled grimly. "That's Jóseph and The Scientific People inside," he said. "Requesting a few words. I'll give 'em an evasive answer." He pounded twice on the hull. "And now a personal message for my wife." His face darkened. He smote the hull angrily and turned away. "Come on. Let's go."

But as they continued the search, the signals followed them. It became apparent that the outer periphery of the asteroid had been abandoned; the tribe had withdrawn to the center. Then, far down a shaft wrought of beaten aluminum, a hatch opened, light blazed forth, and Jóseph appeared in an ancient spacesuit fashioned of glass cloth. He stood in the clumsy sack, his devil face staring, his hands clutched in supplication, his devil mouth making motions.

Foyle stared at the old man, took a step toward him, and then stopped, fists clenched, throat working as fury arose within him. And Jisbella, looking at Foyle, cried out in horror. The old tattooing had returned to his face, blood red against the pallor of the skin, scarlet instead of black, truly a tiger mask in color as well as design.

"Gully!" she cried. "My God! Your face!"

Foyle ignored her and stood glaring at Jóseph while the old man made beseeching gestures, motioned to them to enter the interior of the asteroid, and then disappeared. Only then did Foyle turn to Jisbella and ask: "What? What did you say?"

Through the clear globe of the helmet she could see his face distinctly. And as the rage within Foyle died away, Jisbella saw the blood-red tattooing fade and disappear.

"Did you see that joker?" Foyle demanded. "That was Jóseph. Did you see him begging and pleading after what he did to me . . . ? What did you say?"

"Your face, Gully. I know what's happened to your face."

"What are you talking about?"

"You wanted something that would control you, Gully. Well, you've got it. Your face. It—" Jisbella began to laugh hysterically. "You'll have to learn control now, Gully. You'll never be able to give way to emotion . . . any emotion . . . because—"

But he was staring past her and suddenly he shot up the aluminum shaft with a yell. He jerked to a stop before an open door and began to whoop in triumph. The door opened into a tool locker, four by four by nine. There were shelves in the locker and a jumble of old provisions and discarded containers. It was Foyle's coffin aboard the *Nomad*.

Jóseph and his people had succeeded in sealing the wreck into their asteroid before the holocaust of Foyle's escape had rendered further work impossible. The interior of the ship was virtually untouched. Foyle took Jisbella's arm and dragged her on a quick tour of the ship and finally to the purser's locker where Foyle tore at the windrows of wreckage and debris until he disclosed a massive steel face, blank and impenetrable.

"We've got a choice," he panted. "Either we tear the safe out of the hull and carry it back to Terra where we can work on it, or we open it here. I vote for here. Maybe Dagenham was lying. All depends on what tools Sam has in the Weekender anyway. Come back to the ship, Jiz."

He never noticed her silence and preoccupation until they were back aboard the Weekender and he had finished his urgent search for tools.

"Nothing!" he exclaimed impatiently. "There isn't a hammer or a drill aboard. Nothing but gadgets for opening bottles and rations."

Jisbella didn't answer. She never took her eyes off his face.

"Why are you staring at me like that?" Foyle demanded.

"I'm fascinated," Jisbella answered slowly.

"By what?"

"I'm going to show you something, Gully."

"What?"

"How much I despise you."

Jisbella slapped him thrice. Stung by the blows, Foyle started up furiously. Jisbella picked up a hand mirror and held it before him.

"Look at yourself, Gully," she said quietly. "Look at your face."

He looked. He saw the old tattoo marks flaming blood-red under the skin, turning his face into a scarlet and white tiger mask. He was so chilled by the appalling spectacle that his rage died at once, and simultaneously the mask disappeared.

"My God . . ." he whispered. "Oh my God . . ."

"I had to make you lose your temper to show you," Jisbella said.

"What's it mean, Jiz? Did Baker goof the job?"

"I don't think so. I think you've got scars under the skin, Gully . . . from the original tattooing and then from the bleaching. Needle scars. They don't show normally, but they do show, blood red, when your emotions take over and your heart begins pumping blood . . . when you're furious or frightened or passionate or possessed . . . Do you understand?"

He shook his head, still staring at his face, touching it in bewilderment.

"You said you wished you could carry me in your pocket to stick pins in you when you lose control. You've got something better than that, Gully, or worse, poor darling. You've got your face."

"No!" he said. "No!"

"You can't ever lose control, Gully. You'll never be able to drink too much, eat too much, love too much, hate too much . . . You'll have to hold yourself with an iron grip."

"No!" he insisted desperately. "It can be fixed. Baker can do it, or somebody else. I can't walk around afraid to feel anything because it'll turn me into a freak!"

"I don't think this can be fixed, Gully."

"Skin-graft . . ."

"No. The scars are too deep for graft. You'll never get rid of this stigmata, Gully. You'll have to learn to live with it."

Foyle flung the mirror from him in sudden rage, and again the blood-red mask flared up under his skin. He lunged out of the main cabin to the main hatch where he pulled his spacesuit down and began to squirm into it.

"Gully! Where are you going? What are you going to do?"

"Get tools," he shouted. "Tools for the safe."

"Where?"

"In the asteroid. They've got dozens of warehouses stuffed with tools from wrecked ships. There have to be drills there, everything I need. Don't come with me. There may be trouble. How is my God damned face now? Showing it? By Christ, I hope there *is* trouble!"

He corked his suit and went into the asteroid. He found a hatch separating the habited core from the outer void. He banged on the door. He waited and banged again and continued the imperious summons until at last the hatch was opened. Arms reached out and yanked him in, and the hatch was closed behind him. It had no air lock.

He blinked in the light and scowled at Jóseph and his innocent people gathering before him, their faces hideously decorated. And he knew that his own face must be flaming red and white for he saw Jóseph start, and he saw the devil mouth shape the syllables: NOMAD.

Foyle strode through the crowd, scattering them abruptly. He smashed Jóseph with a backhand blow from his mailed fist. He searched through the inhabited corridors, recognizing them dimly, and he came at last to the chamber, half natural cave, half antique hull, where the tools were stored.

He rooted and ferreted, gathering up drills, diamond bits, acids, thermites, crystallants, dynamite jellies, fuses. In the gently revolving asteroid the gross weight of the equipment was reduced to less than a hundred pounds. He lumped it into a mass, roughly bound it together with cable, and started out of the store-cave.

Jóseph and his Scientific People were waiting for him, like fleas waiting for a wolf. They darted at him and he battered through them, harried, delighted, savage. The armor of his spacesuit protected him from their attacks and he went down the passages searching for a hatch that would lead out into the void.

Jisbella's voice came to him, tinny on the earphones and agitated: "Gully, can you hear me? This is Jiz. Gully, listen to me."

"Go ahead."

"Another ship came up two minutes ago. It's drifting on the other side of the asteroid."

"What!"

"It's marked with yellow and black colors, like a hornet."

"Dagenham's colors!"

"Then we've been followed."

"What else? Dagenham's probably been tailing me ever since we busted out of Gouffre Martel. I was a fool not to think of it. How'd he tail me, Jiz? Through you?"

"Gully!"

"Forget it. Just practicing jokes." He laughed without amusement. "We've got to work fast, Jiz. Cork up in a suit and meet me aboard *Nomad*. The purser's room. Go, girl."

"But Gully . . ."

"Sign off. They may be monitoring our waveband. Go!"

He drove through the asteroid, reached a barred hatch, broke through the guard before it, smashed it open and went into the void of the outer passages. The Scientific People were too desperate getting the hatch closed to stop him. But he knew they would follow him; they were raging.

He hauled the bulk of his equipment through twists and turns to the wreck of the *Nomad*. Jisbella was waiting for him in the purser's room. She made a move to turn on her micro-wave set and Foyle stopped her. He placed his helmet against hers and shouted: "No shortwave. They'll be monitoring and they'll locate us by D/F. You can hear me like this, can't you?"

She nodded.

"All right. We've got maybe an hour before Dagenham locates us. We've got maybe an hour before Jóseph and his mob come after us. We're in a hell of a jam. We've got to work fast."

She nodded again.

"No time to open the safe and transport the bullion."

"If it's there."

"Dagenham's here, isn't he? That's proof it's there. We'll have to cut the whole safe out of the *Nomad* and get it into the Weekender. Then we blast."

"But—"

"Just listen to me and do what I say. Go back to the Weekender. Empty it out. Jettison everything we don't need . . . all supplies except emergency rations."

"Why?"

"Because I don't know how many tons this safe weighs, and the ship may not be able to handle it when we come back to gravity. We've got to make allowances in advance. It'll mean a tough trip back but it's worth it. Strip the ship. Fast! Go, girl. Go!"

He pushed her away and without another glance in her

direction, attacked the safe. It was built into the structural steel of the hull, a massive steel ball some four feet in diameter. It was welded to the strakes and ribs of the *Nomad* at twelve different spots. Foyle attacked each weld in turn with acids, drills, thermite, and refrigerants. He was operating on the theory of structural strain . . . to heat, freeze, and etch the steel until its crystalline structure was distorted and its physical strength destroyed. He was fatiguing the metal.

Jisbella returned and he realized that forty-five minutes had passed. He was dripping and shaking but the globe of the safe hung free of the hull with a dozen rough knobs protruding from its surface. Foyle motioned urgently to Jisbella and she strained her weight against the safe with him. They could not budge its mass together. As they sank back in exhaustion and despair, a quick shadow eclipsed the sunlight pouring through the rents in the *Nomad* hull. They stared up. A spaceship was circling the asteroid less than a quarter of a mile off.

Foyle placed his helmet against Jisbella's. "Dagenham," he gasped. "Looking for us. Probably got a crew down here combing for us too. Soon as they talk to Jóseph they'll be here."

"Oh Gully . . ."

"We've still got a chance. Maybe they won't spot Sam's Weekender until they've made a couple of revolutions. It's hidden in that crater. Maybe we can get the safe aboard in the meantime."

"How, Gully?"

"I don't know, damn it! I don't know." He pounded his fists together in frustration. "I'm finished."

"Couldn't we blast it out?"

"Blast . . . ? What, bombs instead of brains? Is this Mental McQueen speaking?"

"Listen. Blast it with something explosive. That would act like a rocket jet . . . give it a thrust."

"Yes, I've got that. But then what? How do we get it into the ship, girl? Can't keep on blasting. Haven't got time."

"No, we bring the ship to the safe."

"What?"

"Blast the safe straight out into space. Then bring the ship around and let the safe sail right into the main hatch. Like catching a ball in your hat. See?"

He saw. "By God, Jiz, we can do it." Foyle leaped to the pile of equipment and began sorting out sticks of dynamite gelatine, fuses, and caps.

"We'll have to use the short-wave. One of us stays with the safe; one of us pilots the ship. Man with the safe talks the man with the ship into position. Right?"

"Right. You'd better pilot, Gully. I'll do the talking."

He nodded, fixing explosive to the face of the safe, attaching caps and fuses. Then he placed his helmet against hers. "Vacuum fuses, Jiz. Timed for two minutes. When I give the word by short-wave, just pull off the fuse heads and get the hell out of the way. Right?"

"Right."

"Stay with the safe. Once you've talked it into the ship, come right after it. Don't wait for anything. It's going to be close."

He thumped her shoulder and returned to the Weekender. He left the outer hatch open, and the inner door of the airlock as well. The ship's air emptied out immediately. Airless and stripped by Jisbella, it looked dismal and forlorn.

Foyle went directly to the controls, sat down and switched on his micro-wave set. "Stand by," he muttered. "I'm coming out now."

He ignited the jets, blew the laterals for three seconds and then the forwards. The Weekender lifted easily, shaking debris from her back and sides like a whale surfacing. As she slid up and back, Foyle called: "Dynamite, Jiz! Now!"

There was no blast; there was no flash. A new crater opened in the asteroid below him and a flower of rubble sprang upward, rapidly outdistancing a dull steel ball that followed leisurely, turning in a weary spin.

"Ease off." Jisbella's voice came cold and competent over the earphones. "You're backing too fast. And incidentally, trouble's arrived."

He braked with the rear jets, looking down in alarm. The surface of the asteroid was covered with a swarm of hornets. They were Dagenham's crew in yellow and black banded spacesuits. They were buzzing around a single figure in white that dodged and spun and eluded them. It was Jisbella.

"Steady as you go," Jiz said quietly, although he could hear how hard she was breathing. "Ease off a little more . . . Roll a quarter turn."

He obeyed her almost automatically, still watching the struggle below. The flank of the Weekender cut off any view of the trajectory of the safe as it approached him, but he could still see Jisbella and Dagenham's men. She ignited her suit rocket . . . he could see the tiny spurt of flame shoot out from her back . . . and came sailing up from the surface of the asteroid. A score of flames burst out from the backs of Dagenham's men as they followed. Half a dozen dropped the pursuit of Jisbella and came up after the Weekender.

"It's going to be close, Gully," Jisbella was gasping now, but her voice was still steady. "Dagenham's ship came down on the other side, but they've probably signaled him by now and he'll be on his way. Hold your position, Gully. About ten seconds now . . ."

The hornets closed in and engulfed the tiny white suit.

"Foyle! Can you hear me? Foyle!" Dagenham's voice came in fuzzily and finally cleared. "This is Dagenham calling on your band. Come in, Foyle!"

"Jiz! Jiz! Can you get clear of them?"

"Hold your position, Gully. . . . There she goes! It's a hole in one, son!"

A crushing shock racked the Weekender as the safe, moving slowly but massively, rammed into the main hatch. At the same moment the white suited figure broke out of the cluster of yellow wasps. It came rocketing up to the Weekender, hotly pursued.

"Come on, Jiz! Come on!" Foyle howled. "Come, girl! Come!"

As Jisbella disappeared from sight behind the flank of the Weekender, Foyle set controls and prepared for top acceleration.

"Foyle! Will you answer me? This is Dagenham speaking."

"To hell with you, Dagenham," Foyle shouted. "Give me the word when you're aboard, Jiz, and hold on."

"I can't make it, Gully."

"Come on, girl!"

"I can't get aboard. The safe's blocking the hatch. It's wedged in halfway . . ."

"Jiz!"

"There's no way in, I tell you," she cried in despair. "I'm blocked out."

He stared around wildly. Dagenham's men were boarding the hull of the Weekender with the menacing purpose of professional raiders. Dagenham's ship was lifting over the brief horizon of the asteroid on a dead course for him. His head began to spin.

"Foyle, you're finished. You and the girl. But I'll offer a deal . . ."

"Gully, help me. Do something, Gully. I'm lost!"

"Vorga," he said in a strangled voice. He closed his eyes and tripped the controls. The tail jets roared. The Weekender shook and shuddered forward. It broke free of Dagenham's boarders, of Jisbella, of warnings and pleas. It pressed Foyle back into the pilot's chair with the blackout of 10G acceleration, an acceleration that was less pressing, less painful, less treacherous than the passion that drove him.

And as he passed from sight there rose up on his face the blood-red stigmata of his possession.

PART 2

With a heart of furious fancies
 Whereof I am commander,
With a burning spear and a horse of air,
 To the wilderness I wander.
With a knight of ghosts and shadows
 I summoned am to tourney,
Ten leagues beyond the wide world's end—
 Methinks it is no journey.

TOM-A-BEDLAM

CHAPTER
EIGHT

T he old year soured as pestilence poisoned the planets. The war gained momentum and grew from a distant affair of romantic raids and skirmishes in space to a holocaust in the making. It became evident that the last of the World Wars was done and the first of the Solar Wars had begun.

The belligerents slowly massed men and materiel for the havoc. The Outer Satellites introduced universal conscription, and the Inner Planets perforce followed suit. Industries, trades, sciences, skills, and professions were drafted; regulations and oppressions followed. The armies and navies requisitioned and commanded.

Commerce obeyed, for this war (like all wars) was the shooting phase of a commercial struggle. But populations rebelled, and draft-jaunting and labor-jaunting became critical problems. Spy scares and invasion scares spread. The hysterical became informers and lynchers. An ominous foreboding paralyzed every home from Baffin Island to the Falklands. The dying year was enlivened only by the advent of the Four Mile Circus.

This was the popular nickname for the grotesque entourage of Geoffrey Fourmyle of Ceres, a wealthy young buffoon from the largest of the asteroids. Fourmyle of Ceres was enormously rich; he was also enormously amusing. He was the classic *bourgeois gentilhomme*, the upstart *nouveau riche* of all time. His entourage was a cross between a country circus and the comic court of a Bulgarian kinglet, as witness this typical arrival in Green Bay, Wisconsin.

Early in the morning a lawyer, wearing the stovepipe hat of a legal clan, appeared with a list of camp sites in his hand and a small fortune in his pocket. He settled on a four-acre meadow facing Lake Michigan and rented it for an exorbitant fee. He was followed by a gang of surveyors from the Mason & Dixon clan. In twenty minutes the surveyors had laid out a camp site and the word had spread that the Four Mile Circus was arriving. Locals from Wisconsin, Michigan, and Minnesota came to watch the fun.

Twenty roustabouts jaunted in, each carrying a tent pack on his back. There was a mighty overture of bawled orders, shouts, curses, and the tortured scream of compressed air. Twenty giant tents ballooned upward, their lac and latex surfaces gleaming as they dried in the winter sun. The spectators cheered.

A six-motor helicopter drifted down and hovered over a giant trampoline. Its belly opened and a cascade of furnishings came down. Servants, valets, chefs, and waiters jaunted in. They furnished and decorated the tents. The kitchens began smoking and the odor of frying, broiling, and baking pervaded the camp. Fourmyle's private police were already on duty, patrolling the four acres, keeping the huge crowd of spectators back.

Then, by plane, by car, by bus, by truck, by bike, and by jaunte came Fourmyle's entourage. Librarians and books, scientists and laboratories, philosophers, poets, athletes. Racks of swords and sabres were set up, and judo mats and a boxing ring. A fifty-foot pool was sunk in the ground and filled by pump from the lake. An interesting altercation arose between two beefy athletes as to whether the pool should be warmed for swimming or frozen for skating.

Musicians, actors, jugglers, and acrobats arrived. The uproar became deafening. A crew of mechanics melted a greasepit and began revving up Fourmyle's collection of vintage diesel harvesters. Last of all came the camp followers: wives, daughters, mistresses, whores, beggars, chiselers, and grafters. By midmorning the roar of the circus could be heard for four miles, hence the nickname.

At noon, Fourmyle of Ceres arrived with a display of conspicuous transportation so outlandish that it had been known to make seven-year melancholics laugh. A giant amphibian thrummed up from the south and landed on the lake. An LST barge emerged from the plane and droned across the water to the shore. Its forward wall banged down into a drawbridge and out came a twentieth century staff car. Wonder piled on wonder for the delighted spectators, for the staff car drove a matter of twenty yards to the center of camp and then stopped.

"What can possibly come next? Bike?"

"No, roller skates."

"He'll come out on a pogo stick."

Fourmyle capped their wildest speculations. The muzzle of a circus cannon thrust up from the staff car. There was the bang of a black-powder explosion and Fourmyle of Ceres was shot out of the cannon in a graceful arc to the very door of his tent where he was caught in a net by four valets. The applause that greeted him could be heard for six miles. Fourmyle climbed onto his valets' shoulders and motioned for silence.

"Oh, God! It's going to make a speech."

"It? You mean 'he,' don't you?"

"No; it. It can't be human."

"Friends, Romans, Countrymen," Fourmyle began earnestly. "Lend me your ears, Shakespeare. 1564–1616. Damn!" Four white doves shook themselves out of Fourmyle's sleeves and fluttered away. He regarded them with astonishment, then continued. "Friends, greetings, salutations, *bonjour, bon ton, bon vivant, bon voyage, bon*— What the hell?" Fourmyle's pockets caught fire and rocketed forth Roman Candles. He tried to put himself out. Streamers and confetti burst from him. "Friends . . . Shut up! I'll get this speech straight. Quiet! Friends—!" Fourmyle looked down at himself in dismay. His clothes were melting away, revealing lurid scarlet underwear. "Kleinmann!" he bellowed furiously. "Kleinmann! What's happened to your goddamned hypno-training?"

A hairy head thrust out of a tent. "You stoodied for dis sbeech last night, Fourmyle?"

"Damn right. For two hours I stoodied. Never took my head out of the hypno-oven. Kleinmann on Prestidigitation."

"No, no, no!" the hairy man bawled. "How many times must I tell you? Prestidigitation is not sbeechmaking. Is magic. *Dumbkopf!* You haff the wrong hypnosis taken!"

The scarlet underwear began melting. Fourmyle toppled from the shoulders of his shaking valets and disappeared within his tent. There was a roar of laughter and cheering and the Four Mile Circus ripped into high gear. The kitchens sizzled and smoked. There was a perpetuity of eating and drinking. The music never stopped. The vaudeville never ceased.

Inside his tent, Fourmyle changed his clothes, changed his mind, changed again, undressed again, kicked his valets, and called for his tailor in a bastard tongue of French, Mayfair, and affectation. Halfway into a new suit, he recollected he had neglected to bathe. He slapped his tailor, ordered ten gallons of scent to be decanted into the pool, and was stricken with poetic inspiration. He summoned his resident poet.

"Take this down," Fourmyle commanded. "*Le roi est mort, les—* Wait. What rhymes to moon?"

"June," his poet suggested. "Croon, soon, dune, loon, noon, rune, tune, boon . . ."

"I forgot my experiment!" Fourmyle exclaimed. "Dr. Bohun! Dr. Bohun!"

Half-naked, he rushed pell-mell into the laboratory where he blew himself and Dr. Bohun, his resident chemist, halfway across the tent. As the chemist attempted to raise himself from the floor he found himself seized in a most painful and embarrassing strangle hold.

"Nogouchi!" Fourmyle shouted. "Hi! Nogouchi! I just invented a new judo hold."

Fourmyle stood up, lifted the suffocating chemist and jaunted to the judo mat where the little Japanese inspected the hold and shook his head.

"No, please." He hissed politely. "Hfffff. Pressure on windpipe are not perpetually lethal. Hfffff. I show you, please." He seized the dazed chemist, whirled him and deposited him on the mat in a position of perpetual self-strangulation. "You observe, please, Fourmyle?"

But Fourmyle was in the library bludgeoning his librarian over the head with Bloch's *Das Sexual Leben* (eight pounds, nine ounces) because that unhappy man could produce no text on the manufacture of perpetual motion machines. He rushed to his physics laboratory where he destroyed an expensive chronometer to experiment with cog wheels, jaunted to the bandstand where he seized a baton and led the orchestra into confusion, put on skates and fell into the scented swimming pool, was hauled out, swearing fulminously at the lack of ice, and was heard to express a desire for solitude.

"I wish to commute with myself," Fourmyle said, kicking his

valets in all directions. He was snoring before the last of them limped to the door and closed it behind him.

The snoring stopped and Foyle arose. "That ought to hold them for today," he muttered, and went into his dressing room. He stood before a mirror, took a deep breath and held it, meanwhile watching his face. At the expiration of one minute it was still untainted. He continued to hold his breath, maintaining rigid control over pulse and muscle, mastering the strain with iron calm. At two minutes and twenty seconds the stigmata appeared, blood-red. Foyle let out his breath. The tiger mask faded.

"Better," he murmured. "Much better. The old fakir was right, Yoga is the answer. Control. Pulse, breath, bowels, brains."

He stripped and examined his body. He was in magnificent condition, but his skin still showed delicate silver seams in a network from neck to ankles. It looked as though someone had carved an outline of the nervous system into Foyle's flesh. The silver seams were the scars of an operation that had not yet faded.

That operation had cost Foyle a ₡r 200,000 bribe to the chief surgeon of the Mars Commando Brigade and had transformed him into an extraordinary fighting machine. Every nerve plexus had been rewired, microscopic transistors and transformers had been buried in muscle and bone, a minute platinum outlet showed at the base of his spine. To this Foyle affixed a power-pack the size of a pea and switched it on. His body began an internal electronic vibration that was almost mechanical.

"More machine than man," he thought. He dressed, rejected the extravagant apparel of Fourmyle of Ceres for the anonymous black coverall of action.

He jaunted to Robin Wednesbury's apartment in the lonely building amidst the Wisconsin pines. It was the real reason for the advent of the Four Mile Circus in Green Bay. He jaunted and arrived in darkness and empty space and immediately plummeted down. "Wrong co-ordinates!" he thought. "Misjaunted?" The broken end of a rafter dealt him a bruising blow and he landed heavily on a shattered floor upon the putrefying remains of a corpse.

Foyle leaped up in calm revulsion. He pressed hard with his

tongue against his right upper first molar. The operation that had transformed half his body into an electronic machine, had located the control switchboard in his teeth. Foyle pressed a tooth with his tongue and the peripheral cells of his retina were excited into emitting a soft light. He looked down two pale beams at the corpse of a man.

The corpse lay in the apartment below Robin Wednesbury's flat. It was gutted. Foyle looked up. Above him was a ten-foot hole where the floor of Robin's living room had been. The entire building stank of fire, smoke, and rot.

"Jacked," Foyle said softly. "This place has been jacked. What happened?"

The jaunting age had crystallized the hoboes, tramps, and vagabonds of the world into a new class. They followed the night from east to west, always in darkness, always in search of loot, the leavings of disaster, carrion. If earthquake shattered a warehouse, they were jacking it the following night. If fire opened a house or explosion split the defenses of a shop, they jaunted in and scavenged. They called themselves Jack-jaunters. They were jackals.

Foyle climbed up through the wreckage to the corridor on the floor above. The Jack-jaunters had a camp there. A whole calf roasted before a fire which sparked up to the sky through a rent in the roof. There were a dozen men and three women around the fire, rough, dangerous, jabbering in the Cockney rhyming slang of the jackals. They were dressed in mismatched clothes and drinking potato beer from champagne glasses.

An ominous growl of anger and terror met Foyle's appearance as the big man in black came up through the rubble, his intent eyes emitting pale beams of light. Calmly, he strode through the rising mob to the entrance of Robin Wednesbury's flat. His iron control gave him an air of detachment.

"If she's dead," he thought, "I'm finished. I've got to use her. But if she's dead . . ."

Robin's apartment was gutted like the rest of the building. The living room was an oval of floor around the jagged hole in the center. Foyle searched for a body. Two men and a woman were in the bed in the bedroom. The men cursed. The woman shrieked at the apparition. The men hurled themselves at Foyle. He backed a step and pressed his tongue against his upper incisors. Neural circuits buzzed and every sense and response in his body was accelerated by a factor of five.

The effect was an instantaneous reduction of the external world to extreme slow motion. Sound became a deep garble. Color shifted down the spectrum to the red. The two assailants seemed to float toward him with dreamlike languor. To the rest of the world Foyle became a blur of action. He side-stepped the blow inching toward him, walked around the man, raised him and threw him toward the crater in the living room. He threw the second man after the first jackal. To Foyle's accelerated senses their bodies seemed to drift slowly, still in mid-stride, fists inching forward, open mouths emitting heavy clotted sounds.

Foyle whipped to the woman cowering in the bed.

"Wsthrabdy?" the blur asked.

The woman shrieked.

Foyle pressed his upper incisors again, cutting off the acceleration. The external world shook itself out of slow motion back to normal. Sound and color leaped up the spectrum and the two jackals disappeared through the crater and crashed into the apartment below.

"Was there a body?" Foyle repeated gently. "A Negro girl?" The woman was unintelligible. He took her by the hair and shook her, then hurled her through the crater in the living room floor.

His search for a clue to Robin's fate was interrupted by the mob from the hall. They carried torches and makeshift weapons. The Jack-jaunters were not professional killers. They only worried defenseless prey to death. "Don't bother me," Foyle warned quietly, ferreting intently through closets and under overturned furniture.

They edged closer, goaded by a ruffian in a mink suit and a tricornered hat, and inspired by the curses percolating up from the floor below. The man in the tricorne threw a torch at Foyle. It burned him. Foyle accelerated again and the Jack-jaunters were transformed into living statues. Foyle picked up half a chair and calmly clubbed the slow-motion figures. They remained upright. He thrust the man in the tricorne down on the floor and knelt on him. Then he decelerated.

Again the external world came to life. The jackals dropped in their tracks, pole-axed. The man in the tricorne hat and mink suit roared.

"Was there a body in here?" Foyle asked. "Negro girl. Very tall. Very beautiful."

The man writhed and attempted to gouge Foyle's eyes.

"You keep track of bodies," Foyle said gently. "Some of you Jacks like dead girls better than live ones. Did you find her body in here?"

Receiving no satisfactory answer, he picked up a torch and set fire to the mink suit. He followed the Jack-jaunter into the living room and watched him with detached interest. The man howled, toppled over the edge of the crater and flamed down into the darkness below.

"Was there a body?" Foyle called down quietly. He shook his head at the answer. "Not very deft," he murmured. "I've got to learn how to extract information. Dagenham could teach me a thing or two."

He switched off his electronic system and jaunted.

He appeared in Green Bay, smelling so abominably of singed hair and scorched skin that he entered the local Presteign shop (jewels, perfumes, cosmetics, ionics, & surrogates) to buy a deodorant. But the local Mr. Presto had evidently witnessed the arrival of the Four Mile Circus and recognized him. Foyle at once awoke from his detached intensity and became the outlandish Fourmyle of Ceres. He clowned and cavorted, bought a twelve-ounce flagon of *Euge No. 5* at ₵r 100 the ounce, dabbed himself delicately and tossed the bottle into the street to the edification and delight of Mr. Presto.

The record clerk at the County Record Office was unaware of Foyle's identity and was obdurate and uncompromising.

"No, Sir. County Records Are Not Viewed Without Proper Court Order For Sufficient Cause. That Must Be Final."

Foyle examined him keenly and without rancor. "Asthenic type," he decided. "Slender, long-boned, no strength. Epileptoid character. Self-centered, pedantic, single-minded, shallow. Not bribable; too repressed and straitlaced. But repression's the chink of his armor."

An hour later six followers from the Four Mile Circus waylaid the record clerk. They were of the female persuasion and richly endowed with vice. Two hours later, the record clerk, dazed by flesh and the devil, delivered up his information. The apartment building had been opened to Jack-jaunting by a gas explosion two weeks earlier. All tenants had been forced to move. Robin Wednesbury was in protective confinement in Mercy Hospital near the Iron Mountain Proving Grounds.

"Protective confinement?" Foyle wondered. "What for? What's she done?"

It took thirty minutes to organize a Christmas party in the Four Mile Circus. It was made up of musicians, singers, actors, and rabble who knew the Iron Mountain co-ordinates. Led by their chief buffoon, they jaunted up with music, fireworks, firewater, and gifts. They paraded through the town spreading largess and laughter. They blundered into the radar field of the Proving Ground protection system and were driven out with laughter. Fourmyle of Ceres, dressed as Santa Claus, scattering bank notes from a huge sack over his shoulder and leaping in agony as the induction field of the protection system burned his bottom, made an entrancing spectacle. They burst into Mercy Hospital, following Santa Claus who roared and cavorted with the detached calm of a solemn elephant. He kissed the nurses, made drunk the attendants, pestered the patients with gifts, littered the corridors with money, and abruptly disappeared when the happy rioting reached such heights that the police had to be called. Much later it was discovered that a patient had disappeared too, despite the fact that she had been under sedation and was incapable of jaunting. As a matter of fact she departed from the hospital inside Santa's sack.

Foyle jaunted with her over his shoulder to the hospital grounds. There, in a quiet grove of pines under a frosty sky, he helped her out of the sack. She wore severe white hospital pajamas and was beautiful. He removed his own costume, watching the girl intently, waiting to see if she would recognize him and remember him.

She was alarmed and confused; her telesending was like heat lightning: *"My God! Who is he? What's happened? Jacks again? Murder, this time? The music. The uproar. Why kidnapped in a sack? Drunks slurring on trombones. 'Yes, Virginia, there is a Santa Claus.' Adeste Fidelis. There go the rockets. Feu de joi: or feu d'enfer? What's he want from me? Who is he?"*

"I'm Fourmyle of Ceres," Foyle said.

"What? Who? Fourmyle of—? Yes, of course. *The buffoon. The bourgeois gentilhomme. Vulgarity. Imbecility. Obscenity. The Four Mile Circus. My God! Am I telesending? Can you hear me?"*

"I hear you, Miss Wednesbury," Foyle said quietly.

"What have you done? Why? What do you want with me? I—"

"I want you to look at me."

"Bonjour, Madame. In my sack, Madame. Ecco! Look at me. I'm looking," Robin said, trying to control the jangle of her thoughts. She gazed up into his face without recognition. *"It's a face. I've seen so many like it. The faces of men, oh God! The features of masculinity. Everyman in rut. Will God never save us from brute desire?"*

"My rutting season's over, Miss Wednesbury."

"I'm sorry you heard that. I'm terrified, naturally. I—You know me?"

"I know you."

"We've met before?" She scrutinized him closely, but still without recognition. Deep down inside Foyle there was a surge of triumph. If this woman of all women failed to remember him he was safe, provided he kept blood and brains and face under control.

"We've never met," he said. "I've heard of you. I want something from you. That's why we're here; to talk about it. If you don't like my offer you can go back to the hospital."

"You want something? *But I've got nothing . . . nothing. Nothing's left but shame and—Oh God! Why did the suicide fail? Why couldn't I—*"

"So that's it?" Foyle interrupted softly. "You tried to commit suicide, eh? That accounts for the gas explosion that opened the building . . . And your protective confinement. Attempted suicide. Why weren't you hurt in the explosion?"

"So many were hurt. So many died. But I didn't. I'm unlucky, I suppose. I've been unlucky all my life."

"Why suicide?"

"I'm tired. I'm finished. I've lost everything . . . I'm on the army gray list . . . suspected, watched, reported. No job. No family. No—Why suicide? Dear God, what else but suicide?"

"You can work for me."

"I can . . . What did you say?"

"I want you to work for me, Miss Wednesbury."

She burst into hysterical laughter. "For you? *Another camp follower. Another Whore of Babylon in the Circus?* Work for you, Fourmyle?"

"You've got sex on the brain," he said gently. "I'm not looking for tarts. They look for me, as a rule."

"I'm sorry. *I'm obsessed by the brute who destroyed me.* I—I'll try to make sense." Robin calmed herself. "Let me understand you. You've taken me out of the hospital to offer me a job. You've heard of me. That means you want something special. My speciality is telesending."

"And charm."

"What?"

"I want to buy your charm, Miss Wednesbury."

"I don't understand."

"Why," Foyle said mildly. "It ought to be simple for you. I'm the buffoon. I'm vulgarity, imbecility, obscenity. That's got to stop. I want you to be my social secretary."

"You expect me to believe that? You could hire a hundred social secretaries . . . a thousand, with your money. You expect me to believe that I'm the only one for you? That you had to kidnap me from protective confinement to get me?"

Foyle nodded. "That's right, there are thousands, but only one that can telesend."

"What's that got to do with it?"

"You're going to be the ventriloquist; I'm going to be your dummy. I don't know the upper classes; you do. They have their own talk, their own jokes, their own manners. If a man wants to be accepted by them he's got to talk their language. I can't, but you can. You'll talk for me, through my mouth . . ."

"But you can learn."

"No. It would take too long. And charm can't be learned. I want to buy your charm, Miss Wednesbury. Now, about salary. I'll pay you a thousand a month."

Her eyes widened. "You're very generous, Fourmyle."

"I'll clean up this suicide charge for you."

"You're very kind."

"And I'll guarantee to get you off the army gray list. You'll be back on the white list by the time you finish working for me. You can start with a clean slate and a bonus. You can start living again."

Robin's lips trembled and then she began to cry. She sobbed and shook and Foyle had to steady her. "Well," he asked. "Will you do it?"

She nodded. "You're so kind . . . It's . . . I'm not used to kindness any more."

The dull concussion of a distant explosion made Foyle stiffen. "Christ!" he exclaimed in sudden panic. "Another Blue Jaunte. I—"

"No," Robin said. "I don't know what blue jaunte is, but that's the Proving Ground. They—" She looked up at Foyle's face and screamed. The unexpected shock of the explosion and the vivid chain of associations had wrenched loose his iron control. The blood-red scars of tattooing showed under his skin. She stared at him in horror, still screaming.

He touched his face once, then leaped forward and gagged her. Once again he had hold of himself.

"It shows, eh?" he murmured with a ghastly smile. "Lost my grip for a minute. Thought I was back in Gouffre Martel listening to a Blue Jaunte. Yes. I'm Foyle. The brute who destroyed you. You had to know, sooner or later, but I'd hoped it would be later. I'm Foyle, back again. Will you be quiet and listen to me?"

She shook her head frantically, trying to struggle out of his grasp. With detached calm he punched her jaw. Robin sagged. Foyle picked her up, wrapped her in his coat and held her in his arms, waiting for consciousness to return. When he saw her eyelids flutter he spoke again.

"Don't move or you'll be sick. Maybe I didn't pull that punch enough."

"*Brute . . . Beast . . .*"

"I could do this the wrong way," he said. "I could blackmail you. I know your mother and sisters are on Callisto, that you're classed as an alien belligerent by association. That puts you on the black list, *ipso facto*. Is that right? *Ipso facto*. 'By the very fact.' Latin. You can't trust hypno-learning. I could point out that all I have to do is send anonymous information to Central Intelligence and you wouldn't be just suspect any more. They'd be ripping information out of you inside twelve hours . . ."

He felt her shudder. "But I'm not going to do it that way. I'm going to tell you the truth because I want to turn you into a partner. Your mother's in the Inner Planets. She's in the Inner Planets," he repeated. "She may be on Terra."

"Safe?" she whispered.

"I don't know."

"Put me down."

"You're cold."

"Put me down."

He set her on her feet.

"You destroyed me once," she said in choked tones. "Are you trying to destroy me again?"

"No. Will you listen?"

She nodded.

"I was lost in space. I was dead and rotting for six months. A ship came up that could have saved me. It passed me by. It let me die. A ship named *Vorga*. *Vorga*-T:1339. Does that mean anything to you?"

"No."

"Jiz McQueen—a friend of mine who's dead now—once told me to find out why I was left to rot. That would be the answer to who gave the order. So I started buying information about *Vorga*. Any information."

"What's that to do with my mother?"

"Just listen. Information was tough to buy. The *Vorga* records were moved from the Bo'ness & Uig files. I managed to locate three names . . . three out of a standard crew of four officers and twelve men. Nobody knew anything or nobody would talk. And I found this." Foyle took a silver locket from his pocket and handed it to Robin. "It was pawned by some spaceman off the *Vorga*. That's all I could find out."

Robin uttered a cry and opened the locket with trembling fingers. Inside was her picture and the pictures of two other girls. As the locket was opened, the 3D photos smiled and whispered: "Love from Robin, Mama . . . Love from Holly, Mama . . . Love from Wendy, Mama . . ."

"It is my mother's," Robin wept. "It . . . She . . . For pity's sake, where is she? What happened?"

"I don't know," Foyle said steadily. "But I can guess. I think your mother got out of that concentration camp . . . one way or another."

"And my sisters too. She'd never leave them."

"Maybe your sisters too. I think *Vorga* was running refugees out of Callisto. Your family paid with money and jewelry to get aboard and be taken to the Inner Planets. That's how a spaceman off the *Vorga* came to pawn this locket."

"Then where are they?"

"I don't know. Maybe they were dumped on Mars or Venus. Most probably they were sold to a labor camp on the Moon, which is why they haven't been able to get in touch with you. I don't know where they are, but *Vorga* can tell us."

"Are you lying? Tricking me?"

"Is that locket a lie? I'm telling the truth . . . all the truth I know. I want to find out why they left me to die, and who gave the order. The man who gave the order will know where your mother and sisters are. He'll tell you . . . before I kill him. He'll have plenty of time. He'll be a long time dying."

Robin looked at him in horror. The passion that gripped him was making his face once again show the scarlet stigmata. He looked like a tiger closing in for the kill.

"I've got a fortune to spend . . . never mind how I got it. I've got three months to finish the job. I've learned enough maths to compute the probabilities. Three months is the outside before they figure that Fourmyle of Ceres is Gully Foyle. Ninety days. From New Year's to All Fools. Will you join me?"

"You?" Robin cried with loathing. "Join you?"

"All this Four Mile Circus is camouflage. Nobody ever suspects a clown. But I've been studying, learning, preparing for the finish. All I need now is you."

"Why?"

"I don't know where the hunt is going to lead me . . . society or slums. I've got to be prepared for both. The slums I can handle alone. I haven't forgotten the gutter, but I need you for society. Will you come in with me?"

"You're hurting me." Robin wrenched her arm out of Foyle's grasp.

"Sorry. I lose control when I think about *Vorga*. Will you help me find *Vorga* and your family?"

"I hate you," Robin burst out. "I despise you. You're rotten. You destroy everything you touch. Someday I'll pay you back."

"But we work together from New Year's to All Fools?"

"We work together."

CHAPTER
NINE

On New Year's Eve, Geoffrey Fourmyle of Ceres made his onslaught on society. He appeared first in Canberra at the Government House ball, half an hour before midnight. This was a highly formal affair, bursting with color and pageantry, for it was the custom at formals for society to wear the evening dress that had been fashionable the year its clan was founded or its trademark patented.

Thus, the Morses (Telephone and Telegraph) wore nineteenth century frock coats and their women wore Victorian hoop skirts. The Skodas (Powder & Guns) harked back to the late eighteenth century, wearing Regency tights and crinolines. The daring Peenemundes (Rockets & Reactors), dating from the 1920's, wore tuxedos, and their women unashamedly revealed legs, arms, and necks in the décolleté of antique Worth and Mainbocher gowns.

Fourmyle of Ceres appeared in evening clothes, very modern and very black, relieved only by a white sunburst on his shoulder, the trademark of the Ceres clan. With him was Robin Wednesbury in a glittering white gown, her slender waist tight in whalebone, the bustle of the gown accentuating her long, straight back and graceful step.

The black and white contrast was so arresting that an orderly was sent to check the sunburst trademark in the Almanac of Peerages and Patents. He returned with the news that it was of the Ceres Mining Company, organized in 2250 for the exploitation of the mineral resources of Ceres, Pallas, and Vesta. The resources had never manifested themselves and the House of Ceres had gone into eclipse but had never become extinct. Apparently it was now being revived.

"Fourmyle? The clown?"

"Yes. The Four Mile Circus. Everybody's talking about him."

"Is that the same man?"

"Couldn't be. He looks human."

Society clustered around Fourmyle, curious but wary.

"Here they come," Foyle muttered to Robin.

"Relax. They want the light touch. They'll accept anything if it's amusing. Stay tuned."

"Are you that dreadful man with the circus, Fourmyle?"

"Sure you are. Smile."

"I am, madam. You may touch me."

"Why, you actually seem proud. Are you proud of your bad taste?"

"The problem today is to have any taste at all."

"The problem today is to have any taste at all. I think I'm lucky."

"Lucky but dreadfully indecent."

"Indecent but not dull."

"And dreadful but delightful. Why aren't you cavorting now?"

"I'm 'under the influence,' Madam."

"Oh dear. Are you drunk? I'm Lady Shrapnel. When will you be sober again?"

"I'm under your influence, Lady Shrapnel."

"You wicked young man. Charles! Charles, come here and save Fourmyle. I'm ruining him."

"That's Victor of RCA Victor."

"Fourmyle, is it? Delighted. What's that entourage of yours cost?"

"Tell him the truth."

"Forty thousand, Victor."

"Good Lord! A week?"

"A day."

"A day! What on earth d'you want to spend all that money for?"

"The truth!"

"For notoriety, Victor."

"Ha! Are you serious?"

"I told you he was wicked, Charles."

"Damned refreshing. Klaus! Here a moment. This impudent young man is spending forty thousand a day . . . for notoriety, if you please."

"Skoda of Skoda."

"Good evening, Fourmyle. I am much interested in this revival of the name. You are, perhaps, a cadet descendant of the original founding board of Ceres, Inc.?"

"Give him the truth."

"No, Skoda. It's a title by purchase. I bought the company. I'm an upstart."

"Good. Toujours l'audace!"

"My word, Fourmyle! You're frank."

"Told you he was impudent. Very refreshing. There's a parcel of damned upstarts about, young man, but they don't admit it. Elizabeth, come and meet Fourmyle of Ceres."

"Fourmyle! I've been dying to meet you."

"Lady Elizabeth Citroen."

"Is it true you travel with a portable college?"

"The light touch here."

"A portable high school, Lady Elizabeth."

"But why on earth, Fourmyle?"

"Oh, madam, it's so difficult to spend money these days. We have to find the silliest excuses. If only someone would invent a new extravagance."

"You ought to travel with a portable inventor, Fourmyle."

"I've got one. Haven't I, Robin? But he wastes his time on perpetual motion. What I need is a resident spendthrift. Would any of your clans care to lend me a younger son?"

"Welcome, by God! And there's many a clan would pay for the privilege of unloading."

"Isn't perpetual motion spendthrift enough for you, Fourmyle?"

"No. It's a shocking waste of money. The whole point of extravagance is to act like a fool and feel like a fool, but enjoy it. Where's the joy in perpetual motion? Is there any extravagance in entropy? Millions for nonsense but not one cent for entropy. My slogan."

They laughed and the crowd clustering around Fourmyle grew. They were delighted and amused. He was a new toy. Then it was midnight, and as the great clock tolled in the New Year, the gathering prepared to jaunte with midnight around the world.

"Come with us to Java, Fourmyle. Regis Sheffeld's giving a marvelous legal party. We're going to play 'Sober The Judge.'"

"Hong Kong, Fourmyle."

"Tokyo, Fourmyle. It's raining in Hong Kong. Come to Tokyo and bring your circus."

"Thank you, no. Shanghai for me. The Soviet Duomo. I promise an extravagant reward to the first one who discovers the deception of my costume. Meet you all in two hours. Ready, Robin?"

"Don't jaunte. Bad manners. Walk out. Slowly. Languor is chic. Respects to the Governor . . . To the Commissioner . . . Their Ladies . . . Bien. Don't forget to tip the attendants. Not him, idiot! That's the Lieutenant Governor. All right. You made a hit. You're accepted. Now what?"

"Now what we came to Canberra for."

"I thought we came for the ball."

"The ball *and* a man named Forrest."

"Who's that?"

"Ben Forrest, spaceman off the *Vorga*. I've got three leads to the man who gave the order to let me die. Three names. A cook in Rome named Poggi; a quack in Shanghai named Orel; and this man. Forrest. This is a combined operation . . . society and search. Understand?"

"I understand."

"We've got two hours to rip Forrest open. D'you know the co-ordinates of the Aussie Cannery? The company town?"

"I don't want any part of your *Vorga* revenge. I'm searching for my family."

"This is a combined operation . . . every way," he said with such detached savagery that she winced and at once jaunted. When Foyle arrived in his tent in the Four Mile Circus on Jervis Beach, she was already changing into travel clothes. Foyle looked at her. Although he forced her to live in his tent for security reasons, he had never touched her again. Robin caught his glance, stopped changing and waited.

He shook his head. "That's all finished."

"How interesting. You've given up rape?"

"Get dressed," he said, controlling himself. "Tell them they've got two hours to get the camp up to Shanghai."

It was twelve-thirty when Foyle and Robin arrived at the front office of the Aussie Cannery company town. They applied for identification tags and were greeted by the mayor himself.

"Happy New Year," he caroled. "Happy! Happy! Happy! Visiting? A pleasure to drive you around. Permit me." He bundled them into a lush helicopter and took off. "Lots of visitors tonight. Ours is a friendly town. Friendliest company town in the world." The plane circled giant buildings. "That's our ice palace . . . Swimming baths on the left . . . Big dome is the ski jump. Snow all year 'round . . . Tropical gardens under that glass roof. Palms, parrots, orchids, fruit. There's our market . . . theater . . . got our own broadcasting company, too. 3D-5S. Take a look at the football stadium. Two of our boys made All-American this year. Turner at Right Rockne and Otis at Left Thorpe."

"Do tell," Foyle murmured.

"Yessir, we've got everything. Everything. You don't have to jaunte around the world looking for fun. Aussie Cannery brings the world to you. Our town's a little universe. Happiest little universe in the world."

"Having absentee problems, I see."

The mayor refused to falter in his sales pitch. "Look down at the streets. See those bikes? Motorcycles? Cars? We can afford more luxury transportation per capita than any other town on earth. Look at those homes. Mansions. Our people are rich and happy. We keep 'em rich and happy."

"But do you keep them?"

"What d'you mean? Of course we—"

"You can tell us the truth. We're not job prospects. Do you keep them?"

"We can't keep 'em more than six months," the mayor groaned. "It's a hell of a headache. We give 'em everything but we can't hold on to 'em. They get the wanderlust and jaunte. Absenteeism's cut our production by 12 per cent. We can't hold on to steady labor."

"Nobody can."

"There ought to be a law. Forrest, you said? Right here."

He landed them before a Swiss chalet set in an acre of gardens and took off, mumbling to himself. Foyle and Robin stepped before the door of the house, waiting for the monitor to pick them up and announce them. Instead, the door flashed red, and a white skull and crossbones appeared on it. A canned voice spoke: "WARNING. THIS RESIDENCE IS MAN-TRAPPED BY THE LETHAL DEFENSE CORPORATION OF SWEDEN. R:77–23. YOU HAVE BEEN LEGALLY NOTIFIED."

"What the hell?" Foyle muttered. "On New Year's Eve? Friendly fella. Let's try the back."

They walked around the chalet, pursued by the skull and crossbones flashing at intervals, and the canned warning. At one side, they saw the top of a cellar window brightly illuminated and heard the muffled chant of voices: "The Lord is my shepherd, I shall not want . . ."

"Cellar Christians!" Foyle exclaimed. He and Robin peered through the window. Thirty worshippers of assorted faiths were celebrating the New Year with a combined and highly illegal service. The twenty-fifth century had not yet abolished God, but it had abolished organized religion.

"No wonder the house is man-trapped," Foyle said. "Filthy practices like that. Look, they've got a priest and a rabbi, and that thing behind them is a crucifix."

"Did you ever stop to think what swearing is?" Robin asked quietly. "You say 'Jesus' and 'Jesus Christ.' Do you know what that is?"

"Just swearing, that's all. Like 'ouch' or 'damn.'"

"No, it's religion. You don't know it, but there are two thousand years of meaning behind words like that."

"This is no time for dirty talk," Foyle said impatiently. "Save it for later. Come on."

The rear of the chalet was a solid wall of glass, the picture window of a dimly lit, empty living room.

"Down on your face," Foyle ordered. "I'm going in."

Robin lay prone on the marble patio. Foyle triggered his body, accelerated into a lightning blur, and smashed a hole in the glass wall. Far down on the sound spectrum he heard dull concussions. They were shots. Quick projectiles laced toward him. Foyle dropped to the floor and tuned his ears, sweeping from low bass to supersonic until at last he picked up the hum of the Man-Trap control mechanism. He turned his head gently, pin-pointed the location by binaural D/F, wove in through the stream of shots and demolished the mechanism. He decelerated.

"Come in, quick!"

Robin joined him in the living room, trembling. The Cellar Christians were pouring up into the house somewhere, emitting the sounds of martyrs.

"Wait here," Foyle grunted. He accelerated, blurred through the house, located the Cellar Christians in poses of frozen light, and sorted through them. He returned to Robin and decelerated.

"None of them is Forrest," he reported. "Maybe he's upstairs. The back way, while they're going out the front. Come on!"

They raced up the back stairs. On the landing they paused to take bearings.

"Have to work fast," Foyle muttered. "Between the shots and the religion riot, the world and his wife'll be jaunting around asking questions—" He broke off. A low mewling sound came from a door at the head of the stairs. Foyle sniffed.

"Analogue!" he exclaimed. "Must be Forrest. How about that? Religion in the cellar and dope upstairs."

"What are you talking about?"

"I'll explain later. In here. I only hope he isn't on a gorilla kick."

Foyle went through the door like a diesel tractor. They were in a large, bare room. A heavy rope was suspended from the ceiling. A naked man was entwined with the rope midway in the air. He squirmed and slithered up and down the rope, emitting a mewling sound and a musky odor.

"Python," Foyle said. "That's a break. Don't go near him. He'll mash your bones if he touches you."

Voices below began to call: "Forrest! What's all the shooting? Happy New Year, Forrest! Where in hell's the celebration?"

"Here they come," Foyle grunted. "Have to jaunte him out of here. Meet you back at the beach. Go!"

He whipped a knife out of his pocket, cut the rope, swung the squirming man to his back and jaunted. Robin was on the empty Jervis beach a moment before him. Foyle arrived with the squirming man oozing over his neck and shoulders like a python, crushing him in a terrifying embrace. The red stigmata suddenly burst out on Foyle's face.

"Sinbad," he said in a strangled voice. "Old Man of the Sea. Quick girl! Right pockets. Three over. Two down. Sting ampule. Let him have it anywh—" His voice was choked off.

Robin opened the pocket, found a packet of glass beads and took them out. Each bead had a bee-sting end. She thrust the sting of an ampule into the writhing man's neck. He collapsed. Foyle shook him off and arose from the sand.

"Christ!" he muttered, massaging his throat. He took a deep breath. "Blood and bowels. Control," he said, resuming his air of detached calm. The scarlet tattooing faded from his face.

"What was all that horror?" Robin asked.

"Analogue. Psychiatric dope for psychotics. Illegal. A twitch has to release himself somehow, revert back to the primitive. He identifies with a particular kind of animal . . . gorilla, grizzly, brood bull, wolf . . . Takes the dope and turns into the animal he admires. Forrest was queer for snakes, seems as if."

"How do you know all this?"

"Told you I've been studying . . . preparing for *Vorga*. This is one of the things I learned. Show you something else I've learned, if you're not chicken-livered. How to bring a twitch out of Analogue."

Foyle opened another pocket in his battle coveralls and got to work on Forrest. Robin watched for a moment, then uttered a horrified cry, turned and walked to the edge of the water. She stood, staring blindly at the surf and the stars, until the mewling and the twisting ceased and Foyle called to her.

"You can come back now."

Robin returned to find a shattered creature seated upright on the beach gazing at Foyle with dull, sober eyes.

"You're Forrest?"

"Who the hell are you?"

"You're Ben Forrest, leading spaceman. Formerly aboard the Presteign *Vorga*."

Forrest cried out in terror.

"You were aboard the *Vorga* on September 15, 2436."

The man sobbed and shook his head.

"On September sixteen you passed a wreck. Out near the asteroid belt. Wreck of the *Nomad*, your sister ship. She signalled for help. *Vorga* passed her by. Left her to drift and die. Why did *Vorga* pass her by?"

Forrest began to scream hysterically.

"Who gave the order to pass her by?"

"Jesus, no! No! No!"

"The records are all gone from the Bo'ness & Uig files. Someone got to them before me. Who was that? Who was aboard *Vorga*? Who shipped with you? I want officers and crew. Who was in command?"

"No," Forrest screamed. "No!"

Foyle held a sheaf of bank notes before the hysterical man's face. "I'll pay for the information. Fifty thousand. Analogue for the rest of your life. Who gave the order to let me die, Forrest? Who?"

The man smote the bank notes from Foyle's hand, leaped up and ran down the beach. Foyle tackled him at the edge of the surf. Forrest fell headlong, his face in the water. Foyle held him there.

"Who commanded *Vorga*, Forrest? Who gave the order?"

"You're drowning him!" Robin cried.

"Let him suffer a little. Water's easier than vacuum. I suffered for six months. Who gave the order, Forrest?"

The man bubbled and choked. Foyle lifted his head out of the water. "What are you? Loyal? Crazy? Scared? Your kind would sell out for five thousand. I'm offering fifty. Fifty thousand for information, you son of a bitch, or you die slow and hard." The tattooing appeared on Foyle's face. He forced Forrest's head back into the water and held the struggling man. Robin tried to pull him off.

"You're murdering him!"

Foyle turned his terrifying face on Robin. "Get your hands off me, bitch! Who was aboard with you, Forrest? Who gave the order? Why?"

Forrest twisted his head out of the water. "Twelve of us on *Vorga*," he screamed. "Christ save me! There was me and Kemp—"

He jerked spasmodically and sagged. Foyle pulled his body out of the surf.

"Go on. You and who? Kemp? Who else? Talk."

There was no response. Foyle examined the body.

"Dead," he growled.

"Oh my God! My God!"

"One lead shot to hell. Just when he was opening up. What a damned break." He took a deep breath and drew calm about him like an iron cloak. The tattooing disappeared from his face. He adjusted his watch for 120 degrees east longitude. "Almost midnight in Shanghai. Let's go. Maybe we'll have better luck with Sergei Orel, pharmacist's mate off the *Vorga*. Don't look so scared. This is only the beginning. Go, girl. Jaunte!"

Robin gasped. He saw that she was staring over his shoulder with an expression of incredulity. Foyle turned. A flaming figure loomed on the beach, a huge man with burning clothes and a hideously tattooed face. It was himself.

"Christ!" Foyle exclaimed. He took a step toward his burning image, and abruptly it was gone.

He turned to Robin, ashen and trembling. "Did you see that?"

"Yes."

"What was it?"

"You."

"For God's sake! Me? How's that possible? How—"

"It was you."

"But—" He faltered, the strength and furious possession drained out of him. "Was it illusion? Hallucination?"

"I don't know. I saw it too."

"Christ Almighty! To see yourself . . . face to face . . . The clothes were on fire. Did you see that? What in God's name was it?"

"It was Gully Foyle," Robin said, "burning in hell."

"All right," Foyle burst out angrily. "It was me in hell, but I'm still going through with it. If I burn in hell, *Vorga*'ll burn with me." He pounded his palms together, stinging himself back to strength and purpose. "I'm still going through with it, by God! Shanghai next. Jaunte!"

CHAPTER
TEN

At the costume ball in Shanghai, Fourmyle of Ceres electrified society by appearing as Death in Dürer's "Death and the Maiden" with a dazzling blonde creature clad in transparent veils. A Victorian society which stifled its women in purdah, and which regarded the 1920 gowns of the Peenemunde clan as excessively daring, was shocked, despite the fact that Robin Wednesbury was chaperoning the pair. But when Fourmyle revealed that the female was a magnificent android, there was an instant reversal of opinion in his favor. Society was delighted with the deception. The naked body, shameful in humans, was merely a sexless curiosity in androids.

At midnight, Fourmyle auctioned off the android to the gentlemen of the ball.

"The money to go to charity, Fourmyle?"

"Certainly not. You know my slogan: Not one cent for entropy. Do I hear a hundred credits for this expensive and lovely creature? One hundred, gentlemen? She's all beauty and highly adaptable. Two? Thank you. Three and a half? Thank you. I'm bid—Five? Eight? Thank you. Any more bids for this remarkable product of the resident genius of the Four Mile Circus? She walks. She talks. She adapts. She has been conditioned to respond to the highest bidder. Nine? Do I hear any more bids? Are you all done? Are you all through? Sold, to Lord Yale for nine hundred credits."

Tumultuous applause and appalled ciphering: "An android like that must have cost ninety thousand! How can he afford it?"

"Will you turn the money over to the android, Lord Yale? She will respond suitably. Until we meet again in Rome, ladies and gentlemen . . . The Borghese Palace at midnight. Happy New Year."

Fourmyle had already departed when Lord Yale discovered, to the delight of himself and the other bachelors, that a double deception had been perpetrated. The android was, in fact, a living, human creature, all beauty and highly adaptable. She responded magnificently to nine hundred credits. The trick was the smoking room story of the year. The stags waited eagerly to congratulate Fourmyle.

But Foyle and Robin Wednesbury were passing under a sign that read: DOUBLE YOUR JAUNTING OR DOUBLE YOUR MONEY BACK in seven languages, and entering the emporium of DR. SERGEI OREL, CELESTIAL ENLARGER OF CRANIAL CAPABILITIES.

The waiting room was decorated with lurid brain charts demonstrating how Dr. Orel poulticed, cupped, balsamed, and electrolyzed the brain into double its capacity or double your money back. He also doubled your money with anti-febrile purgatives, magnified your morals with tonic roborants, and adjusted all anguished psyches with Orel's Epulotic Vulnerary.

The waiting room was empty. Foyle opened a door at a venture. He and Robin had a glimpse of a long hospital ward. Foyle grunted in disgust.

"A Snow Joint. Might have known he'd be running a dive for hopheads too."

This den catered to Disease Collectors, the most hopeless of neurotic-addicts. They lay in their hospital beds, suffering mildly from illegally induced para-measles, para-flu, para-malaria; devotedly attended by nurses in starched white uniforms, and avidly enjoying their illegal illness and the attention it brought.

"Look at them," Foyle said contemptuously. "Disgusting. If there's anything filthier than a religion-junkey, it's a disease-bird."

"Good evening," a voice spoke behind them.

Foyle shut the door and turned. Dr. Sergei Orel bowed. The good doctor was crisp and sterile in the classic white cap, gown, and surgical mask of the medical clans, to which he belonged by fraudulent assertion only. He was short, swarthy, and olive-eyed, recognizably Russian by his name alone. More than a century of jaunting had so mingled the many populations of the world that racial types were disappearing.

"Didn't expect to find you open for business on New Year's Eve," Foyle said.

"Our Russian New Year comes two weeks later," Dr. Orel answered. "Step this way, please." He pointed to a door and disappeared with a "pop." The door revealed a long flight of stairs. As Foyle and Robin started up the stairs, Dr. Orel appeared above them. "This way, please. Oh . . . one moment." He disappeared and appeared again behind them. "You forgot to close the door." He shut the door and jaunted again. This time he reappeared high at the head of the stairs. "In here, please."

"Showing off," Foyle muttered. "Double your jaunting or double your money back. All the same, he's pretty fast. I'll have to be faster."

They entered the consultation room. It was a glass-roofed penthouse. The walls were lined with gaudy but antiquated medical apparatus: a sedative-bath machine, an electric chair for administering shock treatment to schizophrenics, an EKG analyzer for tracing psychotic patterns, old optical and electronic microscopes.

The quack waited for them behind his desk. He jaunted to the door, closed it, jaunted back to his desk, bowed, indicated chairs, jaunted behind Robin's and held it for her, jaunted to the window and adjusted the shade, jaunted to the light switch and adjusted the lights, then reappeared behind his desk.

"One year ago," he smiled, "I could not jaunte at all. Then I discovered the secret, the Salutiferous Abstersive which . . ."

Foyle touched his tongue to the switchboard wired into the nerve endings of his teeth. He accelerated. He arose without haste, stepped to the slow-motion figure, "Bloo-hwoo-fwaa-mawwing" behind the desk, took out a heavy sap, and scientifically smote Orel across the brow, concussing the frontal lobes and stunning the jaunte center. He picked the quack up and strapped him into the electric chair. All this took approximately five seconds. To Robin Wednesbury it was a blur of motion.

Foyle decelerated. The quack opened his eyes, stirred, discovered where he was, and started in anger and perplexity.

"You're Sergei Orel, pharmacist's mate off the *Vorga*," Foyle said quietly. "You were aboard the *Vorga* on September 16, 2436."

The anger and perplexity turned to terror.

"On September sixteen you passed a wreck. Out near the asteroid belt. It was the wreck of the *Nomad*. She signalled for help and *Vorga* passed her by. You left her to drift and die. Why?"

Orel rolled his eyes but did not answer.

"Who gave the order to pass me by? Who was willing to let me rot and die?"

Orel began to gibber.

"Who was aboard *Vorga*? Who shipped with you? Who was in command? I'm going to get an answer. Don't think I'm not," Foyle said with calm ferocity. "I'll buy it or tear it out of you. Why was I left to die? Who told you to let me die?"

Orel screamed. "I can't talk abou— Wait I'll tell—"

He sagged.

Foyle examined the body.

"Dead," he muttered. "Just when he was ready to talk. Just like Forrest."

"Murdered."

"No. I never touched him. It was suicide." Foyle cackled without humor.

"You're insane."

"No, amused. I didn't kill them; I forced them to kill themselves."

"What nonsense is this?"

"They've been given Sympathetic Blocks. You know about SBs, girl? Intelligence uses them for espionage agents. Take a certain body of information you don't want told. Link it with the sympathetic nervous system that controls automatic respiration and heart beat. As soon as the subject tries to reveal that information, the block comes down, the heart and lungs stop, the man dies, your secret's kept. An agent doesn't have to worry about killing himself to avoid torture; it's been done for him."

"It was done to these men?"

"Obviously."

"But why?"

"How do I know? Refugee running isn't the answer. *Vorga* must have been operating worse rackets than that to take this precaution. But we've got a problem. Our last lead is Poggi in Rome. Angelo Poggi, chef's assistant off the *Vorga*. How are we going to get information out of him without—" He broke off.

His image stood before him, silent, ominous, face burning blood-red, clothes flaming.

Foyle was paralyzed. He took a breath and spoke in a shaking voice. "Who are you? What do you—"

The image disappeared.

Foyle turned to Robin, moistening his lips. "Did you see it?" Her expression answered him. "Was it real?"

She pointed to Sergei Orel's desk, alongside which the image had stood. Papers on the desk had caught fire and were burning briskly. Foyle backed away, still frightened and bewildered. He passed a hand across his face. It came away wet.

Robin rushed to the desk and tried to beat out the flames. She picked up wads of paper and letters and slammed helplessly. Foyle did not move.

"I can't stop it," she gasped at last. "We've got to get out of here."

Foyle nodded, then pulled himself together with power and resolution. "Rome," he croaked. "We jaunte to Rome. There's got to be some explanation for this. I'll find it, by God! And in the meantime I'm not quitting. Rome. Go, girl. Jaunte!"

∞

Since the Middle Ages the Spanish Stairs have been the center of corruption in Rome. Rising from the Piazza di Spagna to the gardens of the Villa Borghese in a broad, long sweep, the Spanish Stairs are, have been, and always will be swarming with vice. Pimps lounge on the stairs, whores, perverts, lesbians, catamites. Insolent and arrogant, they display themselves and jeer at the respectables who sometimes pass.

The Spanish Stairs were destroyed in the fission wars of the late twentieth century. They were rebuilt and destroyed again in the war of the World Restoration in the twenty-first century. Once more they were rebuilt and this time covered over with blast-proof crystal, turning the stairs into a stepped Galleria. The dome of the Galleria cut off the view from the death chamber in Keats's house. No longer would visitors peep through the narrow window and see the last sight that met the dying poet's eyes. Now they saw the smoky dome of the Spanish Stairs, and through it the distorted figures of corruption below.

The Galleria of the Stairs was illuminated at night, and this New Year's Eve was chaotic. For a thousand years Rome has welcomed the New Year with a bombardment . . . firecrackers, rockets, torpedoes, gunshots, bottles, shoes, old pots and pans. For months Romans save junk to be hurled out of top-floor windows when midnight strikes. The roar of fireworks inside the Stairs, and the clatter of debris clashing on the Galleria roof, were deafening as Foyle and Robin Wednesbury climbed down from the carnival in the Borghese Palace.

They were still in costume: Foyle in the livid crimson-and-black tights and doublet of Cesare Borgia, Robin wearing the silver-encrusted gown of Lucrezia Borgia. They wore grotesque velvet masks. The contrast between their Renaissance costumes and the modern clothes around them brought forth jeers and cat-calls. Even the Lobos who frequented the Spanish Stairs, the unfortunate habitual criminals who had had a quarter of their brains burned out by prefrontal lobotomy, were aroused from their dreary apathy to stare. The job seethed around the couple as they descended the Galleria.

"Poggi," Foyle called quietly. "Angelo Poggi?"

A bawd bellowed anatomical adjurations at him.

"Poggi? Angelo Poggi?" Foyle was impassive. "I'm told he can be found on the Stairs at night. Angelo Poggi?"

A whore maligned his mother.

"Angelo Poggi? Ten credits to anyone who brings me to him."

Foyle was ringed with extended hands, some filthy, some scented, all greedy. He shook his head. "Show me, first."

Roman rage crackled around him.

"Poggi? Angelo Poggi?"

∞

After six weeks of loitering on the Spanish Stairs, Captain Peter Y'ang-Yeovil at last heard the words he had hoped to hear. Six weeks of tedious assumption of the identity of one Angelo Poggi, chef's assistant off the *Vorga*, long dead, was finally paying off. It had been a gamble, first risked when Intelligence had brought the news to Captain Y'ang-Yeovil that someone was making cautious inquiries about the crew of the Presteign *Vorga*, and paying heavily for information.

"It's a long shot," Y'ang-Yeovil had said, "But Gully Foyle, AS-128/127:006, *did* make that lunatic attempt to blow up *Vorga*. And twenty pounds of PyrE is worth a long shot."

Now he waddled up the stairs toward the man in the Renaissance costume and mask. He had put on forty pounds weight with glandular shots. He had darkened his complexion with diet manipulation. His features, never of an Oriental cast but cut more along the hawklike lines of the ancient American Indian, easily fell into an unreliable pattern with a little muscular control.

The Intelligence man waddled up the Spanish Stairs, a gross cook with a larcenous countenance. He extended a package of soiled envelopes toward Foyle.

"Filthy pictures, signore? Cellar Christians, kneeling, praying, singing psalms, kissing cross? Very naughty. Very smutty, signore. Entertain your friends . . . Excite the ladies."

"No," Foyle brushed the pornography aside. "I'm looking for Angelo Poggi."

Y'ang-Yeovil signalled microscopically. His crew on the stairs began photographing and recording the interview without ceasing its pimping and whoring. The Secret Speech of the Intelligence Tong of the Inner Planets Armed Forces wig-wagged around Foyle and Robin in a hail of tiny tics, sniffs, gestures, attitudes, motions. It was the ancient Chinese sign language of eyelids, eyebrows, fingertips, and infinitesimal body motions.

"Signore?" Y'ang-Yeovil wheezed.

"Angelo Poggi?"

"Si, signore. I am Angelo Poggi."

"Chef's assistant off the *Vorga*?" Expecting the same start of terror manifested by Forrest and Orel, which he at last understood, Foyle shot out a hand and grabbed Y'ang-Yeovil's elbow. "Yes?"

"Si, signore," Y'ang-Yeovil replied tranquilly. "How can I serve your worship?"

"Maybe this one can come through," Foyle murmured to Robin. "He's not scared. Maybe he knows a way around the Block. I want information from you, Poggi."

"Of what nature, signore, and at what price?"

"I want to buy all you've got. Anything you've got. Name your price."

"But signore! I am a man full of years and experience. I am not to be bought in wholesale lots. I must be paid item by item. Make your selection and I will name the price. What do you want?"

"You were aboard the *Vorga* on September 16, 2436?"

"The cost of that item is ₢r 10."

Foyle smiled mirthlessly and paid.

"I was, signore."

"I want to know about a ship you passed out near the asteroid belt. The wreck of the *Nomad*. You passed her on September 16. *Nomad* signalled for help and *Vorga* passed her by. Who gave that order?"

"Ah, signore!"

"Who gave you that order, and why?"

"Why do you ask, signore?"

"Never mind why I ask. Name the price and talk."

"I must know why a question is asked before I answer, signore." Y'ang-Yeovil smiled greasily. "And I will pay for my caution by cutting the price. Why are you interested in *Vorga* and *Nomad* and this shocking abandonment in space? Were you, perhaps, the unfortunate who was so cruelly treated?"

"He's not Italian! His accent's perfect, but the speech pattern's all wrong. No Italian would frame sentences like that."

Foyle stiffened in alarm. Y'ang-Yeovil's eyes, sharpened to detect and deduce from minutiae, caught the change in attitude. He realized at once that he had slipped somehow. He signalled to his crew urgently.

A white-hot brawl broke out on the Spanish Stairs. In an instant, Foyle and Robin were caught up in a screaming, struggling mob. The crews of the Intelligence Tong were past masters of this OP-I maneuver, designed to outwit a jaunting world. Their split-second timing could knock any man off balance and strip him for identification. Their success was based on the simple fact that between unexpected assault and defensive response there must always be a recognition lag. Within the space of that lag, the Intelligence Tong guaranteed to prevent any man from saving himself.

In three-fifths of a second Foyle was battered, kneed, hammered across the forehead, dropped to the steps and spread-eagled. The mask was plucked from his face, portions of his clothes torn away, and he was ripe and helpless for the rape of the identification cameras. Then, for the first time in the history of the tong, their schedule was interrupted.

A man appeared, straddling Foyle's body . . . a huge man with a hideously tattooed face and clothes that smoked and flamed. The apparition was so appalling that the crew stopped dead and stared. A howl went up from the crowd on the Stairs at the dreadful spectacle.

"The Burning Man! Look! The Burning Man!"

"But *that's* Foyle," Y'ang-Yeovil whispered.

For perhaps a quarter of a minute the apparition stood, silent, burning, staring with blind eyes. Then it disappeared. The man spread-eagled on the ground disappeared too. He turned into a lightning blur of action that whipped through the crew, locating and destroying cameras, recorders, all identification apparatus. Then the blur seized the girl in the Renaissance gown and vanished.

The Spanish Stairs came to life again, painfully, as though struggling out of a nightmare. The bewildered Intelligence crew clustered around Y'ang-Yeovil.

"What in God's name was that, Yeo?"

"I think it was our man. Gully Foyle. You saw that tattooed face."

"And the burning clothes! Christ Almighty!"

"Looked like a witch at the stake."

"But if that burning man was Foyle, who in hell were we wasting our time on?"

"I don't know. Does the Commando Brigade have an Intelligence service they haven't bothered to mention to us?"

"Why the Commandos, Yeo?"

"You saw the way he accelerated, didn't you? He destroyed every record we made."

"I still can't believe my eyes."

"Oh, you can believe what you didn't see, all right. That was top secret Commando technique. They take their men apart and rewire and regear them. I'll have to check with Mars HQ and find out whether Commando Brigade's running a parallel investigation."

"Does the army tell the navy?"

"They'll tell Intelligence," Y'ang-Yeovil said angrily. "This case is critical enough without jurisdictional hassles. And another thing: there was no need to manhandle that girl in the maneuver. It was undisciplined and unnecessary." Y'ang-Yeovil paused, for once unaware of the significant glances passing around him. "I must find out who she is," he added dreamily.

"If she's been regeared too, it'll be real interesting, Yeo," a bland voice, markedly devoid of implication, said. "Boy Meets Commando."

Y'ang-Yeovil flushed. "All right," he blurted. "I'm transparent."

"Just repetitious, Yeo. All your romances start the same way. 'There's no need to manhandle that girl . . . ' And then—Dolly Quaker, Jean Webster, Gwynn Roget, Marion—"

"No names, please!" a shocked voice interrupted. "Does Romeo tell Juliet?"

"You're all going on latrine assignment tomorrow," Y'ang-Yeovil said. "I'm damned if I'll stand for this salacious insubordination. No, not tomorrow; but as soon as this case is closed." His hawk face darkened. "My God, what a mess! Will you ever forget Foyle standing there like a burning brand? But where is he? What's he up to? What's it all mean?"

CHAPTER
ELEVEN

Presteign of Presteign's mansion in Central Park was ablaze for the New Year. Charming antique electric bulbs with zig-zag filaments and pointed tips shed yellow light. The jaunte-proof maze had been removed and the great door was open for the special occasion. The interior of the house was protected from the gaze of the crowd outside by a jeweled screen just inside the door.

The sightseers buzzed and exclaimed as the famous and near-famous of clan and sept arrived by car, by coach, by litter, by every form of luxurious transporation. Presteign of Presteign himself stood before the door, iron gray, handsome, smiling his basilisk smile, and welcomed society to his open house. Hardly had a celebrity stepped through the door and disappeared behind the screen when another, even more famous, came clattering up in a vehicle even more fabulous.

The Colas arrived in a band wagon. The Esso family (six sons, three daughters) was magnificent in a glass-topped Greyhound bus. But Greyhound arrived (in an Edison electric runabout) hard on their heels and there was much laughter and chaffing at the door. But when Edison of Westinghouse dismounted from his Esso-fueled gasoline buggy, completing the circle, the laughter on the steps turned into a roar.

Just as the crowd of guests turned to enter Presteign's home, a distant commotion attracted their attention. It was a rumble, a fierce chatter of pneumatic punches, and an outrageous metallic bellowing. It approached rapidly. The outer fringe of sightseers opened a broad lane. A heavy truck rumbled down the lane. Six men were tumbling baulks of timber out the back of the truck. Following them came a crew of twenty arranging the baulks neatly in rows.

Presteign and his guests watched with amazement. A giant machine, bellowing and pounding, approached, crawling over the ties. Behind it were deposited parallel rails of welded steel. Crews with sledges and pneumatic punches spiked the rails to the timber ties. The track was laid to Presteign's door in a sweeping arc and then curved away. The bellowing engine and crews disappeared into the darkness.

"Good God!" Presteign was distinctly heard to stay. Guests poured out of the house to watch.

A shrill whistle sounded in the distance. Down the track came a man on a white horse, carrying a large red flag. Behind him panted a steam locomotive drawing a single observation car.

The train stopped before Presteign's door. A conductor swung down from the car followed by a Pullman porter. The porter arranged steps. A lady and gentleman in evening clothes descended.

"Shan't be long," the gentleman told the conductor. "Come back for me in an hour."

"Good God!" Presteign exclaimed again.

The train puffed off. The couple mounted the steps.

"Good evening, Presteign," the gentleman said. "Terribly sorry about that horse messing up your grounds, but the old New York franchise still insists on the red flag in front of trains."

"Fourmyle!" the guests shouted.

"Fourmyle of Ceres!" the sightseers cheered.

Presteign's party was now an assured success.

Inside the vast velvet and plush reception hall, Presteign examined Fourmyle curiously. Foyle endured the keen iron-gray gaze with equanimity, meanwhile nodding and smiling to the enthusiastic admirers he had acquired from Canberra to New York.

"Control," he thought. *"Blood, bowels and brains. He grilled me in his office for one hour after that crazy attempt I made on Vorga. Will he recognize me?* Your face is familiar, Presteign," Fourmyle said. "Have we met before?"

"I have not had the honor of meeting a Fourmyle until tonight," Presteign answered ambiguously. Foyle had trained himself to read men, but Presteign's hard, handsome face was inscrutable. Standing face to face, the one detached and compelled, the other reserved and indomitable, they looked like a pair of brazen statues at white heat on the verge of running molten.

"I'm told that you boast of being an upstart, Fourmyle."

"Yes. I've patterned myself after the first Presteign."

"Indeed?"

"You will remember that he boasted of starting the family fortune in the plasma blackmarket during the third World War."

"It was the second war, Fourmyle. But the hypocrites of our clan never acknowledge him. The name was Payne then."

"I hadn't known."

"And what was your unhappy name before you changed it to Fourmyle?"

"It was Presteign."

"Indeed?" The basilisk smile acknowledged the hit. "You claim a relationship with our clan?"

"I will claim it in time."

"Of what degree?"

"Let's say . . . a blood relationship."

"How interesting. I detect a certain fascination for blood in you, Fourmyle."

"No doubt a family weakness, Presteign."

"You're pleased to be cynical," Presteign said, not without cynicism, "but you speak the truth. We have always had a fatal weakness for blood and money. It is our vice. I admit it."

"And I share it."

"A passion for blood and money?"

"Indeed I do. Most passionately."

"Without mercy, without forgiveness, without hypocrisy?"

"Without mercy, without forgiveness, without hypocrisy."

"Fourmyle, you are a young man after my own heart. If you do not claim a relationship with our clan I shall be forced to adopt you."

"You're too late, Presteign. I've already adopted you."

Presteign took Foyle's arm. "You must be presented to my daughter, Lady Olivia. Will you allow me?"

They crossed the reception hall. Triumph surged within Foyle. *He doesn't know. He'll never know.* Then doubt came: *But I'll never know if he does know. He's crucible steel. He could teach me a thing or two about control.*

Acquaintances hailed Fourmyle.

"Wonderful deception you worked in Shanghai."

"Marvelous carnival in Rome, wasn't it? Did you hear about the burning man who appeared on the Spanish Stairs?"

"We looked for you in London."

"What a heavenly entrance that was," Harry Sherwin-Williams called. "Outdid us all, Fourmyle. Made us look like a pack of damned pikers."

"You forget yourself, Harry," Presteign said coldly. "You know I permit no profanity in my home."

"Sorry, Presteign. Where's the circus now, Fourmyle?"

"I don't know," Foyle said. "Just a moment."

A crowd gathered, grinning in anticipation of the latest Fourmyle folly. He took out a platinum watch and snapped open the case. The face of a valet appeared on the dial.

"Ahhh . . . whatever your name is . . . Where are we staying just now?"

The answer was tiny and tinny. "You gave orders to make New York your permanent residence, Fourmyle."

"Oh? Did I? And?"

"We bought St. Patrick's Cathedral, Fourmyle."

"And where is that?"

"Old St. Patrick's, Fourmyle. On Fifth Avenue and what was formerly 50th Street. We've pitched the camp inside."

"Thank you." Fourmyle closed the platinum Hunter. "My address is Old St. Patrick's, New York. There's one thing to be said for the outlawed religions . . . At least they built churches big enough to house a circus."

Olivia Presteign was seated on a dais, surrounded by admirers.

She was a Snow Maiden, an Ice Princess with coral eyes and coral lips, imperious, mysterious, unattainable. Foyle looked at her once and lowered his eyes in confusion before the blind gaze that could only see him as electromagnetic waves and infrared light. His heart began to beat faster.

"Don't be a fool!" he thought desperately. *"Control yourself. Stop dreaming. This can be dangerous . . ."*

He was introduced; was addressed in a husky, silvery voice; was given a cool, slim hand; but the hand seemed to explode within his with an electric shock. It was almost a start of mutual recognition . . . almost a joining of emotional impact.

"This is insane. *She's a symbol. The Dream Princess . . . The Unattainable . . . Control!*"

He was fighting so hard that he scarcely realized he had been dismissed, graciously and indifferently. He could not believe it. He stood, gaping like a lout.

"What? Are you still here, Fourmyle?"

"I couldn't believe I'd been dismissed, Lady Olivia."

"Hardly that, but I'm afraid you *are* in the way of my friends."

"I'm not used to being dismissed. *(No. No. All wrong!)* At least by someone I'd like to count as a friend."

"Don't be tedious, Fourmyle. Do step down."

"How have I offended you?"

"Offended me? Now you're being ridiculous."

"Lady Olivia . . . *(Christ! Can't I say anything right? Where's Robin?)* Can we start again, please?"

"If you're trying to be gauche, Fourmyle, you're succeeding admirably."

"Your hand again, please. Thank you. I'm Fourmyle of Ceres."

"All right." She laughed. "I'll concede you're a clown. Now do step down. I'm sure you can find someone to amuse."

"What's happened this time?"

"Really, sir, are you trying to make me angry?"

"No. *(Yes, I am. Trying to touch you somehow . . . cut through the ice.)* The first time our handclasp was . . . violent. Now it's nothing. What happened?"

"Fourmyle," Olivia said wearily, "I'll concede that you're amusing, original, witty, fascinating . . . anything, if you will only go away."

He stumbled off the dais. *"Bitch. Bitch. Bitch. No. She's the dream just as I dreamed her. The icy pinnacle to be stormed and taken. To lay siege . . . invade . . . ravish . . . force to her knees . . ."*

He came face to face with Saul Dagenham.

He stood paralyzed, coercing blood and bowels.

"Ah, Fourmyle," Presteign said. "This is Saul Dagenham. He can only give us thirty minutes and he insists on spending one of them with you."

"Does he know? Did he send for Dagenham to make sure? Attack. Toujours audace. What happened to your face, Dagenham?" Fourmyle asked with detached curiosity.

The death's head smiled. "And I thought I was famous. Radiation poisoning. I'm hot. Time was when they said 'Hotter than a pistol.' Now they say 'Hotter than Dagenham.'" The deadly eyes raked Foyle. "What's behind that circus of yours?"

"A passion for notoriety."

"I'm an old hand at camouflage myself. I recognize the signs. What's your larceny?"

"Did Dillinger tell Capone?" Foyle smiled back, beginning to relax, restraining his triumph. *I've outfaced them both.* "You look happier, Dagenham." Instantly he realized the slip.

Dagenham picked it up in a flash. "Happier than when? Where did we meet before?"

"Not happier than when; happier than me." Foyle turned to Presteign. "I've fallen desperately in love with Lady Olivia."

"Saul, your half hour's up."

Dagenham and Presteign, on either side of Foyle, turned. A tall woman approached, stately in an emerald evening gown, her red hair gleaming. It was Jisbella McQueen. Their glances met. Before the shock could seethe into his face, Foyle turned, ran six steps to the first door he saw, opened it and darted through.

The door slammed behind him. He was in a short blind corridor. There was a click, a pause, and then a canned voice spoke courteously: "You have invaded a private portion of this residence. Please retire."

Foyle gasped and struggled with himself.

"You have invaded a private portion of this residence. Please retire."

"I never knew . . . Thought she was killed out there . . . She recognized me . . ."

"You have invaded a private portion of this residence. Please retire."

"I'm finished . . . She'll never forgive me . . . Must be telling Dagenham and Presteign now."

The door from the reception hall opened, and for a moment Foyle thought he saw his flaming image. Then he realized he was looking at Jisbella's flaming hair. She made no move, just stood and smiled at him in furious triumph. He straightened.

"By God, I won't go down whining."

Without haste, Foyle sauntered out of the corridor, took Jisbella's arm and led her back to the reception hall. He never bothered to look around for Dagenham or Presteign. They would present themselves, with force and arms, in due time. He smiled at Jisbella; she smiled back, still in triumph.

"Thanks for running away, Gully. I never dreamed it could be so satisfying."

"Running away? My dear Jiz!"

"Well?"

"I can't tell you how lovely you're looking tonight. We've come a long way from Gouffre Martel, haven't we?" Foyle motioned to the ballroom. "Dance?"

Her eyes widened in surprise at his composure. She permitted him to escort her to the ballroom and take her in his arms.

"By the way, Jiz, how did you manage to keep out of Gouffre Martel?"

"Dagenham arranged it. So you dance now, Gully?"

"I dance, speak four languages miserably, study science and philosophy, write pitiful poetry, blow myself up with idiotic experiments, fence like a fool, box like a buffoon . . . In short, I'm the notorious Fourmyle of Ceres."

"No longer Gully Foyle."

"Only to you, dear, and whoever you've told."

"Just Dagenham. Are you sorry I blew your secret?"

"You couldn't help yourself any more than I could."

"No, I couldn't. Your name just popped out of me. What would you have paid me to keep my mouth shut?"

"Don't be a fool, Jiz. This accident's going to earn you about ₵r 17,980,000."

"What d'you mean?"

"I told you I'd give you whatever was left over after I finished *Vorga*."

"You've finished *Vorga*?" she said in surprise.

"No, dear, you've finished me. But I'll keep my promise."

She laughed. "Generous Gully Foyle. Be real generous, Gully. Make a run for it. Entertain me a little."

"Squealing like a rat? I don't know how, Jiz. I'm trained for hunting, nothing else."

"And I killed the tiger. Give me one satisfaction, Gully. Say you were close to *Vorga*. I ruined you when you were half a step from the finish. Yes?"

"I wish I could, Jiz, but I can't. I'm nowhere. I was trying to pick up another lead here tonight."

"Poor Gully. Maybe I can help you out of this jam. I can say . . . oh . . . that I made a mistake . . . or a joke . . . that you really aren't Gully Foyle. I know how to confuse Saul. I can do it, Gully . . . if you still love me."

He looked down at her and shook his head. "It's never been love between us, Jiz. You know that. I'm too one-track to be anything but a hunter."

"Too one-track to be anything but a fool!"

"What did you mean, Jiz . . . Dagenham arranged to keep you out of Gouffre Martel . . . You know how to confuse Saul Dagenham? What have you got to do with him?"

"I work for him. I'm one of his couriers."

"You mean he's blackmailing you? Threatening to send you back if you don't . . ."

"No. We hit it off the minute we met. He started off capturing me; I ended up capturing him."

"How do you mean?"

"Can't you guess?"

He stared at her. Her eyes were veiled, but he understood. "Jiz! With *him?*"

"Yes."

"But how? He—"

"There are precautions. It's . . . I don't want to talk about it, Gully."

"Sorry. He's a long time returning."

"Returning?"

"Dagenham. With his army."

"Oh. Yes, of course." Jisbella laughed again, then spoke in a low, furious tone. "You don't know what a tightrope you've been walking, Gully. If you'd begged or bribed or tried to romance me . . . By God, I'd have ruined you. I'd have told the world who you were . . . Screamed it from the housetops . . ."

"What are you talking about?"

"Saul isn't returning. He doesn't know. You can go to hell on your own."

"I don't believe you."

"D'you think it would take him *this* long to get you? Saul Dagenham?"

"But why didn't you tell him? After the way I ran out on you . . ."

"Because I don't want him going to hell with you. I'm not talking about *Vorga*. I mean something else. PyrE. That's why they hunted you. That's what they're after. Twenty pounds of PyrE."

"What's that?"

"When you got the safe open was there a small box in it? Made of ILI . . . Inert Lead Isotope?"

"Yes."

"What was inside the ILI box?"

"Twenty slugs that looked like compressed iodine crystals."

"What did you do with the slugs?"

"Sent two out for analysis. No one could find out what they are. I'm trying to run an analysis on a third in my lab . . . when I'm not clowning for the public."

"Oh, you are, are you? Why?"

"I'm growing up, Jiz," Foyle said gently. "It didn't take much to figure out *that* was what Presteign and Dagenham were after."

"Where have you got the rest of the slugs?"

"In a safe place."

"They're not safe. They can't ever be safe. I don't know what PyrE is, but I know it's the road to hell, and I don't want Saul walking it."

"You love him that much?"

"I respect him that much. He's the first man that ever showed me an excuse for the double standard."

"Jiz, what is PyrE? You know."

"I've guessed. I've pieced together the hints I've heard. I've got an idea. And I could tell you, Gully, but I won't." The fury in her face was luminous. "I'm running out on *you*, this time. I'm leaving you to hang helpless in the dark. See what it feels like, boy! Enjoy!"

She broke away from him and swept across the ballroom floor. At that moment the first bombs fell.

They came in like meteor swarms; not so many, but far more deadly. They came in on the morning quadrant, that quarter of the globe in darkness from midnight to dawn. They collided head on with the forward side of the earth in its revolution around the sun. They had been traveling a distance of four hundred million miles.

Their excessive speed was matched by the rapidity of the Terran defense computors which traced and intercepted these New Year gifts from the Outer Satellites within the space of microseconds. A multitude of fierce new stars prickled in the sky and vanished; they were bombs detected and detonated five hundred miles above their target.

But so narrow was the margin between speed of defense and speed of attack that many got through. They shot through the aurora level, meteor level, the twilight limit, the stratosphere, and down to earth. The invisible trajectories ended in titanic convulsions.

The first atomic explosion which destroyed Newark shook the Presteign mansion with an unbelievable quake. Floors and walls shuddered and the guests were thrown in heaps along with furniture and decorations. Quake followed quake as the random shower descended around New York. They were deafening, numbing, chilling. The sounds, the shocks, the flares of lurid light on the horizon were so enormous, that reason was stripped from humanity, leaving nothing but flayed animals to shriek, cower, and run. Within the space of five seconds Presteign's New Year party was transformed from elegance into anarchy.

Foyle arose from the floor. He looked at the struggling bodies on the ballroom parquet, saw Jisbella fighting to free herself, took a step toward her and then stopped. He revolved his head, dazedly, feeling it was no part of him. The thunder never ceased. He saw Robin Wednesbury in the reception hall, reeling and battered. He took a step toward her and then stopped again. He knew where he must go.

He accelerated. The thunder and lightning dropped down the spectrum to grinding and flickering. The shuddering quakes turned into greasy undulations. Foyle blurred through the giant house, searching, until at last he found her, standing in the garden, standing tiptoe on a marble bench looking like a marble statue to his accelerated senses . . . the statue of exaltation.

He decelerated. Sensation leaped up the spectrum again and once more he was buffeted by that bigger-than-death size bombardment.

"Lady Olivia," he called.

"Who is that?"

"The clown."

"Fourmyle?"

"Yes."

"And you came searching for me? I'm touched, really touched."

"You're insane to be standing out here like this. I beg you to let me—"

"No, no, no. It's beautiful . . . Magnificent!"

"Let me jaunte with you to some place that's safe."

"Ah, you see yourself as a knight in armor? Chivalry to the rescue. It doesn't suit you, my dear. You haven't the flair for it. You'd best go."

"I'll stay."

"As a beauty lover?"

"As a lover."

"You're still tedious, Fourmyle. Come, be inspired. This is Armageddon . . . Flowering Monstrosity. Tell me what you see."

"There's nothing much," he answered, looking around and wincing. "There's light all over the horizon. Quick clouds of it. Above, there's a . . . a sort of sparkling effect. Like Christmas lights twinkling."

"Oh, you see so little with your eyes. See what I see! There's a dome in the sky, a rainbow dome. The colors run from deep tang to brilliant burn. That's what I've named the colors I see. What would that dome be?"

"The radar screen," Foyle muttered.

"And then there are vasty shafts of fire thrusting up and swaying, weaving, dancing, sweeping. What are they?"

"Interceptor beams. You're seeing the whole electronic defense system."

"And I can see the bombs coming down too . . . quick streaks of what you call red. But not your red; mine. Why can I see them?"

"They're heated by air friction, but the inert lead casing doesn't show the color to us."

"See how much better you're doing as Galileo than Galahad. Oh! There's one coming down in the east. Watch for it! It's coming, coming, coming . . . Now!"

A flare of light on the eastern horizon proved it was not her imagination.

"There's another to the north. Very close. Very. Now!"

A shock tore down from the north.

"And the explosions, Fourmyle . . . They're not just clouds of light. They're fabrics, webs, tapestries of meshing colors. So beautiful. Like exquisite shrouds."

"Which they are, Lady Olivia."

"Are you afraid?"

"Yes."

"Then run away."

"No."

"Ah, you're defiant."

"I don't know what I am. I'm scared, but I won't run."

"Then you're brazening it out. Making a show of knightly courage." The husky voice sounded amused. "Just think, Fourmyle. How long does it take to jaunte? You could be safe in seconds . . . in Mexico, Canada, Alaska. So safe. There must be millions there now. We're probably the last left in the city."

"Not everybody can jaunte so far and so fast."

"Then we're the last left who count. Why don't you leave me? Be safe. I'll be killed soon. No one will ever know your pretense turned tail."

"Bitch!"

"Ah, you're angry. What shocking language. It's the first sign of weakness. Why don't you exercise your better judgment and carry me off? That would be the second sign."

"Damn you!"

He stepped close to her, clenching his fists in rage. She touched his cheek with a cool, quiet hand, but once again there was that electric shock.

"No, it's too late, my dear," she said quietly. "Here comes a whole cluster of red streaks . . . down, down, down . . . directly at us. There'll be no escaping this. Quick, now! Run! Jaunte! Take me with you. Quick! Quick!"

He swept her off the bench. "Bitch! Never!"

He held her, found the soft coral mouth and kissed her; bruised her lips with his, waiting for the final blackout.

The concussion never came.

"Tricked!" he exclaimed. She laughed. He kissed her again and at last forced himself to release her. She gasped for breath, then laughed again, her coral eyes blazing.

"It's over," she said.

"It hasn't begun yet."

"What d'you mean?"

"The war between us."

"Make it a human war," she said fiercely. "You're the first not to be deceived by my looks. Oh God! The boredom of the chivalrous knights and their milk-warm passion for the fairy tale princess. But I'm not like that . . . inside. I'm not. I'm not. Never. Make it a savage war between us. Don't win me . . . destroy me!"

Suddenly she was Lady Olivia again, the gracious snow maiden. "I'm afraid the bombardment has finished, my dear Fourmyle. The show is over. But what an exciting prelude to the New Year. Good night."

"Good night?" he echoed incredulously.

"Good night," she repeated. "Really, my dear Fourmyle, are you so gauche that you never know when you're dismissed? You may go now. Good night."

He hesitated, searched for words, and at last turned and lurched out of the house. He was trembling with elation and confusion. He walked in a daze, scarcely aware of the confusion and disaster around him. The horizon now was lit with the light of red flames. The shock waves of the assault had stirred the atmosphere so violently that winds still whistled in strange gusts. The tremor of the explosions had shaken the city so hard that brick, cornice, glass, and metal were tumbling and crashing. And this despite the fact that no direct hit had been made on New York.

The streets were empty; the city was deserted. The entire population of New York, of every city, had jaunted in a desperate search for safety . . . to the limit of their ability . . . five miles, fifty miles, five hundred miles. Some had jaunted into the center of a direct hit. Thousands died in jaunte-explosions, for the public jaunte stages had never been designed to accommodate the crowding of mass exodus.

Foyle became aware of white-armored Disaster Crews appearing on the streets. An imperious signal directed at him warned him that he was about to be summarily drafted for disaster work. The problem of jaunting was not to get populations out of cities, but to force them to return and restore order. Foyle had no intention of spending a week fighting fire and looters. He accelerated and evaded the Disaster Crew.

At Fifth Avenue he decelerated; the drain of acceleration on his energy was so enormous that he was reluctant to maintain it for more than a few moments. Long periods of acceleration demanded days of recuperation.

The looters and Jack-jaunters were already at work on the avenue, singly, in swarms, furtive yet savage; jackals rending the body of a living but helpless animal. They descended on Foyle. Anything was their prey tonight.

"I'm not in the mood," he told them. "Play with somebody else."

He emptied the money out of his pockets and tossed it to them. They snapped it up but were not satisfied. They desired entertainment and he was obviously a helpless gentleman. Half a dozen surrounded Foyle and closed in to torment him.

"Kind gentleman," they smiled. "We're going to have a party."

Foyle had once seen the mutilated body of one of their party guests. He sighed and detached his mind from visions of Olivia Presteign.

"All right, jackals," he said. "Let's have a party."

They prepared to send him into a screaming dance. Foyle tripped the switchboard in his mouth and became for twelve devastating seconds the most murderous machine ever devised . . . the Commando killer. It was done without conscious thought or violation; his body merely followed the directive taped into muscle and reflex. He left six bodies stretched on the street.

Old St. Pat's still stood, unblemished, eternal, the distant fires flickering on the green copper of its roof. Inside, it was deserted. The tents of the Four Mile Circus filled the nave, illuminated and furnished, but the circus personnel was gone. Servants, chefs, valets, athletes, philosophers, camp followers, and crooks had fled.

"But they'll be back to loot," Foyle murmured.

He entered his own tent. The first thing he saw was a figure in white, crouched on a rug, crooning sunnily to itself. It was Robin Wednesbury, her gown in tatters, her mind in tatters.

"Robin!"

She went on crooning wordlessly. He pulled her up, shook her, and slapped her. She beamed and crooned. He filled a syringe and gave her a tremendous shot of Niacin. The sobering wrench of the drug on her pathetic flight from reality was ghastly. Her satin skin turned ashen. The beautiful face twisted. She recognized Foyle, remembered what she had tried to forget, screamed and sank to her knees. She began to cry.

"That's better," he told her. "You're a great one to escape, aren't you? First suicide. Now this. What's next?"

"*Go away.*"

"Probably religion. I can see you joining a cellar sect with passwords like *Pax Vobiscum.* Bible smuggling and martyrdom for the faith. Can't you ever face up to anything?"

"*Don't you ever run away?*"

"Never. Escape is for cripples. Neurotics."

"*Neurotics. The favorite word of the Johnny-Come-Lately educated. You're so educated, aren't you? So poised. So balanced. You've been running away all your life.*"

"Me? Never. I've been hunting all my life."

"*You've been running. Haven't you ever heard of Attack-Escape? To run away from reality by attacking it . . . denying it . . . destroying it? That's what you've been doing.*"

"Attack-Escape?" Foyle was brought up with a jolt. "You mean I've been running away from something?"

"*Obviously.*"

"From what?"

"*From reality. You can't accept life as it is. You refuse. You attack it . . . try to force it into your own pattern. You attack and destroy everything that stands in the way of your own insane pattern.*" She lifted her tearstained face. "I can't stand it any more. I want you to let me go."

"Go? Where?"

"To live my own life."

"What about your family?"

"And find them my own way."

"Why? What now?"

"It's too much . . . you *and* the war . . . because you're as bad as the war. Worse. What happened to me tonight is what happens to me every moment I'm with you. I can stand one or the other; not both."

"No," he said. "I need you."

"I'm prepared to buy my way out."

"How?"

"You've lost all your leads to *Vorga*, haven't you?"

"And?"

"I've found another."

"Where?"

"Never mind where. Will you agree to let me go if I turn it over to you?"

"I can take it from you."

"Go ahead. Take it." Her eyes flashed. "If you know what it is, you won't have any trouble."

"I can make you give it to me."

"Can you? After the bombing tonight? Try."

He was taken aback by her defiance. "How do I know you're not bluffing?"

"I'll give you one hint. Remember the man in Australia?"

"Forrest?"

"Yes. He tried to tell you the names of the crew. Do you remember the only name he got out?"

"Kemp."

"He died before he could finish it. The name is Kempsey."

"That's your lead?"

"Yes. Kempsey. Name and address. In return for your promise to let me go."

"It's a sale," he said. "You can go. Give it to me."

She went at once to the travel dress she had worn in Shanghai. From the pocket she took out a sheet of partially burned paper.

"I saw this on Sergei Orel's desk when I was trying to put the fire out . . . the fire the Burning Man started . . ."

She handed him the sheet of paper. It was a fragment of a begging letter. It read:

> ... *do anything to get out of these bacteria fields. Why should a man just because he can't jaunte get treated like a dog? Please help me, Serg. Help an old shipmate off a ship we don't mention. You can spare Ȼr 100. Remember all the favors I done you? Send Ȼr 100 or even Ȼr 50. Don't let me down.*
>
>
>
> Rodg Kempsey
> Barrack 3
> Bacteria, Inc.
> Mare Nubium
> Moon
>

"By God!" Foyle exclaimed. "This *is* the lead. We can't fail this time. We'll know what to do. He'll spill everything . . . everything." He grinned at Robin. "We leave for the moon tomorrow night. Book passage. No, there'll be trouble on account of the attack. Buy a ship. They'll be unloading them cheap anyway."

"We?" Robin said. "You mean you."

"I mean we," Foyle answered. "We're going to the moon. Both of us."

"I'm leaving."

"You're not leaving. You're staying with me."

"But you swore you'd—"

"Grow up, girl. I had to swear to anything to get this. I need you more than ever now. Not for *Vorga*. I'll handle *Vorga* myself. For something much more important."

He looked at her incredulous face and smiled ruefully. "It's too bad, girl. If you'd given me this letter two hours ago I'd have kept my word. But it's too late now. I need a Romance Secretary. I'm in love with Olivia Presteign."

She leaped to her feet in a blaze of fury. *"You're in love with her? Olivia Presteign? In love with that white corpse!"* The bitter fury of her telesending was a startling revelation to him. *"Ah, now you have lost me. Forever. Now I'll destroy you!"*

She disappeared.

CHAPTER
TWELVE

Captain Peter Y'ang-Yeovil was handling reports at Central Intelligence Hq. in London at the rate of six per minute. Information was phoned in, wired in, cabled in, jaunted in. The bombardment picture unfolded rapidly.

ATTACK SATURATED N & S AMERICA FROM 60° TO 120° WEST LONGITUDE . . . LABRADOR TO ALASKA IN N . . . RIO TO ECUADOR IN S . . . ESTIMATED TEN PER CENT (10%)

MISSILES PENETRATED INTERCEPTION SCREEN . . . ESTI-MATED POPULATION LOSS: TEN TO TWELVE MILLION . . .

"Thank God for jaunting," Y'ang-Yeovil said. "Or the losses would have been five times that. All the same, it's close to a knockout. One more punch like that and Terra's finished."

He addressed this to the assistants jaunting in and out of his office, appearing and disappearing, dropping reports on his desk and chalking results and equations on the glass blackboard that covered one entire wall. Informality was the rule, and Y'ang-Yeovil was surprised and suspicious when an assistant knocked on his door and entered with elaborate formality.

"What larceny now?" he asked.

"Lady to see you, Yeo."

"Is this the time for comedy?" Y'ang-Yeovil said in exasper-ated tones. He pointed to the Whitehead equations spelling disas-ter on the transparent blackboard. "Read that and weep on the way out."

"Very special lady, Yeo. Your Venus from the Spanish Stairs."

"Who? What Venus?"

"Your Congo Venus."

"Oh? That one?" Y'ang-Yeovil hesitated. "Send her in."

"You'll interview her in private, of course."

"Of course nothing. There's a war on. Keep those reports coming, but tip everybody to switch to Secret Speech if they have to talk to me."

Robin Wednesbury entered the office, still wearing the torn white evening gown. She had jaunted immediately from New York to London without bothering to change. Her face was strained, but lovely. Y'ang-Yeovil gave her a split-second inspec-tion and realized that his first appreciation of her had not been mistaken. Robin returned the inspection and her eyes dilated. "But you're the cook from the Spanish Stairs! Angelo Poggi!"

As an Intelligence Officer, Y'ang-Yeovil was prepared to deal with this crisis. "Not a cook, madam. I haven't had time to change back to my usual fascinating self. Please sit here, Miss . . . ?"

"Wednesbury. Robin Wednesbury."

"Charmed. I'm Captain Y'ang-Yeovil. How nice of you to come and see me, Miss Wednesbury. You've saved me a long hard search."

"B-But I don't understand. What were you doing on the Spanish Stairs? Why were you hunting—?"

Y'ang-Yeovil saw that her lips weren't moving. "Ah? You're a telepath, Miss Wednesbury? How is that possible? I thought I knew every telepath in the system."

"I'm not a full telepath. I'm a telesend. I can only send . . . not receive."

"Which, of course, makes you worthless to the world. I see." Y'ang-Yeovil cocked a sympathetic eye at her. "What a dirty trick, Miss Wednesbury . . . to be saddled with all the disadvantages of telepathy, and be deprived of all the advantages. I do sympathize. Believe me."

"Bless him! He's the first ever to realize that without being told."

"Careful, Miss Wednesbury, I'm receiving you. Now, about the Spanish Stairs?"

He paused, listening intently to her agitated telesending: *"Why was he hunting? Me? Alien Bellig—Oh God! Will they hurt me? Cut and— Information. I—"*

"My dear girl," Y'ang-Yeovil said gently. He took her hands and held them sympathetically. "Listen to me a moment. You're alarmed over nothing. Apparently you're an Alien Belligerent. Yes?"

She nodded.

"That's unfortunate, but we won't worry about it now. About Intelligence cutting and slicing information out of people . . . that's all propaganda."

"Propaganda?"

"We're not maladroits, Miss Wednesbury. We know how to extract information without being medieval. But we spread the legend to soften people up in advance, so to speak."

"Is that true? He's lying. It's a trick."

"It's true, Miss Wednesbury. I do finesse, but there's no need now. Not when you've evidently come of your own free will to offer information."

"He's too adroit . . . too quick . . . He—"

"You sound as though you've been badly tricked recently, Miss Wednesbury . . . Badly burned."

"I have. God, I have. *By myself, mostly. I'm a fool. A hateful fool.*"

"Never a fool, Miss Wednesbury, and never hateful. I don't know what's happened to shatter your opinion of yourself, but I hope to restore it. So . . . you've been deceived, have you? By yourself, mostly? We all do that. But you've been helped by someone. Who?"

"I'm betraying him."

"Then don't tell me."

"But I've got to find my mother and sisters . . . I can't trust him any more . . . I've got to do it myself." Robin took a deep breath. "I want to tell you about a man named Gulliver Foyle."

Y'ang-Yeovil at once got down to business.

∞

"Is it true he arrived by railroad?" Olivia Presteign asked. "In a locomotive and observation car? What wonderful audacity."

"Yes, he's a remarkable young man," Presteign answered. He stood, iron gray and iron hard, in the reception hall of his home, alone with his daughter. He was guarding honor and life while he waited for servants and staff to return from their panic-stricken jaunte to safety. He chatted imperturbably with Olivia, never once permitting her to realize their grave danger.

"Father, I'm exhausted."

"It's been a trying night, my dear. But please don't retire yet."

"Why not?'

Presteign refrained from telling her that she would be safer with him. "I'm lonely, Olivia. We'll talk for a few minutes."

"I did a daring thing, Father. I watched the attack from the garden."

"My dear! Alone?"

"No. With Fourmyle."

A heavy pounding began to shake the front door which Presteign had closed.

"What's that?"

"Looters," Presteign answered calmly. "Don't be alarmed, Olivia. They won't get in." He stepped to a table on which he had laid out an assortment of weapons as neatly as a game of patience. "There's no danger, my love." He tried to distract her. "You were telling me about Fourmyle. . . ."

"Oh, yes. We watched together . . . describing the bombing to each other."

"Unchaperoned? That wasn't discreet, Olivia."

"I know. I know. I behaved disgracefully. He seemed so big, so sure of himself, that I gave him the Lady Hauteur treatment. You remember Miss Post, my governess, who was so dignified and aloof that I called her Lady Hauteur? I acted like Miss Post. He was furious, Father. That's why he came looking for me in the garden."

"And you permitted him to remain? I'm shocked, dear."

"I am too. I think I was half out of my mind with excitement. What's he like, Father? Tell me. What's he look like to you?"

"He *is* big. Tall, very dark, rather enigmatic. Like a Borgia. He seems to alternate between assurance and savagery."

"Ah, he is savage, then? I could see it myself. He glows with danger. Most people just shimmer . . . he looks like a lightning bolt. It's terribly fascinating."

"My dear," Presteign remonstrated gently. "Unmarried females are too modest to talk like that. It would displease me, my love, if you were to form a romantic attachment for a parvenu like Fourmyle of Ceres."

The Presteign staff jaunted into the reception hall, cooks, waitresses, footmen, pages, coachmen, valets, maids. All were shaken and hang-dog after their flight from death.

"You have deserted your posts. It will be remembered," Presteign said coldly. "My safety and honor are again in your hands. Guard them. Lady Olivia and I will retire."

He took his daughter's arm and led her up the stairs, savagely protective of his ice-pure princess. "Blood and money," Presteign murmured.

"What, Father?"

"I was thinking of a family vice, Olivia. I was thanking the Deity that you have not inherited it."

"What vice is that?"

"There's no need for you to know. It's one that Fourmyle shares."

"Ah, he's wicked? I knew it. Like a Borgia, you said. A wicked Borgia with black eyes and lines in his face. That must account for the pattern."

"Pattern, my dear?"

"Yes. I can see a strange pattern over his face . . . not the usual electricity of nerve and muscle. Something laid over that. It fascinated me from the beginning."

"What sort of pattern do you mean?"

"Fantastic . . . Wonderfully evil. I can't describe it. Give me something to write with. I'll show you."

They stopped before a six-hundred-year-old Chippendale cabinet. Presteign took out a silver-mounted slab of crystal and handed it to Olivia. She touched it with her fingertip; a black dot appeared. She moved her finger and the dot elongated into a line. With quick strokes she sketched the hideous swirls and blazons of a devil mask.

∞

Saul Dagenham left the darkened bedroom. A moment later it was flooded with light as one wall illuminated. It seemed as though a giant mirror reflected Jisbella's bedroom, but with one odd quirk. Jisbella lay in the bed alone, but in the reflection Saul Dagenham sat on the edge of the bed alone. The mirror was, in fact, a sheet of lead glass separating identical rooms. Dagenham had just illuminated his.

"Love by the clock." Dagenham's voice came through a speaker. "Disgusting."

"No, Saul. Never."

"Frustrating."

"Not that, either."

"But unhappy."

"No. You're greedy. Be content with what you've got."

"God knows, it's more than I ever had. You're magnificent."

"You're extravagant. Now go to sleep, darling. We're skiing tomorrow."

"No, there's been a change of plan. I've got to work."

"Oh Saul . . . you promised me. No more working and fretting and running. Aren't you going to keep your promise?"

"I can't with a war on."

"To hell with the war. You sacrificed enough up at Tycho Sands. They can't ask any more of you."

"I've got one job to finish."

"I'll help you finish it."

"No. You'd best keep out of this, Jisbella."

"You don't trust me."

"I don't want you hurt."

"Nothing can hurt us."

"Foyle can."

"W-What?"

"Fourmyle is Foyle. You know that. I know you know."

"But I never—"

"No, you never told me. You're magnificent. Keep faith with me the same way, Jisbella."

"Then how did you find out?"

"Foyle slipped."

"How?"

"The name."

"Fourmyle of Ceres? He bought the Ceres company."

"But Geoffrey Fourmyle?"

"He invented it."

"He thinks he invented it. He remembered it. Geoffrey Fourmyle is the name they use in the megalomania test down in Combined Hospital in Mexico City. I used the Megal Mood on Foyle when I tried to open him up. The name must have stayed buried in his memory. He dredged it up and thought it was original. That tipped me."

"Poor Gully."

Dagenham smiled. "Yes, no matter how we defend ourselves against the outside we're always licked by something from the inside. There's no defense against betrayal, and we all betray ourselves."

"What are you going to do, Saul?"

"Do? Finish him, of course."

"For twenty pounds of PyrE?"

"No. To win a lost war."

"What?" Jisbella came to the glass wall separating the rooms. "You, Saul? Patriotic?"

He nodded, almost guiltily. "It's ridiculous. Grotesque. But I am. You've changed me completely. I'm a sane man again."

He pressed his face to the wall too, and they kissed through three inches of lead glass.

$$\infty$$

Mare Nubium was ideally suited to the growth of anaerobic bacteria, soil organisms, phage, rare moulds, and all those microscopic life forms, essential to medicine and industry, which required airless culture. Bacteria, Inc. was a huge mosaic of culture fields traversed by catwalks spread around a central clump of barracks, offices, and plant. Each field was a giant glass vat, one hundred feet in diameter, twelve inches high and no more than two molecules thick.

A day before the sunrise line, creeping across the face of the moon, reached Mare Nubium, the vats were filled with culture medium. At sunrise, abrupt and blinding on the airless moon, the vats were seeded, and for the next fourteen days of continuous sun they were tended, shielded, regulated, nurtured . . . the field workers trudging up and down the catwalks in spacesuits. As the sunset line crept toward Mare Nubium, the vats were harvested and then left to freeze and sterilize in the two week frost of the lunar night.

Jaunting was of no use in this tedious step-by-step cultivation. Hence Bacteria, Inc. hired unfortunates incapable of jaunting and paid them slave wages. This was the lowest form of labor, the dregs and scum of the Solar System; and the barracks of Bacteria, Inc. resembled an inferno during the two week lay-off period. Foyle discovered this when he entered Barrack 3.

He was met by an appalling spectacle. There were two hundred men in the giant room; there were whores and their hard-eyed pimps, professional gamblers and their portable tables, dope peddlers, money lenders. There was a haze of acrid smoke and the stench of alcohol and Analogue. Furniture, bedding, clothes, unconscious bodies, empty bottles, rotting food were scattered on the floor.

A roar challenged Foyle's appearance, but he was equipped to handle this situation. He spoke to the first hairy face thrust into his.

"Kempsey?" he asked quietly. He was answered outrageously. Nevertheless he grinned and handed the man a Cr 100 note. "Kempsey?" he asked another. He was insulted. He paid again and continued his saunter down the barracks distributing Cr 100 notes in calm thanks for insult and invective. In the center of the barracks he found his key man, the obvious barracks bully, a monster of a man, naked, hairless, fondling two bawds and being fed whiskey by sycophants.

"Kempsey?" Foyle asked in the old gutter tongue. "I'm diggin' Rodger Kempsey."

"I'm diggin' you for broke," the man answered, thrusting out a huge paw for Foyle's money. "Gimmie."

There was a delighted howl from the crowd. Foyle smiled and spat in his eye. There was an abject hush. The hairless man dumped the bawds and surged up to annihilate Foyle. Five seconds later he was groveling on the floor with Foyle's foot planted on his neck.

"Still diggin' Kempsey," Foyle said gently. "Diggin' hard, man. You better finger him, man, or you're gone, is all."

"Washroom!" the hairless man howled. "Holed up. Washroom."

"Now you broke me," Foyle said. He dumped the rest of his money on the floor before the hairless man and walked quickly to the washroom.

Kempsey was cowering in the corner of a shower, face pressed to the wall, moaning in a dull rhythm that showed he had been at it for hours.

"Kempsey?"

The moaning answered him.

"What's a matter, you?"

"Clothes," Kempsey wept. "Clothes. All over, clothes. Like filth, like sick, like dirt. Clothes. All over, clothes."

"Up, man. Get up."

"Clothes. All over, clothes. Like filth, like sick, like dirt . . ."

"Kempsey, mind me, man. Orel sent me."

Kempsey stopped weeping and turned his sodden countenance to Foyle. "Who? Who?"

"Sergei Orel sent me. I've bought your release. You're free. We'll blow."

"When?"

"Now."

"Oh God! God bless him. Bless him!" Kempsey began to caper in weary exultation. The bruised and bloated face split into a facsimile of laughter. He laughed and capered and Foyle led him out of the washroom. But in the barracks he screamed and wept again, and as Foyle led him down the long room, the naked bawds swept up armfuls of dirty clothes and shook them before his eyes. Kempsey foamed and gibbered.

"What's a matter, him?" Foyle inquired of the hairless man in the gutter patois.

The hairless man was now a respectful neutral if not a friend.

"Guesses for grabs," he answered. "Always like that, him. Show old clothes and he twitch. Man!"

"For why, already?"

"For why? Crazy, is all."

At the main-office airlock, Foyle got Kempsey and himself corked in suits and then led him out to the rocket field where a score of anti-grav beams pointed their pale fingers upward from pits to the gibbous earth hanging in the night sky. They entered a pit, entered Foyle's yawl and uncorked. Foyle took a bottle and a sting ampule from a cabinet. He poured a drink and handed it to Kempsey. He hefted the ampule in his palm, smiling.

Kempsey drank the whiskey, still dazed, still exulting. "Free," he muttered. "God bless him! Free. Christ, what I've been through." He drank again. "I still can't believe it. It's like a dream. Why don't you take off, man? I—" Kempsey choked and dropped the glass, staring at Foyle in horror. "Your face!" he exclaimed. "My God, your face! What happened to it?"

"You happened to it, you son of a bitch!" Foyle cried. He leaped up, his tiger face burning, and flung the ampule like a knife. It pierced Kempsey's neck and hung quivering. Kempsey toppled.

Foyle accelerated, blurred to the body, picked it up in mid-fall and carried it aft to the starboard stateroom. There were two main staterooms in the yawl, and Foyle had prepared both of them in advance. The starboard room had been stripped and turned into a surgery. Foyle strapped the body on the operating table, opened a case of surgical instruments, and began the delicate operation he had learned by hypno-training that morning . . . an operation made possible only by his five-to-one acceleration.

He cut through skin and fascia, sawed through the rib cage, exposed the heart, dissected it out and connected veins and arteries to the intricate blood pump alongside the table. He started the pump. Twenty seconds, objective time, had elapsed. He placed an oxygen mask over Kempsey's face and switched on the alternating suction and ructation of the oxygen pump.

Foyle decelerated, checked Kempsey's temperature, shot an anti-shock series into his veins and waited. Blood gurgled through the pump and Kempsey's body. After five minutes, Foyle removed the oxygen mask. The respiration reflex continued. Kempsey was without a heart, yet alive. Foyle sat down alongside the operating table and waited. The stigmata still showed on his face.

Kempsey remained unconscious.

Foyle waited.

Kempsey awoke, screaming.

Foyle leaped up, tightened the straps and leaned over the heartless man.

"Hallo, Kempsey," he said.

Kempsey screamed.

"Look at yourself, Kempsey. You're dead."

Kempsey fainted. Foyle brought him to with the oxygen mask.

"Let me die, for God's sake!"

"What's the matter? Does it hurt? I died for six months, and I didn't whine."

"Let me die."

"In time, Kempsey. Your sympathetic block's been bypassed, but I'll let you die in time, if you behave. You were aboard *Vorga* on September 16, 2436?"

"For Christ's sake, let me die."

"You were aboard *Vorga?*"

"Yes."

"You passed a wreck out in space. Wreck of the *Nomad*. She signalled for help and you passed her by. Yes?"

"Yes."

"Why?"

"Christ! Oh Christ help me!"

"Why?"

"Oh Jesus!"

"I was aboard *Nomad*, Kempsey. Why did you leave me to rot?"

"Sweet Jesus help me! Christ, deliver me!"

"I'll deliver you, Kempsey, if you answer questions. Why did you leave me to rot?"

"Couldn't pick you up."

"Why not?"

"Reffs aboard."

"Oh? I guessed right, then. You were running refugees in from Callisto?"

"Yes."

"How many?"

"Six hundred."

"That's a lot, but you could have made room for one more. Why didn't you pick me up?"

"We were scuttling the reffs."

"What!" Foyle cried.

"Overboard . . . all of them . . . six hundred . . . Stripped 'em . . . took their clothes, money, jewels, baggage . . . Put 'em through the airlock in batches. Christ! The clothes all over the ship . . . The shrieking and the—Jesus! If I could only forget! The naked women . . . blue . . . busting wide open . . . spinning behind us . . . The clothes all over the ship . . . Six hundred . . . Scuttled!"

"You son of a bitch! It was a racket? You took their money and never intended bringing them to earth?"

"It was a racket."

"And that's why you didn't pick me up?"

"Would have had to scuttle you anyway."

"Who gave the order?"

"Captain."

"Name?"

"Joyce. Lindsey Joyce."

"Address?"

"Skoptsy Colony, Mars."

"What!" Foyle was thunderstruck. "He's a Skoptsy? You mean after hunting him for a year, I can't touch him . . . hurt him . . . make him feel what I felt?" He turned away from the tortured man on the table, equally tortured himself by frustration. "A Skoptsy! The one thing I never figured on . . . After preparing that port stateroom for him . . . What am I going to do? What, in God's name, am I going to do?" he roared in fury, the stigmata showing livid on his face.

He was recalled by a desperate moan from Kempsey. He returned to the table and bent over the dissected body. "Let's get it straight for the last time. This Skoptsy, Lindsey Joyce, gave the order to scuttle the reffs?"

"Yes."

"And to let me rot?"

"Yes. Yes. Yes. For God's sake, that's enough. Let me die."

"Live, you pig-man . . . filthy heartless bastard! Live without a heart. Live and suffer. I'll keep you alive forever, you—"

A lurid flash of light caught Foyle's eye. He looked up. His burning image was peering through the large square porthole of the stateroom. As he leaped to the porthole, the burning man disappeared.

Foyle left the stateroom and darted forward to main controls where the observation bubble gave him two hundred and seventy degrees of vision. The Burning Man was nowhere in sight.

"It's not real," he muttered. "It couldn't be real. It's a sign, a good luck sign . . . a Guardian Angel. It saved me on the Spanish Stairs. It's telling me to go ahead and find Lindsey Joyce."

He strapped himself into the pilot chair, ignited the yawl's jets, and slammed into full acceleration.

"Lindsey Joyce, Skoptsy Colony, Mars," he thought as he was thrust back deep into the pneumatic chair. "A Skoptsy . . . Without senses, without pleasure, without pain. The ultimate in Stoic escape. How am I going to punish him? Torture him? Put him in the port stateroom and make him feel what I felt aboard *Nomad?* Damnation! It's as though he's dead. He *is* dead. And I've got to figure how to beat a dead body and make it feel pain. To come so close to the end and have the door slammed in your face . . . The damnable frustration of revenge. Revenge is for dreams . . . never for reality."

An hour later he released himself from the acceleration and his fury, unbuckled himself from the chair, and remembered Kempsey. He went aft to the surgery. The extreme acceleration of the take-off had choked the blood pump enough to kill Kempsey. Suddenly Foyle was overcome with a novel passionate revulsion for himself. He fought it helplessly.

"What's a matter, you?" he whispered. "Think of the six hundred, scuttled . . . Think of yourself . . . Are you turning into a white-livered Cellar Christian turning the other cheek and whining forgiveness? Olivia, what are you doing to me? Give me strength, not cowardice . . ."

Nevertheless he averted his eyes as he scuttled the body.

CHAPTER
THIRTEEN

ALL PERSONS KNOWN TO BE IN THE EMPLOY
OF FOURMYLE OF CERES OR ASSOCIATED WITH
HIM IN ANY CAPACITY TO BE HELD FOR QUESTION-
ING. Y-Y: CENTRAL INTELLIGENCE.

ALL EMPLOYEES OF THIS COMPANY TO
MAINTAIN STRICT WATCH FOR ONE FOURMYLE
OF CERES, AND REPORT AT ONCE TO LOCAL MR.
PRESTO. PRESTEIGN.

ALL COURIERS WILL ABANDON PRESENT AS-
SIGNMENTS AND REPORT FOR REASSIGNMENT TO
FOYLE CASE. DAGENHAM.

A BANK HOLIDAY WILL BE DECLARED IMMEDI-
ATELY IN THE NAME OF THE WAR CRISIS TO CUT
FOURMYLE OFF FROM ALL FUNDS. Y-Y: CENTRAL
INTELLIGENCE.

ANYONE MAKING INQUIRIES RE: S.S. *VORGA* TO
BE TAKEN TO CASTLE PRESTEIGN FOR EXAMINA-
TION. PRESTEIGN.

ALL PORTS AND FIELDS IN INNER PLANETS TO
BE ALERTED FOR ARRIVAL OF FOURMYLE. QUAR-
ANTINE AND CUSTOMS TO CHECK ALL LANDINGS.
Y-Y: CENTRAL INTELLIGENCE.

OLD ST. PATRICK'S TO BE SEARCHED AND
WATCHED. DAGENHAM.

THE FILES OF BO'NESS & UIG TO BE CHECKED
FOR NAMES OF OFFICERS AND MEN OF *VORGA* TO
ANTICIPATE, IF POSSIBLE, FOYLE'S NEXT MOVE.
PRESTEIGN.

WAR CRIMES COMMISSION TO MAKE UP LIST
OF PUBLIC ENEMIES GIVING FOYLE NUMBER ONE
SPOT. Y-Y: CENTRAL INTELLIGENCE.

ÇR 1,000,000 REWARD OFFERED FOR INFORMA-
TION LEADING TO APPREHENSION OF FOURMYLE
OF CERES, ALIAS GULLIVER FOYLE, ALIAS GULLY
FOYLE, NOW AT LARGE IN THE INNER PLANETS. PRI-
ORITY! URGENT! DANGEROUS!

After two centuries of colonization, the air struggle on Mars
was still so critical that the V-L Law, the Vegetative-Lynch Law,
was still in effect. It was a killing offense to endanger or destroy

any plant vital to the transformation of Mars' carbon dioxide atmosphere into an oxygen atmosphere. Even blades of grass were sacred. There was no need to erect KEEP OFF THE GRASS neons. The man who wandered off a path onto a lawn would be instantly shot. The woman who picked a flower would be killed without mercy. Two centuries of sudden death had inspired a reverence for green growing things that almost amounted to a religion.

Foyle remembered this as he raced up the center of the causeway leading to Mars St. Michele. He had jaunted direct from the Syrtis airport to the St. Michele stage at the foot of the causeway which stretched for a quarter of a mile through green fields to Mars St. Michele. The rest of the distance had to be traversed on foot.

Like the original Mont St. Michele on the French coast, Mars St. Michele was a majestic Gothic cathedral of spires and buttresses looming on a hill and yearning toward the sky. Ocean tides surrounded Mont St. Michele on earth. Green tides of grass surrounded Mars St. Michele. Both were fortresses. Mont St. Michele had been a fortress of faith before organized religion was abolished. Mars St. Michele was a fortress of telepathy. Within it lived Mars's sole full telepath, Sigurd Magsman.

"Now these are the defenses protecting Sigurd Magsman," Foyle chanted, halfway between hysteria and litany. "Firstly, the Solar System; secondly, martial law; thirdly, Dagenham-Presteign & Co.; fourthly, the fortress itself; fifthly, the uniformed guards, attendants, servants, and admirers of the bearded sage we all know so well, Sigurd Magsman, selling his awesome powers for awesome prices. . . ."

Foyle laughed immoderately: "But there's a Sixthly that I know: Sigurd Magsman's Achilles' Heel . . . For I've paid ₵r 1,000,000 to Sigurd III . . . or was he IV?"

He passed through the outer labyrinth of Mars St. Michele with his forged credentials and was tempted to bluff or proceed directly by commando action to an audience with the Great Man himself, but time was pressing and his enemies were closing in and he could not afford to satisfy his curiosity. Instead, he accelerated, blurred, and found a humble cottage set in a walled garden within the Mars St. Michele home farm. It had drab windows and a thatched roof and might have been mistaken for a stable. Foyle slipped inside.

The cottage was a nursery. Three pleasant nannies sat motionless in rocking chairs, knitting poised in their frozen hands. The blur that was Foyle came up behind them and quietly stung them with ampules. Then he decelerated. He looked at the ancient, ancient child; the wizened, shriveled boy who was seated on the floor playing with electronic trains.

"Hello, Sigurd," Foyle said.

The child began to cry.

"Crybaby! What are you afraid of? I'm not going to hurt you."

"You're a bad man with a bad face."

"I'm your friend, Sigurd."

"No, you're not. You want me to do b-bad things."

"I'm your friend. Look, I know all about those big hairy men who pretend to be you, but I won't tell. Read me and see."

"You're going to hurt him and y-you want me to tell him."

"Who?"

"The captain-man. The Skl— Skot—" The child fumbled with the word, wailing louder. *"Go away. You're bad. Badness in your head and burning mens and—"*

"Come here, Sigurd."

"No. NANNIE! NAN-N-I-E!"

"Shut up, you little bastard!"

Foyle grabbed the seventy-year-old child and shook it. "This is going to be a brand new experience for you, Sigurd. The first time you've ever been walloped into anything. Understand?"

The ancient child read him and howled.

"Shut up! We're going on a trip to the Skoptsy Colony. If you behave yourself and do what you're told, I'll bring you back safe and give you a lolly or whatever the hell they bribe you with. If you don't behave, I'll beat the living daylights out of you."

"*No, you won't. . . . You won't. I'm Sigurd Magsman. I'm Sigurd the telepath. You wouldn't dare.*"

"Sonny, I'm Gully Foyle, Solar Enemy Number One. I'm just a step away from the finish of a year-long hunt . . . I'm risking my neck because I need you to settle accounts with a son of a bitch who—Sonny, I'm Gully Foyle. There isn't anything I wouldn't dare."

The telepath began broadcasting terror with such an uproar that alarms sounded all over Mars St. Michele. Foyle took a firm grip on the ancient child, accelerated and carried him out of the fortress. Then he jaunted.

> URGENT. SIGURD MAGSMAN KIDNAPED BY
> MAN TENTATIVELY IDENTIFIED AS GULLIVER FOYLE,
> ALIAS FOURMYLE OF CERES, SOLAR ENEMY NUM-
> BER ONE. DESTINATION TENTATIVELY FIXED. ALERT
> COMMANDO BRIGADE. INFORM CENTRAL INTELLI-
> GENCE. URGENT! URGENT! URGENT!

The ancient Skoptsy sect of White Russia, believing that sex was the root of all evil, practiced an atrocious self-castration to extirpate the root. The modern Skoptsys, believing that sensation was the root of all evil, practiced an even more barbaric custom. Having entered the Skoptsy Colony and paid a fortune for the privilege, the initiates submitted joyously to an operation that severed the sensory nervous system, and lived out their days without sight, sound, speech, smell, taste, or touch.

When they first entered the monastery, the initiates were shown elegant ivory cells in which it was intimated they would spend the remainder of their lives in rapt contemplation, lovingly tended. In actuality, the senseless creatures were packed in catacombs where they sat on rough stone slabs and were fed and exercised once a day. For twenty-three out of twenty-four hours they sat alone in the dark, untended, unguarded, unloved.

"The living dead," Foyle muttered. He decelerated, put Sigurd Magsman down, and switched on the retinal light in his eyes, trying to pierce the wombgloom. It was midnight above ground. It was permanent midnight down in the catacombs. Sigurd Magsman was broadcasting terror and anguish with such a telepathic bray that Foyle was forced to shake the child again.

"Shut up!" he whispered. "You can't wake these dead. Now find me Lindsey Joyce."

"They're sick . . . all sick . . . like worms in their heads . . . worms and sickness and—"

"Christ, don't I know it. Come on, let's get it over with. There's worse to come."

They went down the twisting labyrinth of the catacombs. The stone slabs shelved the walls from floor to ceiling. The Skoptsys, white as slugs, mute as corpses, motionless as Buddhas, filled the caverns with the odor of living death. The telepathic child wept and shrieked. Foyle never relaxed his relentless grip on him; he never relaxed the hunt.

"Johnson, Wright, Keeley, Graff, Nastro, Underwood . . . God, there's thousands here." Foyle read off the bronze identification plates attached to the slabs. "Reach out, Sigurd. Find Lindsey Joyce for me. We can't go over them name by name. Regal, Cone, Brady, Vincent— What in the—?"

Foyle started back. One of the bone-white figures had cuffed his brow. It was swaying and writhing, its face twitching. All the white slugs on their shelves were squirming and writhing. Sigurd Magsman's constant telepathic broadcast of anguish and terror was reaching them and torturing them.

"Shut up!" Foyle snapped. "Stop it. Find Lindsey Joyce and we'll get out of here. Reach out and find him."

"Down there." Sigurd wept. *"Straight down there. Seven, eight, nine shelves down. I want to go home. I'm sick. I—"*

Foyle went pell-mell down the catacombs with Sigurd, reading off identification plates until at last he came to: "LINDSEY JOYCE. BOUGAINVILLE. VENUS."

This was his enemy, the instigator of his death and the deaths of the six hundred from Callisto. This was the enemy for whom he had planned vengeance and hunted for months. This was the enemy for whom he had prepared the agony of the port stateroom aboard his yawl. This was *Vorga*. It was a woman.

Foyle was thunderstruck. In these days of the double standard, with women kept in purdah, there were many reported cases of women masquerading as men to enter the worlds closed to them, but he had never yet heard of a woman in the merchant marine . . . masquerading her way to top officer rank.

"This?" he exclaimed furiously. "This is Lindsey Joyce? Lindsey Joyce off the *Vorga*? Ask her."

"I don't know what Vorga *is."*

"Ask her!"

"But I don't— She was . . . She like gave orders."

"Captain?"

"I don't like what's inside her. It's all sick and dark. It hurts. I want to go home."

"Ask her. Was she captain of the *Vorga*?"

"Yes. Please, please, please don't make me go inside her any more. It's twisty and hurts. I don't like her."

"Tell her I'm the man she wouldn't pick up on September 16, 2436. Tell her it's taken a long time but I've finally come to settle the account. Tell her I'm going to pay her back."

"I d-don't understand. Don't understand."

"Tell her I'm going to kill her, slow and hard. Tell her I've got a stateroom aboard my yawl, fitted up just like my locker aboard *Nomad* where I rotted for six months . . . where she ordered *Vorga* to leave me to die. Tell her she's going to rot and die just like me. Tell her!" Foyle shook the wizened child furiously. "Make her feel it. Don't let her get away by turning Skoptsy. Tell her I kill her filthy. Read me and tell her!"

"She . . . Sh-She didn't give that order."

"What!"

"I c-can't understand her."

"She didn't give the order to scuttle me?"

"I'm afraid to go in."

"Go in, you little son of a bitch, or I'll take you apart. What does she mean?"

The child wailed; the woman writhed; Foyle fumed. "Go in! Go in! Get it out of her. Jesus Christ, why does the only telepath on Mars have to be a child? Sigurd! Sigurd, listen to me. Ask her: Did she give the order to scuttle the reffs?"

"No. No!"

"No she didn't or no you won't?"

"She didn't."

"Did she give the order to pass *Nomad* by?"

"She's twisty and sicky. Oh please! NAN-N-I-E! I want to go home. Want to go."

"Did she give the order to pass *Nomad* by?"

"No."

"She didn't?"

"No. Take me home."

"Ask her who did."

"I want my Nannie."

"Ask her who could give her an order. She was captain aboard her own ship. Who could command her? Ask her!"

"I want my Nannie."

"Ask her!"

"No. No. No. I'm afraid. She's sick. She's dark and black. She's bad. I don't understand her. I want my Nannie. I want to go home."

The child was shrieking and shaking; Foyle was shouting. The echoes thundered. As Foyle reached for the child in a rage, his eyes were blinded by brilliant light. The entire catacomb was illuminated by the Burning Man. Foyle's image stood before him, face hideous, clothes on fire, the blazing eyes fixed on the convulsing Skoptsy that had been Lindsey Joyce.

The Burning Man opened his tiger mouth. A grating sound emerged. It was like flaming laughter.

"She hurts," he said.

"Who are you?" Foyle whispered.

The Burning Man winced. "Too bright," he said. "Less light."

Foyle took a step forward. The Burning Man clapped hands over his ears in agony. "Too loud," he cried. "Don't move so loud."

"Are you my guardian angel?"

"You're blinding me. Shhh!" Suddenly he laughed again. "Listen to her. She's screaming. Begging. She doesn't want to die. She doesn't want to be hurt. Listen to her."

Foyle trembled.

"She's telling us who gave the order. Can't you hear? Listen with your eyes." The Burning Man pointed a talon finger at the writhing Skoptsy. "She says Olivia."

"What!"

"She says Olivia. Olivia Presteign. Olivia Presteign. Olivia Presteign."

The Burning Man vanished.

The catacombs were dark again.

Colored lights and cacophonies whirled around Foyle. He gasped and staggered. "Blue jaunte," he muttered. "Olivia. No. Not. Never. Olivia. I—"

He felt a hand reach for his. "Jiz?" he croaked.

He became aware that Sigurd Magsman was holding on to his hand and weeping. He picked the boy up.

"*I hurt,*" Sigurd whimpered.

"I hurt too, son."

"*Want to go home.*"

"I'll take you home."

Still holding the boy in his arms, he blundered through the catacombs.

"The living dead," he mumbled.

And then: "I've joined them."

He found the stone steps that led up from the depths to the monastery cloister above ground. He trudged up the steps, tasting death and desolation. There was bright light above him, and for a moment he imagined that dawn had come already. Then he realized that the cloister was brilliantly lit with artificial light. There was the tramp of shod feet and the low growl of commands. Halfway up the steps, Foyle stopped and mustered himself.

"Sigurd," he whispered. "Who's above us? Find out."

"*Sogers,*" the child answered.

"Soldiers? What soldiers?"

"*Commando sogers.*" Sigurd's crumpled face brightened. "*They come for me. To take me home to Nannie. HERE I AM! HERE I AM!*"

The telepathic clamor brought a shout from overhead. Foyle accelerated and blurred up the rest of the steps to the cloister. It was a square of Romanesque arches surrounding a green lawn. In the center of the lawn was a giant cedar of Lebanon. The flagged walks swarmed with Commando search parties, and Foyle came face to face with his match; for an instant after they saw his blur whip up from the catacombs they accelerated too, and all were on even terms.

But Foyle had the boy. Shooting was impossible. Cradling Sigurd in his arms, he wove through the cloister like a broken-field runner hurtling toward a goal. No one dared block him, for at plus-five acceleration a head-on collision between two bodies would be instantly fatal to both. Objectively, this break-neck skirmish looked like a five second zigzag of lightning.

Foyle broke out of the cloister, went through the main hall of the monastery, passed through the labyrinth, and reached the public jaunte stage outside the main gate. There he stopped, decelerated and jaunted to the monastery airfield, half a mile distant. The field, too, was ablaze with lights and swarming with Commandos. Every anti-grav pit was occupied by a Brigade ship. His own yawl was under guard.

A fifth of a second after Foyle arrived at the field, the pursuers from the monastery jaunted in. He looked around, desperately. He was surrounded by half a regiment of Commandos, all under acceleration, all geared for lethal-action, all his equal or better. The odds were impossible.

And then the Outer Satellites altered the odds. Exactly one week after the saturation raid on Terra, they struck at Mars.

Again the missiles came down on the midnight to dawn quadrant. Again the heavens twinkled with interceptions and detonations, and the horizon exploded great puffs of light while the ground shook. But this time there was a ghastly variation, for a brilliant nova burst overhead, flooding the nightside of the planet with garish light. A swarm of fission heads had struck Mars's tiny satellite, Phobos, instantly vaporizing it into a sunlet.

The recognition lag of the Commandos to this appalling attack gave Foyle his opportunity. He accelerated again and burst through them to his yawl. He stopped before the main hatch and saw the stunned guard party hesitate between a continuance of the old action and a response to the new. Foyle hurled the frozen body of Sigurd Magsman up into the air like a Scotsman tossing the caber. As the guard party rushed to catch the boy, Foyle dove through them into his yawl, slammed the hatch, and dogged it.

Still under acceleration, never pausing to see if anyone was inside the yawl, he shot forward to controls, tripped the release lever, and as the yawl started to float up the anti-grav beam, threw on full 10-G propulsion. He was not strapped into the pilot chair. The effect of the 10-G drive on his accelerated and unprotected body was monstrous.

A creeping force took hold of him and spilled him out of the chair. He inched back toward the rear wall of the control chamber like a sleepwalker. The wall appeared, to his accelerated senses, to approach him. He thrust out both arms, palms flat against the wall to brace himself. The sluggish power thrusting him back split his arms apart and forced him against the wall, gently at first, then harder and harder until face, jaw, chest, and body were crushed against the metal.

The mounting pressure became agonizing. He tried to trip the switchboard in his mouth with his tongue, but the propulsion crushing him against the wall made it impossible for him to move his distorted mouth. A burst of explosions, so far down the sound spectrum that they sounded like sodden rock slides, told him that the Commando Brigade was bombarding him with shots from below. As the yawl tore up into the blue-black of outer space, he began to scream in a bat screech before he mercifully lost consciousness.

CHAPTER
FOURTEEN

Foyle awoke in darkness. He was decelerated, but the exhaustion of his body told him he had been under acceleration while he had been unconscious. Either his power pack had run out or . . . He inched a hand to the small of his back. The pack was gone. It had been removed.

He explored with trembling fingers. He was in a bed. He listened to the murmur of ventilators and refrigerants and the click and buzz of servo-mechanisms. He was aboard a ship. He was strapped to the bed. The ship was in free fall.

Foyle unfastened himself, pressed his elbows against the mattress and floated up. He drifted through the darkness searching for a light switch or a call button. His hands brushed against a water carafe with raised letters on the glass. He read them with his fingertips. SS, he felt. V, O, R, G, A. *Vorga*. He cried out.

The door of the stateroom opened. A figure drifted through the door, silhouetted against the light of a luxurious private lounge behind it.

"This time we picked you up," a voice said.

"Olivia?"

"Yes."

"Then it's true?"

"Yes, Gully."

Foyle began to cry.

"You're still weak," Olivia Presteign said gently. "Come and lie down."

She urged him into the lounge and strapped him into a chaise longue. It was still warm from her body. "You've been like this for six days. We never thought you'd live. Everything was drained out of you before the surgeon found that battery on your back."

"Where is it?" he croaked.

"You can have it whenever you want it. Don't fret, my dear."

He looked at her for a long moment, his Snow Maiden, his beloved Ice Princess . . . the white satin skin, the blind coral eyes and exquisite coral mouth. She touched his moist eyelids with a scented handkerchief.

"I love you," he said.

"Shhh. I know, Gully."

"You've known all about me. For how long?"

"I knew Gully Foyle was my enemy from the beginning. I never knew he was Fourmyle until we met. Ah, if only I'd known before. How much would have been saved."

"You knew and you've been laughing at me."

"No."

"Standing by and shaking with laughter."

"Standing by and loving you. No, don't interrupt. I'm trying to be rational and it's not easy." A flush cascaded across the marble face. "I'm not playing with you now. I . . . I betrayed you to my father. I did. Self-defense, I thought. Now that I've met him at last I can see he's too dangerous. An hour later I knew it was a mistake because I realized I was in love with you. I'm paying for it now. You need never have known."

"You expect me to believe that?"

"Then why am I here?" She trembled slightly. "Why did I follow you? That bombing was ghastly. You'd have been dead in another minute when we picked you up. Your yawl was a wreck. . . ."

"Where are we now?"

"What difference does it make?"

"I'm stalling for time."

"Time for what?"

"Not for time . . . I'm stalling for courage."

"We're orbiting Terra."

"How did you follow me?"

"I knew you'd be after Lindsey Joyce. I took over one of my father's ships. It happened to be *Vorga* again."

"Does he know?"

"He never knows. I live my own private life."

He could not take his eyes off her, and yet it hurt him to look at her. He was yearning and hating . . . yearning for the reality to be undone, hating the truth for what it was. He discovered that he was stroking her handkerchief with tremulous fingers.

"I love you, Olivia."

"I love you, Gully, my enemy."

"For God's sake!" he burst out. "Why did you do it?"

"What?" she lashed back. "Are you demanding apologies?"

"I'm demanding an explanation."

"You'll get none from me!"

"Blood and money, your father said. He was right. Oh . . . Bitch! Bitch! Bitch!"

"Blood and money, yes; and unashamed."

"I'm drowning, Olivia. Throw me a lifeline."

"Then drown. Nobody ever saved me. No— No . . . This is wrong, all wrong. Wait, my dear. Wait." She composed herself and began speaking very tenderly. "I could lie, Gully dear, and make you believe it, but I'm going to be honest. There's a simple explanation. I live my own private life. We all do. You do."

"What's yours?"

"No different from yours . . . from the rest of the world. I cheat, I lie, I destroy . . . like all of us. I'm criminal . . . like all of us."

"Why? For money? You don't need money."

"No."

"For control . . . power?"

"Not for power."

"Then why?"

She took a deep breath, as though this truth was the first truth and was crucifying her. "For hatred . . . To pay you back, all of you."

"For what?"

"For being blind," she said in a smoldering voice. "For being cheated. For being helpless . . . They should have killed me when I was born. Do you know what it's like to be blind . . . to receive life secondhand? To be dependent, begging, crippled? 'Bring them down to your level,' I told my secret life. 'If you're blind make them blinder. If you're helpless, cripple them. Pay them back . . . all of them.'"

"Olivia, you're insane."

"And you?"

"I'm in love with a monster."

"We're a pair of monsters."

"No!"

"No? Not you?" she flared. "What have you been doing but paying the world back, like me? What's your revenge but settling your own private account with bad luck? Who wouldn't call you a crazy monster? I tell you, we're a pair, Gully. We couldn't help falling in love."

He was stunned by the truth of what she said. He tried on the shroud of her revelation and it fit, clung tighter than the tiger mask tattooed on his face.

"'Remorseless,'" he said. "'Lecherous, treacherous, kindless villain.' It's true. I'm no better than you. Worse. But before God I never murdered six hundred."

"You're murdering six million."

"What?"

"Perhaps more. You've got something they need to end the war, and you're holding out."

"You mean PyrE?"

"Yes."

"What is it, this bringer of peace, this twenty pounds of miracle that they're fighting for?"

"I don't know, but I know they need it, and I don't care. Yes, I'm being honest now. I don't care. Let millions be murdered. It makes no difference to us. Not to us, Gully, because we stand apart. We stand apart and shape our own world. We're the strong."

"We're the damned."

"We're the blessed. We've found each other." Suddenly she laughed and held out her arms. "I'm arguing when there's no need for words. Come to me, my love. . . . Wherever you are, come to me. . . ."

He touched her and then put his arms around her. He found her mouth and devoured her. But he was forced to release her.

"What is it, Gully darling?"

"I'm not a child any more," he said wearily. "I've learned to understand that nothing is simple. There's never a simple answer. You can love someone and loathe them."

"Can you, Gully?"

"And you're making me loathe myself."

"No, my dear."

"I've been a tiger all my life. I trained myself . . . educated myself . . . pulled myself up by my stripes to make me a stronger tiger with a longer claw and a sharper tooth . . . quick and deadly. . . ."

"And you are. You are. The deadliest."

"No. I'm not. I went too far. I went beyond simplicity. I turned myself into a thinking creature. I look through your blind eyes, my love whom I loathe, and I see myself. The tiger's gone."

"There's no place for the tiger to go. You're trapped, Gully; by Dagenham, Intelligence, my father, the world."

"I know."

"But you're safe with me. We're safe together, the pair of us. They'll never dream of looking for you near me. We can plan together, fight together, destroy them together. . . ."

"No. Not together."

"What is it?" she flared again. "Are you still hunting me? Is that what's wrong? Do you still want revenge? Then take it. Here I am. Go ahead . . . destroy me."

"No. Destruction's finished for me."

"Ah, I know what it is." She became tender again in an instant. "It's your face, poor darling. You're ashamed of your tiger face, but I love it. You burn so brightly for me. You burn through the blindness. Believe me . . ."

"My God! What a pair of loathsome freaks we are."

"What's happened to you?" she demanded. She broke away from him, her coral eyes glittering. "Where's the man who watched the raid with me? Where's the unashamed savage who—"

"Gone, Olivia. You've lost him. We both have."

"Gully!"

"He's lost."

"But why? What have I done?"

"You don't understand, Olivia."

"Where are you?" she reached out, touched him and then clung to him. "Listen to me, darling. You're tired. You're exhausted. That's all. Nothing is lost." The words tumbled out of her. "You're right. Of course you're right. We've been bad, both of us. Loathsome. But all that's gone now. Nothing is lost. We were wicked because we were alone and unhappy. But we've found each other; we can save each other. Be my love, darling. Always. Forever. I've looked for you so long, waited and hoped and prayed . . ."

"No. You're lying, Olivia, and you know it."

"For God's sake, Gully!"

"Put *Vorga* down, Olivia."

"Land?"

"Yes."

"On Terra?"

"Yes."

"What are you going to do? You're insane. They're hunting you . . . waiting for you . . . watching. What are you going to do?"

"Do you think this is easy for me?" he said. "I'm doing what I have to do. I'm still driven. No man ever escapes from that. But there's a different compulsion in the saddle, and the spurs hurt, damn it. They hurt like hell."

He stifled his anger and controlled himself. He took her hands and kissed her palms.

"It's all finished, Olivia," he said gently. "But I love you. Always. Forever."

∞

"I'll sum it up," Dagenham rapped. "We were bombed the night we found Foyle. We lost him on the Moon and found him a week later on Mars. We were bombed again. We lost him again. He's been lost for a week. Another bombing's due. Which one of the Inner Planets? Venus? The Moon? Terra again? Who knows. But we all know this: one more raid without retaliation and we're lost."

He glanced around the table. Against the ivory-and-gold background of the Star Chamber of Castle Presteign, his face, all three faces, looked strained. Y'ang-Yeovil slitted his eyes in a frown. Presteign compressed his thin lips.

"And we know this too," Dagenham continued. "We can't retaliate without PyrE and we can't locate the PyrE without Foyle."

"My instructions were," Presteign interposed, "that PyrE was not to be mentioned in public."

"In the first place, this is not public," Dagenham snapped. "It's a private information pool. In the second place, we've gone beyond property rights. We're discussing survival, and we've all got equal rights in that. Yes, Jiz?"

Jisbella McQueen had jaunted into the Star Chamber, looking intent and furious.

"Still no sign of Foyle."

"Old St. Pat's still being watched?"

"Yes."

"Commando Brigade's report in from Mars yet?"

"No."

"That's my business and Most Secret," Y'ang-Yeovil objected mildly.

"You've got as few secrets from me as I have from you." Dagenham grinned mirthlessly. "See if you can beat Central Intelligence back here with that report, Jiz. Go."

She disappeared.

"About property rights," Y'ang-Yeovil murmured. "May I suggest to Presteign that Central Intelligence will guarantee full payment to him for his right, title, and interest in PyrE?"

"Don't coddle him, Yeovil."

"This conference is being recorded," Presteign said, coldly. "The Captain's offer is now on file." He turned his basilisk face to Dagenham. "You are in my employ, Mr. Dagenham. Please control your references to myself."

"And to your property?" Dagenham inquired with a deadly smile. "You and your damned property. All of you and all of your damned property have put us in this hole. The system's on the edge of total annihilation for the sake of your property. I'm not exaggerating. It will be a shooting war to end all wars if we can't stop it."

"We can always surrender," Presteign answered.

"No," Y'ang-Yeovil said. "That's already been discussed and discarded at HQ. We know the post-victory plans of the Outer Satellites. They involve total exploitation of the Inner Planets. We're to be gutted and worked until nothing's left. Surrender would be as disastrous as defeat."

"But not for Presteign," Dagenham added.

"Shall we say . . . present company excluded?" Yang-Yeovil replied gracefully.

"All right, Presteign," Dagenham swiveled in his chair. "Give."

"I beg your pardon, sir?"

"Let's hear all about PyrE. I've got an idea how we can bring Foyle out into the open and locate the stuff, but I've got to know all about it first. Make your contribution."

"No," Presteign answered.

"No, what?"

"I have decided to withdraw from this information pool. I will reveal nothing about PyrE."

"For God's sake, Presteign! Are you insane? What's got into you? Are you fighting Regis Sheffield's Liberal party again?"

"It's quite simple, Dagenham," Y'ang-Yeovil interposed. "My information about the surrender-defeat situation has shown Presteign a way to better his position. No doubt he intends negotiating a sale to the enemy in return for . . . property advantages."

"Can nothing move you?" Dagenham asked Presteign scornfully. "Can nothing touch you? Are you all property and nothing else? Go away, Jiz! The whole thing's fallen apart."

Jisbella had jaunted into the Star Chamber again. "Commando Brigade's reported," she said. "We know what happened to Foyle."

"What?"

"Presteign's got him."

"What!" Both Dagenham and Y'ang-Yeovil started to their feet.

"He left Mars in a private yawl, was shot up, and was observed being picked up by the Presteign S.S. *Vorga*."

"Damn you, Presteign," Dagenham snapped. "So that's why you've been—"

"Wait," Y'ang-Yeovil commanded. "It's news to him too, Dagenham. Look at him."

Presteign's handsome face had gone the color of ashes. He tried to rise and fell back stiffly in his chair. "Olivia . . ." he whispered. "With him . . . That scum . . ."

"Presteign?"

"My daughter, gentlemen, has . . . for some time been engaged in . . . certain activities. The family vice. Blood and— I . . . have managed to close my eyes to it . . . Had almost convinced myself that I was mistaken. I . . . But Foyle! Dirt! Filth! He must be destroyed!" Presteign's voice soared alarmingly. His head twisted back like a hanged man's and his body began to shudder.

"What in the—?"

"Epilepsy," Y'ang-Yeovil said. He pulled Presteign out of the chair onto the floor. "A spoon, Miss McQueen. Quick!" He levered Presteign's teeth open and placed a spoon between them to protect the tongue. As suddenly as it had begun, the seizure was over. The shuddering stopped. Presteign opened his eyes.

"*Petit mal*," Y'ang-Yeovil murmured, withdrawing the spoon. "But he'll be dazed for a while."

Suddenly Presteign began speaking in a low monotone. "PyrE is a pyrophoric alloy. A pyrophore is a metal which emits sparks when scraped or struck. PyrE emits energy, which is why E, the energy symbol, was added to the prefix Pyr. PyrE is a solid solution of transplutonian isotopes, releasing thermonuclear energy on the order of stellar Phoenix action. Its discoverer was of the opinion that he had produced the equivalent of the primordial protomatter which exploded into the Universe."

"My God!" Jisbella exclaimed.

Dagenham silenced her with a gesture and bent over Presteign. "How is it brought to critical mass, Presteign? How is the energy released?"

"As the original energy was generated in the beginning of time," Presteign droned. "Through Will and Idea."

"I'm convinced he's a Cellar Christian," Dagenham muttered to Y'ang-Yeovil. He raised his voice. "Will you explain, Presteign?"

"Through Will and Idea," Presteign repeated. "PyrE can only be exploded by psychokinesis. Its energy can only be released by thought. It must be willed to explode and the thought directed at it. That is the only way."

"There's no key? No formula?"

"No. Only Will and Idea are necessary." The glazed eyes closed.

"God in heaven!" Dagenham mopped his brow. "Will this give the Outer Satellites pause, Yeovil?"

"It'll give us all pause."

"It's the road to hell," Jisbella said.

"Then let's find it and get off the road. Here's my idea, Yeovil. Foyle was tinkering with that hell brew in his lab in Old St. Pat's, trying to analyze it."

"I told you that in strict confidence," Jisbella said furiously.

"I'm sorry, dear. We're past honor and the decencies. Now look, Yeovil, there must be some fragments of the stuff lying about . . . as dust, in solution, in precipitates . . . We've got to detonate those fragments and blow the hell out of Foyle's circus."

"Why?"

"To bring him running. He must have the bulk of the PyrE hidden there somewhere. He'll come to salvage it."

"What if it blows up too?"

"It can't, not inside an Inert Lead Isotope safe."

"Maybe it's not all inside."

"Jiz says it is . . . at least so Foyle reported."

"Leave me out of this," Jisbella said

"Anyway, we'll have to gamble."

"Gamble!" Y'ang-Yeovil exclaimed. "On a Phoenix action? You'll gamble the solar system into a brand new nova."

"What else can we do? Pick any other road . . . and it's the road to destruction too. Have we got any choice?"

"We can wait," Jisbella said.

"For what? For Foyle to blow us up himself with his tinkering?"

"We can warn him."

"We don't know where he is."

"We can find him."

"How soon? Won't that be a gamble too? And what about that stuff lying around waiting for someone to think it into energy? Suppose a Jack-jaunter gets in and cracks the safe, looking for goodies? And then we don't just have dust waiting for an accidental thought, but twenty pounds."

Jisbella turned pale. Dagenham turned to the Intelligence man. "You make the decision, Yeovil. Do we try it my way or do we wait?"

Y'ang-Yeovil sighed. "I was afraid of this," he said. "Damn all scientists. I'll have to make my decision for a reason you don't know, Dagenham. The Outer Satellites are on to this too. We've got reason to believe that they've got agents looking for Foyle in the worst way. If we wait they may pick him up before us. In fact, they may have him now."

"So your decision is . . . ?"

"The blow-up. Let's bring Foyle running if we can."

"No!" Jisbella cried.

"How?" Dagenham asked, ignoring her.

"Oh, I've got just the one for the job. A one-way telepath named Robin Wednesbury."

"When?"

"At once. We'll clear the entire neighborhood. We'll get full news coverage and do a full broadcast. If Foyle's anywhere in the Inner Planets, he'll hear about it."

"Not *about* it," Jisbella said in despair. "He'll *hear* it. It'll be the last thing any of us hear."

"Will and Idea," Presteign whispered.

∞

As always, when he returned from a stormy civil court session in Leningrad, Regis Sheffield was pleased and complacent, rather like a cocky prizefighter who's won a tough fight. He stopped off at Blekmann's in Berlin for a drink and some war talk, had a second and more war talk in a legal hangout on the Quai D'Orsay, and a third session in the Skin & Bones opposite Temple Bar. By the time he arrived in his New York office he was pleasantly illuminated.

As he strode through the clattering corridors and outer rooms, he was greeted by his secretary with a handful of memo-beads.

"Knocked Djargo-Dantchenko for a loop," Sheffield reported triumphantly. "Judgment and full damages. Old DD's sore as a boil. This makes the score eleven to five, my favor." He took the beads, juggled them, and then began tossing them into unlikely receptacles all over the office, including the open mouth of a gaping clerk.

"Really, Mr. Sheffield! Have you been drinking?"

"No more work today. The war news is too damned gloomy. Have to do something to stay cheerful. What say we brawl in the streets?"

"Mr. Sheffield!"

"Anything waiting for me that can't wait another day?"

"There's a gentleman in your office."

"He made you let him get that far?" Sheffield looked impressed. "Who is he? God, or somebody?"

"He won't give his name. He gave me this."

The secretary handed Sheffield a sealed envelope. On it was scrawled: "URGENT." Sheffield tore it open, his blunt features crinkling with curiosity. Then his eyes widened. Inside the envelope were two ₡r 50,000 notes. Sheffield turned without a word and burst into his private office. Foyle arose from his chair.

"These are genuine," Sheffield blurted.

"To the best of my knowledge."

"Exactly twenty of these notes were minted last year. All are on deposit in Terran treasuries. How did you get hold of these two?"

"Mr. Sheffield?"

"Who else? How did you get hold of these notes?"

"Bribery."

"Why?"

"I thought at the time that it might be convenient to have them available."

"For what? More bribery?"

"If legal fees are bribery."

"I set my own fees," Sheffield said. He tossed the notes back to Foyle. "You can produce them again *if* I decide to take your case and *if* I decide I've been worth that to you. What's your problem?"

"Criminal."

"Don't be too specific yet. And . . . ?"

"I want to give myself up."

"To the police?"

"Yes."

"For what crime?"

"Crimes."

"Name two."

"Robbery and rape."

"Name two more."

"Blackmail and murder."

"Any other items?"

"Treason and genocide."

"Does that exhaust your catalogue?"

"I think so. We may be able to unveil a few more when we get specific."

"Been busy, haven't you? Either you're the Prince of Villains or insane."

"I've been both, Mr. Sheffield."

"Why do you want to give yourself up?"

"I've come to my senses," Foyle answered bitterly.

"I don't mean that. A criminal never surrenders while he's ahead. You're obviously ahead. What's the reason?"

"The most damnable thing that ever happened to a man. I picked up a rare disease called conscience."

Sheffield snorted. "That can often turn fatal."

"It is fatal. I've realized that I've been behaving like an animal."

"And now you want to purge yourself?"

"No, it isn't that simple," Foyle said grimly. "That's why I've come to you . . . for major surgery. The man who upsets the morphology of society is a cancer. The man who gives his own decisions priority over society is a criminal. But there are chain reactions. Purging yourself with punishment isn't enough. Everything's got to be set right. I wish to God everything could be cured just by sending me back to Gouffre Martel or shooting me . . ."

"Back?" Sheffield cut in keenly.

"Shall I be specific?"

"Not yet. Go on. You sound as though you've got ethical growing pains."

"That's it exactly." Foyle paced in agitation, crumpling the banknotes with nervous fingers. "This is one hell of a mess, Sheffield. There's a girl that's got to pay for a vicious, rotten crime. The fact that I love her— No, never mind that. She has a cancer that's got to be cut out . . . like me. Which means I'll have to add informing to my catalogue. The fact that I'm giving myself up too doesn't make any difference."

"What *is* all this mish-mash?"

Foyle turned on Sheffield. "One of the New Year's bombs has just walked into your office, and it's saying: 'Put it all right. Put me together again and send me home. Put together the city I flattened and the people I shattered.' That's what I want to hire you for. I don't know how most criminals feel, but—"

"Sensible, matter-of-fact, like good businessmen who've had bad luck," Sheffield answered promptly. "That's the usual attitude of the professional criminal. It's obvious you're an amateur, if you're a criminal at all. My dear sir, do be sensible. You come here, extravagantly accusing yourself of robbery, rape, murder, genocide, treason, and God knows what else. D'you expect me to take you seriously?"

Bunny, Sheffield's assistant, jaunted into the private office. "Chief!" he shouted in excitement. "Something brand new's turned up. A lech-jaunte! Two society kids bribed a C-class tart to— Ooop. Sorry. Didn't realize you had—" Bunny broke off and stared. "Fourmyle!" he exclaimed.

"What? Who?" Sheffield demanded.

"Don't you know him, Chief?" Bunny stammered. "That's Fourmyle of Ceres. Gully Foyle."

More than a year ago, Regis Sheffield had been hypnotically fulminated and triggered for this moment. His body had been prepared to respond without thought, and the response was lightning. Sheffield struck Foyle in half a second; temple, throat, and groin. It had been decided not to depend on weapons since none might be available.

Foyle fell. Sheffield turned on Bunny and battered him back across the office. Then he spat into his palm. It had been decided not to depend on drugs since drugs might not be available. Sheffield's salivary glands had been prepared to respond with an anaphylaxis secretion to the stimulus. He ripped open Foyle's sleeve, dug a nail deep into the hollow of Foyle's elbow and slashed. He pressed his spittle into the ragged cut and pinched the skin together.

A strange cry was torn from Foyle's lips; the tattooing showed livid on his face. Before the stunned law assistant could make a move, Sheffield swung Foyle up to his shoulder and jaunted.

He arrived in the middle of the Four Mile Circus in Old St. Pat's. It was a daring but calculated move. This was the last place he would be expected to go, and the first place where he might expect to locate the PyrE. He was prepared to deal with anyone he might meet in the cathedral, but the interior of the circus was empty.

The vacant tents ballooning up in the nave looked tattered;

they had already been looted. Sheffield plunged into the first he saw. It was Fourmyle's traveling library, filled with hundreds of books and thousands of glittering novel-beads. The Jack-jaunters were not interested in literature. Sheffield threw Foyle down on the floor. Only then did he take a gun from his pocket.

Foyle's eyelids fluttered; his eyes opened.

"You're drugged," Sheffield said rapidly. "Don't try to jaunte. And don't move. I'm warning you, I'm prepared for anything."

Dazedly, Foyle tried to rise. Sheffield instantly fired and seared his shoulder. Foyle was slammed back against the stone flooring. He was numbed and bewildered. There was a roaring in his ears and a poison coursing through his blood.

"I'm warning you," Sheffield repeated. "I'm prepared for anything."

"What do you want?" Foyle whispered.

"Two things. Twenty pounds of PyrE, and you. You most of all."

"You lunatic! You damned maniac! I came into your office to give it up . . . hand it over . . ."

"To the O.S.?"

"To the . . . what?"

"The Outer Satellites? Shall I spell it for you?"

"No . . ." Foyle muttered. "I might have known. The patriot, Sheffield, an O.S. agent. I should have known. I'm a fool."

"You're the most valuable fool in the world, Foyle. We want you even more than the PyrE. That's an unknown to us, but we know what you are."

"What are you talking about?"

"My God! You don't know, do you? You still don't know. You haven't an inkling."

"Of what?"

"Listen to me," Sheffield said in a pounding voice. "I'm taking you back two years to *Nomad*. Understand? Back to the death of the *Nomad*. One of our raiders finished her off and they found you aboard the wreck. The last man alive."

"So an O.S. ship did blast *Nomad?*"

"Yes. You don't remember?"

"I don't remember anything about that. I never could."

"I'm telling you why. The raider got a clever idea. They'd turn you into a decoy . . . a sitting duck, understand? You were half dead, but they took you aboard and patched you up. They put you into a spacesuit and cast you adrift with your micro-wave on. You were broadcasting distress signals and mumbling for help on every wave band. The idea was, they'd lurk nearby and pick off the IP ships that came to rescue you."

Foyle began to laugh. "I'm getting up," he said recklessly. "Shoot again, you son of a bitch, but I'm getting up." He struggled to his feet, clutching his shoulder. "So *Vorga* shouldn't have picked me up anyway," Foyle laughed. "I was a decoy. Nobody should have come near me. I was a shill, a lure, death bait . . . Isn't that the final irony? *Nomad* didn't have any right to be rescued in the first place. I didn't have any right to revenge."

"You still don't understand," Sheffield pounded. "They were nowhere near *Nomad* when they set you adrift. They were six hundred thousand miles from *Nomad*."

"Six hundred thous—?"

"*Nomad* was too far out of the shipping lanes. They wanted you to drift where ships would pass. They took you six hundred thousand miles sunward and set you adrift. They put you through the air lock and backed off, watching you drift. Your suit lights were blinking and you were moaning for help on the micro-wave. Then you disappeared."

"Disappeared?"

"You were gone. No more lights, no more broadcast. They came back to check. You were gone without a trace. And the next thing we learned . . . you got back aboard *Nomad*."

"Impossible."

"Man, you space-jaunted!" Sheffield said savagely. "You were patched and delirious, but you space-jaunted. You space-jaunted six hundred thousand miles through the void back to the wreck of the *Nomad*. You did something that's never been done before. God knows how. You don't even know yourself, but we're going to find out. I'm taking you out to the Satellites with me and we'll get that secret out of you if we have to tear it out."

He took Foyle's throat in his powerful hand and hefted the gun in the other. "But first I want the PyrE. You'll produce it, Foyle. Don't think you won't." He lashed Foyle across the forehead with the gun. "I'll do anything to get it. Don't think I won't." He smashed Foyle again, coldly, efficiently. "If you're looking for a purge, man, you've found it!"

∞

Bunny leaped off the public jaunte stage at Five-Points and streaked into the main entrance of Central Intelligence's New York Office like a frightened rabbit. He shot past the outermost guard cordon, through the protective labyrinth, and into the inner offices. He acquired a train of excited pursuers and found himself face to face with the more seasoned guards who had calmly jaunted to positions ahead of him and were waiting.

Bunny began to shout: "Yeovil! Yeovil! Yeovil!"

Still running, he dodged around desks, kicked over chairs, and created an incredible uproar. He continued his yelling: "Yeovil! Yeovil! Yeovil!" Just before they were about to put him out of his misery, Y'ang-Yeovil appeared.

"What's all this?" he snapped. "I gave orders that Miss Wednesbury was to have absolute quiet."

"Yeovil!" Bunny shouted.

"Who's that?"

"Sheffield's assistant."

"What . . . Bunny?"

"Foyle!" Bunny howled. "Gully Foyle."

Y'ang-Yeovil covered the fifty feet between them in exactly one-point-six-six seconds. "What about Foyle?"

"Sheffield's got him," Bunny gasped.

"Sheffield? When?"

"Half an hour ago."

"Why didn't he bring him here?"

"Don't know . . . Got an idea . . . May be an O.S. agent."

"Why didn't you come at once?"

"Sheffield jaunted with Foyle. . . . Knocked him stiffer'n a mackerel and disappeared. I went looking. All over. Took a chance. Must have made fifty jaunts in twenty minutes. . . ."

"Amateur!" Y'ang-Yeovil exclaimed in exasperation. "Why didn't you leave that to the pros?"

"Found 'em."

"You found them? Where?"

"Old St. Pat's. Sheffield's after the—"

But Y'ang-Yeovil had turned on his heel and was tearing back up the corridor, shouting: "Robin! Robin! Stop! Stop!"

And then their ears were bruised by the bellow of thunder.

CHAPTER
FIFTEEN

L ike widening rings in a pond, the Will and the Idea spread,
searching out, touching and tripping the delicate subatomic
trigger of PyrE. The thought found particles, dust, smoke, vapor, motes, molecules. The Will and the Idea transformed them all.

In Sicily, where Dott. Franco Torre had worked for an ex-
hausting month attempting to unlock the secret of one slug of
PyrE, the residues and the precipitates had been dumped down a
drain which led to the sea. For many months the Mediterranean

currents had drifted these residues across the sea bottom. In an instant a hump-backed mound of water towering fifty feet high traced the courses, northeast to Sardinia and southwest to Tripoli. In a micro-second the surface of the Mediterranean was raised into the twisted casting of a giant earthworm that wound around the islands of Pantelleria, Lampedusa, Linosa, and Malta.

Some of the residues had been burned off; had gone up the chimney with smoke and vapor to drift for hundreds of miles before settling. These minute particles showed where they had finally settled in Morocco, Algeria, Libya, and Greece with blinding pin-point explosions of incredible minuteness and intensity. And some motes, still drifting in the stratosphere, revealed their presence with brilliant gleams like daylight stars.

In Texas, where Prof. John Mantley had had the same baffling experience with PyrE, most of the residues had gone down the shaft of an exhausted oil well which was also used to accommodate radioactive wastes. A deep water table had absorbed much of the matter and spread it slowly over an area of some ten square miles. Ten square miles of Texas flats shook themselves into corduroy. A vast untapped deposit of natural gas at last found a vent and came shrieking up to the surface where sparks from flying stones ignited it into a roaring torch, two hundred feet high.

A milligram of PyrE deposited on a disk of filter paper long since discarded, forgotten, rounded up in a waste paper drive and at last pulped into a mold for type metal, destroyed the entire late night edition of the *Glasgow Observer*. A fragment of PyrE spattered on a lab smock long since converted into rag paper, destroyed a Thank You note written by Lady Shrapnel, and destroyed an additional ton of first class mail in the process.

A shirt cuff, inadvertently dipped into an acid solution of PyrE, long abandoned along with the shirt, and now worn under his mink suit by a Jack-jaunter, blasted off the wrist and hand of the Jack-jaunter in one fiery amputation. A decimilligram of PyrE, still adhering to a former evaporation crystal now in use as an ash tray, kindled a fire that scorched the office of one Baker, dealer in freaks and purveyor of monsters.

Across the length and breadth of the planet were isolated explosions, chains of explosions, traceries of fire, pin points of fire, meteor flares in the sky, great craters and narrow channels plowed in the earth, exploded in the earth, vomited forth from the earth.

In Old St. Pat's nearly a tenth of a gram of PyrE was exposed in Fourmyle's laboratory. The rest was sealed in its Inert Lead Isotope safe, protected from accidental and intentional psychokinetic ignition. The blinding blast of energy generated from that tenth of a gram blew out the walls and split the floors as though an internal earthquake had convulsed the building. The buttresses held the pillars for a split second and then crumbled. Down came towers, spires, pillars, buttresses, and roof in a thundering avalanche to hesitate above the yawning crater of the floor in a tangled, precarious equilibrium. A breath of wind, a distant vibration, and the collapse would continue until the crater was filled solid with pulverized rubble.

The star-like heat of the explosion ignited a hundred fires and melted the ancient thick copper of the collapsed roof. If a milligram more of PyrE had been exposed to detonation, the heat would have been intense enough to vaporize the metal immediately. Instead, it glowed white and began to flow. It streamed off the wreckage of the crumbled roof and began searching its way downward through the jumbled stone, iron, wood, and glass, like some monstrous molten mold creeping through a tangled web.

Dagenham and Y'ang-Yeovil arrived almost simultaneously. A moment later Robin Wednesbury appeared and then Jisbella McQueen. A dozen Intelligence operatives and six Dagenham couriers arrived along with Presteign's Jaunte Watch and the police. They formed a cordon around the blazing block, but there were very few spectators. After the shock of the New Year's Eve raid, that single explosion had frightened half New York into another wild jaunte for safety.

The uproar of the fire was frightful, and the massive grind of tons of wreckage in uneasy balance was ominous. Everyone was forced to shout and yet was fearful of the vibrations. Y'ang-Yeovil bawled the news about Foyle and Sheffield into Dagenham's ear. Dagenham nodded and displayed his deadly smile.

"We'll have to go in," he shouted.

"Fire suits," Y'ang-Yeovil shouted.

He disappeared and reappeared with a pair of white Disaster Crew fire suits. At the sight of these, Robin and Jisbella began shouting hysterical objections. The two men ignored them, wriggled into the Inert Isomer armor and inched into the inferno.

Within Old St. Pat's it was as though a monstrous hand had churned a log jam of wood, stone, and metal. Through every interstice crawled tongues of molten copper, slowly working downward, igniting wood, crumbling stone, shattering glass. Where the copper flowed it merely glowed, but where it poured it spattered dazzling droplets of white hot metal.

Beneath the log jam yawned a black crater where formerly the floor of the cathedral had been. The explosion had split the flagstone asunder, revealing the cellars, subcellars, and vaults deep below the building. These too were filled with a snarl of stones, beams, pipes, wire, the remnants of the Four Mile circus tents; all fitfully lit small fires. Then the first of the copper dripped down into the crater and illuminated it with a brilliant molten splash.

Dagenham pounded Y'ang-Yeovil's shoulder to attract his attention and pointed. Halfway down the crater, in the midst of the tangle, lay the body of Regis Sheffield, drawn and quartered by the explosion. Y'ang-Yeovil pounded Dagenham's shoulder and pointed. Almost at the bottom of the crater lay Gully Foyle, and as the blazing spatter of molten copper illuminated him, they saw him move. The two men at once turned and crawled out of the cathedral for a conference.

"He's alive."

"How's it possible?"

"I can guess. Did you see the shreds of tent wadded near him? It must have been a freak explosion up at the other end of the cathedral and the tents in between cushioned Foyle. Then he dropped through the floor before anything else could hit him."

"I'll buy that. We've got to get him out. He's the only man who knows where the PyrE is."

"Could it still be here . . . unexploded?"

"If it's in the ILI safe, yes. That stuff is inert to anything. Never mind that now. How are we going to get him out?"

"Well we can't work down from above."

"Why not?"

"Isn't it obvious? One false step and the whole mess will collapse."

"Did you see that copper flowing down?"

"God, yes!"

"Well if we don't get him out in ten minutes, he'll be at the bottom of a pool of molten copper."

"What can we do?"

"I've got a long shot."

"What?"

"The cellars of the old RCA buildings across the street are as deep as St. Pat's."

"And?"

"We'll go down and try to hole through. Maybe we can pull Foyle out from the bottom."

A squad broke into the ancient RCA buildings, abandoned and sealed up for two generations. They went down into the cellar arcades, crumbling museums of the retail stores of centuries past. They located the ancient elevator shafts and dropped through them into the subcellars filled with electric installations, heat plants, and refrigeration systems. They went down into the sump cellars, waist deep in water from the streams of prehistoric Manhattan Island, streams that still flowed beneath the streets that covered them.

As they waded through the sump cellars, bearing east-northeast to bring up opposite the St. Pat's vaults, they suddenly discovered that the pitch dark was illuminated by a fiery flickering up ahead. Dagenham shouted and flung himself forward. The explosion that had opened the subcellars of St. Pat's had split the septum between its vaults and those of the RCA buildings. Through a jagged rent in stone and earth they could peer into the bottom of the inferno.

Fifty feet inside was Foyle, trapped in a labyrinth of twisted beams, stones, pipe, metal, and wire. He was illuminated by a roaring glow from above him and fitful flames around him. His clothes were on fire and the tattooing was livid on his face. He moved feebly, like a bewildered animal in a maze.

"My God!" Y'ang-Yeovil exclaimed. "The Burning Man!"

"What?"

"The Burning Man I saw on the Spanish Stairs. Never mind that now. What can we do?"

"Go in, of course."

A brilliant white gob of copper suddenly oozed down close to Foyle and splashed ten feet below him. It was followed by a second, a third, a slow steady stream. A pool began to form. Dagenham and Y'ang-Yeovil sealed the face plates of their armor and crawled through the break in the septum. After three minutes of agonized struggling they realized that they could not get through the labyrinth to Foyle. It was locked to the outside but not from the inside. Dagenham and Y'ang-Yeovil backed up to confer.

"We can't get to him," Dagenham shouted, "but he can get out."

"How? He can't jaunte, obviously, or he wouldn't be there."

"No, he can climb. Look. He goes left, then up, reverses, makes a turn along that beam, slides under it and pushes through that tangle of wire. The wire can't be pushed in, which is why we can't get to him, but it *can* push out, which is how he can get out. It's a one-way door."

The pool of molten copper crept up toward Foyle.

"If he doesn't get out soon he'll be roasted alive."

"We'll have to talk him out . . . Tell him what to do."

The men began shouting: "Foyle! Foyle! Foyle!"

The Burning Man in the maze continued to move feebly. The downpour of sizzling copper increased.

"Foyle! Turn left. Can you hear me? Foyle! Turn left and

climb up. You can get out if you'll listen to me. Turn left and climb up. Then— Foyle!"

"He's not listening. Foyle! Gully Foyle! Can you hear us?"

"Send for Jiz. Maybe he'll listen to her."

"No, Robin. She'll telesend. He'll have to listen."

"But will she do it? Save *him* of all people?"

"She'll have to. This is bigger than hatred. It's the biggest damned thing the world's ever encountered. I'll get her." Y'ang-Yeovil started to crawl out. Dagenham stopped him.

"Wait, Yeo. Look at him. He's flickering."

"Flickering?"

"Look! He's . . . blinking like a glow-worm. Watch! Now you see him and now you don't."

The figure of Foyle was appearing, disappearing, and reappearing in rapid succession, like a firefly caught in a flaming trap.

"What's he doing now? What's he trying to do? What's happening?"

∞

He was trying to escape. Like a trapped firefly or some seabird caught in the blazing brazier of a naked beacon fire, he was beating about in a frenzy . . . a blackened, burning creature, dashing himself against the unknown.

Sound came as sight to him, as light in strange patterns. He saw the sound of his shouted name in vivid rhythms:

```
F O Y L E    F O Y L E    F O Y L E
F O Y L E    F O Y L E    F O Y L E
F O Y L E    F O Y L E    F O Y L E
F O Y L E    F O Y L E    F O Y L E
F O Y L E    F O Y L E    F O Y L E
```

Motion came as sound to him. He heard the writhing of the flames, he heard the swirls of smoke, he heard the flickering, jeering shadows . . . all speaking deafeningly in strange tongues:

"BURUU GYARR RWAWW JERRMAKING?" the steam asked.

"Asha. Asha, rit-kit-dit-zit m'gid," the quick shadows answered.

"Ohhh. Ahhh. Heee. Teee. Oooo. Ahhh," the heat ripples clamored. "Ahhh. Maaa. Paaa. Laaaaaaaaaaaaa!"

Even the flames smoldering on his own clothes roared gibberish in his ears. "MANTERGEISTMANN!" they bellowed. "UNVERTRACKINSTEIGN GANZELSSFURSTINLASTENBRUGG!"

Color was pain to him . . . heat, cold, pressure; sensations of intolerable heights and plunging depths, of tremendous accelerations and crushing compressions:

RED RECEDED FROM HIM

GREEN LIGHT ATTACKED

INDIGO UNDULATED WITH SICKENING SPEED LIKE A SHIVERING SNAKE

Touch was taste to him . . . the feel of wood was acrid and chalky in his mouth, metal was salt, stone tasted sour-sweet to the touch of his fingers, and the feel of glass cloyed his palate like over-rich pastry.

∞

Smell was touch . . . Hot stone smelled like velvet caressing his cheek. Smoke and ash were harsh tweeds rasping his skin, almost the feel of wet canvas. Molten metal smelled like blows hammering his heart, and the ionization of the PyrE explosion filled the air with ozone that smelled like water trickling through his fingers.

∞

He was not blind, not deaf, not senseless. Sensation came to him, but filtered through a nervous system twisted and short-circuited by the shock of the PyrE concussion. He was suffering from synesthesia, that rare condition in which perception receives messages from the objective world and relays these messages to the brain, but there in the brain the sensory perceptions are confused with one another. So, in Foyle, sound registered as sight, motion registered as sound, colors became pain sensations, touch became taste, and smell became touch. He was not only trapped within the labyrinth of the inferno under Old St. Pat's; he was trapped in the kaleidoscope of his own cross-senses.

Again desperate, on the ghastly verge of extinction, he abandoned all disciplines and habits of living; or, perhaps, they were stripped from him. He reverted from a conditioned product of environment and experience to an inchoate creature craving escape and survival and exercising every power it possessed. And again the miracle of two years ago took place. The undivided energy of an entire human organism, of every cell, fiber, nerve, and muscle empowered that craving, and again Foyle space-jaunted.

He went hurtling along the geodesical space lines of the curving universe at the speed of thought, far exceeding that of light. His spatial velocity was so frightful that his time axis was twisted from the vertical line drawn from the Past through Now to the

Future. He went flickering along the new near-horizontal axis, this new space-time geodesic, driven by the miracle of a human mind no longer inhibited by concepts of the impossible.

Again he achieved what Helmut Grant and Enzio Dandridge and scores of other experimenters had failed to do, because his blind panic forced him to abandon the spatio-temporal inhibitions that had defeated previous attempts. He did not jaunte to Elsewhere, but to Elsewhen. But most important, the fourth dimensional awareness, the complete picture of the Arrow of Time and his position on it which is born in every man but deeply submerged by the trivia of living, was in Foyle close to the surface. He jaunted along the space-time geodesics to Elsewheres and Elsewhens, translating "i," the square root of minus one, from an imaginary number into reality by a magnificent act of imagination.

He jaunted.

He was aboard *Nomad*, drifting in the empty frost of space.

He stood in the door to nowhere.

The cold was the taste of lemons and the vacuum was a rake of talons on his skin. The sun and the stars were a shaking ague that racked his bones.

"GLOMMHA FREDNIS THE CLOMOHAMAGENSIN!" motion roared in his ears.

It was a figure with its back to him vanishing down the corridor; a figure with a copper cauldron of provisions over its shoulder; a figure darting, floating, squirming through free fall. It was Gully Foyle.

"MEEHAT JESSROT TO CRONAGAN BUT FLIMMCORK," the sight of his motion bellowed.

"Aha! Oh-ho! M'git not to kak," the flicker of light and shade answered.

"Oooooooh? Soooooo? Noooooo. Ahhhhhh!" the whirling raffle of debris in his wake murmured.

The lemon taste in his mouth became unbearable. The rake of talons on his skin was torture.

He jaunted.

He reappeared in the furnace beneath Old St. Pat's less than a second after he had disappeared from there. He was drawn, as the seabird is drawn, again and again to the flames from which it is struggling to escape. He endured the roaring torture for only another moment.

He jaunted.

He was in the depths of Gouffre Martel.

The velvet black darkness was bliss, paradise, euphoria.

"Ah!" he cried in relief.

"AH!" came the echo of his voice, and the sound was translated into a blinding pattern of light.

```
AHAHAHAHAHAHAHAHAH
HAHAHAHAHAHAHAHAHA
AHAHAHAHAHAHAHAHAH
HAHAHAHAHAHAHAHAHA
AHAHAHAHAHAHAHAHAH
HAHAHAHAHAHAHAHAHA
```

The Burning Man winced. "Stop!" he called, blinded by the noise. Again came the dazzling pattern of the echo:

```
StOpStOpStOp
OpStOpStOpStOp
StOpStOpStOpStOp
OpStOpStOpStOpStop
OpStOpStOpStOpSt
OpStOpStOpStOp
OpStOpStOpSt
```

A distant clatter of steps came to his eyes in soft patterns of vertical borealis streamers:

```
c       c       c       c       c       c
 l       l       l       l       l       l
  a       a       a       a       a       a
  t       t       t       t       t       t
 t       t       t       t       t       t
 e       e       e       e       e       e
   r       r       r       r       r       r
```

ALFRED BESTER

THERE CAME A SHOUT LIKE A ZIGZAG OF LIGHTNING

A BEAM OF LIGHT ATTACKED

It was the search party from the Gouffre Martel hospital, tracking Foyle and Jisbella McQueen by geophone. The Burning

238

Man disappeared, but not before he had unwittingly decoyed the searchers from the trail of the vanished fugitives.

He was back under Old St. Pat's, reappearing only an instant after his last disappearance. His wild beatings into the unknown sent him stumbling up geodesic space-time lines that inevitably brought him back to the Now he was trying to escape, for in the inverted saddle curve of space-time, his Now was the deepest depression in the curve.

He could drive himself up, up, up the geodesic lines into the past or future, but inevitably he must fall back into his own Now, like a thrown ball hurled up the sloping walls of an infinite pit, to land, hang poised for a moment, and then roll back into the depths.

But still he beat into the unknown in his desperation.

Again he jaunted.

He was on Jervis beach on the Australian coast.

The motion of the surf was bawling: "LOGGERMIST CROTEHAVEN JALL. LOOGERMISK MOTESLAVEN DOOL."

The churning of the surf blinded him with the lights of batteries of footlights:

Gully Foyle and Robin Wednesbury stood before him. The body of a man lay on the sand which felt like vinegar in the Burning Man's mouth. The wind brushing his face tasted like brown paper.

Foyle opened his mouth and exclaimed. The sound came out in burning star-bubbles.

Foyle took a step. "GRASH?" the motion blared.

The Burning Man jaunted.

He was in the office of Dr. Sergei Orel in Shanghai.

Foyle was again before him, speaking in light patterns:

```
W A Y          W A Y   W A Y
  H R O       H R O       H R O
  O  E U    O  E U       O  E U
```

He flickered back to the agony of Old St. Pat's and jaunted again.

> HE WAS ON THE BRAWLING SPANISH STAIRS. HE WAS ON THE BRAWLING SPANISH STAIRS. HE WAS ON THE BRAWLING SPANISH STAIRS. HE WAS ON THE BRAWLING SPANISH STAIRS. HE WAS ON THE BRAWLING SPANISH STAIRS. HE WAS ON THE BRAWLING SPANISH STAIRS. HE WAS ON THE BRAWLING SPANISH STAIRS. HE WAS ON THE BRAWLING SPANISH STAIRS.

The Burning Man jaunted.

It was cold again, with the taste of lemons, and vacuum raked his skin with unspeakable talons. He was peering through the porthole of a silvery yawl. The jagged mountains of the Moon towered in the background. Through the porthole he could see the jangling racket of blood pumps and oxygen pumps and hear the uproar of the motion Gully Foyle made toward him. The clawing of the vacuum caught his throat in an agonizing grip.

The geodesic lines of space-time rolled him back to Now under Old St. Pat's, where less than two seconds had elapsed since he first began his frenzied struggle. Once more, like a burning spear, he hurled himself into the unknown.

He was in the Skoptsy Catacomb on Mars. The white slug that was Lindsey Joyce was writhing before him.

THE STARS MY DESTINATION

"NO! NO! NO!" her motion screamed. "DON'T HURT ME. DON'T KILL ME. NO PLEASE . . . PLEASE . . . PLEASE . . ."

The Burning Man opened his tiger mouth and laughed. "She hurts," he said. The sound of his voice burned his eyes.

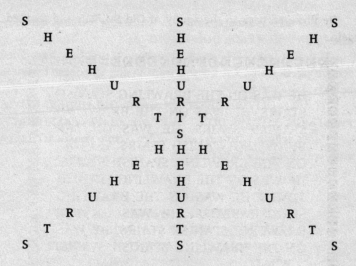

"Who are you?" Foyle whispered.

```
WWWWWWWWWWWWWWWWWWWW
HHHHHHHHHHHHHH
                HHHHH
OOOOOOOOOOOOOO
                OOOOO
AREAREAREAREAREARE
AREAREAREAREAREARE
AREAREAREAREAREARE
YYYYYYYYYYYYY
                YYYYY
OOOOOOOOOOOOOO
                OOOOO
UUUUUUUUUUUUUU
                UUUUU
```

The Burning Man winced. "Too bright," he said. "Less light."

Foyle took a step forward. "BLAA-GAA-DAA-MAWW-FRAA-MISHINGLISTONVISTA!" the motion roared.

The Burning Man clapped his hands over his ears in agony. "Too loud," he cried. "Don't move so loud."

The writhing Skoptsy's motion was still screaming, beseeching: "DON'T HURT ME. DON'T HURT ME."

The Burning Man laughed again. "Listen to her. She's screaming. Begging. She doesn't want to die. She doesn't want to be hurt. Listen to her."

"IT WAS OLIVIA PRESTEIGN GAVE THE ORDER. OLIVIA PRESTEIGN. NOT ME. DON'T HURT ME. OLIVIA PRESTEIGN."

"She's telling who gave the order. Can't you hear? Listen with your eyes. She says Olivia."

WHAT?   WHAT?   WHAT?
    WHAT?   WHAT?   WHAT?
WHAT?   WHAT?   WHAT?
    WHAT?   WHAT?   WHAT?
WHAT?   WHAT?   WHAT?

The checkerboard glitter of Foyle's question was too much for him.

"She says Olivia. Olivia Presteign. Olivia Presteign. Olivia Presteign."

He jaunted.

He fell back into the pit under Old St. Pat's, and suddenly his confusion and despair told him he was dead. This was the finish of Gully Foyle. This was eternity, and hell was real. What he had seen was the past passing before his crumbling senses in the final moment of death. What he was enduring he must endure through all time. He was dead. He knew he was dead.

He refused to submit to eternity.

He beat again into the unknown.

The Burning Man jaunted.

THE STARS MY DESTINATION

He was in a scintillating mist

a snowflake cluster of stars

a shower   of liquid diamonds.

There was the touch of butterfly wings on his skin

There was the taste of a strand of cool pearls in his mouth

His crossed kaleidoscopic senses could not tell him where he was, but he knew he wanted to remain in this Nowhere forever.

"Hello, Gully."

"Who's that?"

"This is Robin."

"Robin?"

"Robin Wednesbury that was."

"That was?"

"Robin Yeovil that is."

"I don't understand. Am I dead?"

"No, Gully."

"Where am I?"

"*A long, long way from Old St. Pat's.*"

"But where?"

"*I can't take the time to explain, Gully. You've only got a few moments here.*"

"Why?"

"*Because you haven't learned how to jaunte through space-time yet. You've got to go back and learn.*"

"But I do know. I must know. Sheffield said I space-jaunted to *Nomad* . . . six hundred thousand miles."

"*That was an accident then, Gully, and you'll do it again . . . after you teach yourself . . . But you're not doing it now. You don't know how to hold on yet . . . how to turn any Now into reality. You'll tumble back into Old St. Pat's in a moment.*"

"Robin, I've just remembered. I have bad news for you."

"*I know, Gully.*"

"Your mother and sisters are dead."

"*I've known for a long time, Gully.*"

"How long?"

"*For thirty years.*"

"That's impossible."

"*No it isn't. This is a long, long way from Old St. Pat's. I've been waiting to tell you how to save yourself from the fire, Gully. Will you listen?*"

"I'm not dead?"

"*No.*"

"I'll listen."

"*Your senses are all confused. It'll pass soon, but I won't give the directions in left and right or up and down. I'll tell you what you can understand now.*"

"Why are you helping me . . . after what I've done to you?"

"*That's all forgiven and forgotten, Gully. Now listen to me. When you get back to Old St. Pat's, turn around until you're facing the loudest shadows. Got that?*"

"Yes."

"*Go toward the noise until you feel a deep prickling on your skin. Then stop.*"

"Then stop."

"Make a half turn into compression and a feeling of falling. Follow that."

"Follow that."

"You'll pass through a solid sheet of light and come to the taste of quinine. That's really a mass of wire. Push straight through the quinine until you see something that sounds like trip hammers. You'll be safe."

"How do you know all this, Robin?"

"I've been briefed by an expert, Gully." There was the sensation of laughter. *"You'll be falling back into the past any moment now. Peter and Saul are here. They say au revoir and good luck. And Jiz Dagenham too. Good luck, Gully dear . . ."*

"The past? This is the future?"

"Yes, Gully."

"Am I here? Is . . . Olivia—?"

And then he was tumbling down, down, down the space-time lines back into the dreadful pit of Now.

CHAPTER
SIXTEEN

His senses uncrossed in the ivory-and-gold star chamber of Castle Presteign. Sight became sight and he saw the high mirrors and stained glass windows, the gold tooled library with android librarian on library ladder. Sound became sound and he heard the android secretary tapping the manual bead-recorder at the Louis Quinze desk. Taste became taste as he sipped the cognac that the robot bartender handed him.

He knew he was at bay, faced with the decision of his life. He ignored his enemies and examined the perpetual beam carved in the robot face of the bartender, the classic Irish grin.

"Thank you," Foyle said.

"My pleasure, sir," the robot replied and awaited its next cue.

"Nice day," Foyle remarked.

"Always a lovely day somewhere, sir," the robot beamed.

"Awful day," Foyle said.

"Always a lovely day somewhere, sir," the robot responded.

"Day," Foyle said.

"Always a lovely day somewhere, sir," the robot said.

Foyle turned to the others. "That's me," he said, motioning to the robot. "That's all of us. We prattle about free will, but we're nothing but response . . . mechanical reaction in prescribed grooves. So . . . here I am, here I am, waiting to respond. Press the buttons and I'll jump." He aped the canned voice of the robot. "My pleasure to serve, sir." Suddenly his tone lashed them. "What do you want?"

They stirred with uneasy purpose. Foyle was burned, beaten, chastened . . . and yet he was taking control of all of them.

"We'll stipulate the threats," Foyle said. "I'm to be hung, drawn, and quartered, tortured in hell if I don't . . . What? What do you want?"

"I want my property," Presteign said, smiling coldly.

"Eighteen and some odd pounds of PyrE. Yes. What do you offer?"

"I make no offer, sir. I demand what is mine."

Y'ang-Yeovil and Dagenham began to speak. Foyle silenced them. "One button at a time, gentlemen. Presteign is trying to make me jump at present." He turned to Presteign. "Press harder, blood and money, or find another button. Who are you to make demands at this moment?"

Presteign tightened his lips. "The law . . ." he began.

"What? Threats?" Foyle laughed. "Am I to be frightened into anything? Don't be imbecile. Speak to me the way you did New Year's Eve, Presteign . . . without mercy, without forgiveness, without hypocrisy."

Presteign bowed, took a breath, and ceased to smile. "I offer you power," he said. "Adoption as my heir, partnership in Presteign Enterprises, the chieftainship of clan and sept. Together we can own the world."

"With PyrE?"

"Yes."

"Your proposal is noted and declined. Will you offer your daughter?"

"Olivia?" Presteign choked and clenched his fists.

"Yes, Olivia. Where is she?"

"You scum!" Presteign cried. "Filth . . . Common thief . . . You dare to . . ."

"Will you offer your daughter for the PyrE?"

"Yes," Presteign answered, barely audible.

Foyle turned to Dagenham. "Press your button, death's-head," he said.

"If the discussion's to be conducted on this level . . ." Dagenham snapped.

"It is. Without mercy, without forgiveness, without hypocrisy. What do you offer?"

"Glory."

"Ah?"

"We can't offer money or power. We can offer honor. Gully Foyle, the man who saved the Inner Planets from annihilation. We can offer security. We'll wipe out your criminal record, give you an honored name, guarantee a niche in the hall of fame."

"No," Jisbella McQueen cut in sharply. "Don't accept. If you want to be a savior, destroy the secret. Don't give PyrE to anyone."

"What is PyrE?"

"Quiet!" Dagenham snapped.

"It's a thermonuclear explosive that's detonated by thought alone . . . by psychokinesis," Jisbella said.

"What thought?"

"The desire of anyone to detonate it, directed at it. That brings it to critical mass if it's not insulated by Inert Lead Isotope."

"I told you to be quiet," Dagenham growled.

"If we're all to have a chance at him, I want mine."

"This is bigger than idealism."

"Nothing's bigger than idealism."

"Foyle's secret is," Y'ang-Yeovil murmured. "I know how relatively unimportant PyrE is just now." He smiled at Foyle. "Sheffield's law assistant overheard part of your little discussion in Old St. Pat's. We know about the space-jaunting."

There was a sudden hush.

"Space-jaunting," Dagenham exclaimed. "Impossible. You don't mean it."

"I do mean it. Foyle's demonstrated that space-jaunting is not impossible. He jaunted six hundred thousand miles from an O.S. raider to the wreck of the *Nomad*. As I said, this is far bigger than PyrE. I should like to discuss that matter first."

"Everyone's been telling what they want," Robin Wednesbury said slowly. "What do you want, Gully Foyle?"

"Thank you," Foyle answered. "I want to be punished."

"What?"

"I want to be purged," he said in a suffocated voice. The stigmata began to appear on his bandaged face. "I want to pay for what I've done and settle the account. I want to get rid of this damnable cross I'm carrying . . . this ache that's cracking my spine. I want to go back to Gouffre Martel. I want a lobo, if I deserve it . . . and I know I do. I want—"

"You want escape," Dagenham interrupted. "There's no escape."

"I want release!"

"Out of the question," Y'ang-Yeovil said. "There's too much of value locked up in your head to be lost by lobotomy."

"We're beyond easy childish things like crime and punishment," Dagenham added.

"No," Robin objected. "There must always be sin and forgiveness. We're never beyond that."

"Profit and loss, sin and forgiveness, idealism and realism," Foyle smiled. "You're all so sure, so simple, so single-minded. I'm the only one in doubt. Let's see how sure you really are. You'll give up Olivia, Presteign? To me, yes? Will you give her up to the law? She's a killer."

Presteign tried to rise, and then fell back in his chair.

"There must be forgiveness, Robin? Will you forgive Olivia Presteign? She murdered your mother and sisters."

Robin turned ashen. Y'ang-Yeovil tried to protest.

"The Outer Satellites don't have PyrE, Yeovil. Sheffield revealed that. Would you use it on them anyway? Will you turn my name into common anathema . . . like Lynch and Boycott?"

Foyle turned to Jisbella. "Will your idealism take you back to Gouffre Martel to serve out your sentence? And you, Dagenham, will you give her up? Let her go?"

He listened to the outcries and watched the confusion for a moment, bitter and constrained.

"Life is so simple," he said. "This decision is so simple, isn't it? Am I to respect Presteign's property rights? The welfare of the planets? Jisbella's ideals? Dagenham's realism? Robin's conscience? Press the button and watch the robot jump. But I'm not a robot. I'm a freak of the universe . . . a thinking animal . . . and I'm trying to see my way clear through this morass. Am I to turn PyrE over to the world and let it destroy itself? Am I to teach the world how to space-jaunte and let us spread our freak show from galaxy to galaxy through all the universe? What's the answer?"

The bartender robot hurled its mixing glass across the room with a resounding crash. In the amazed silence that followed, Dagenham grunted: "Damn! My radiation's disrupted your dolls again, Presteign."

"The answer is yes," the robot said, quite distinctly.

"What?" Foyle asked, taken aback.

"The answer to your question is yes."

"Thank you," Foyle said.

"My pleasure, sir," the robot responded. "A man is a member of society first, and an individual second. You must go along with society, whether it chooses destruction or not."

"Completely haywire," Dagenham said impatiently. "Switch it off, Presteign."

"Wait," Foyle commanded. He looked at the beaming grin engraved in the steel robot face. "But society can be so stupid. So confused. You've witnessed this conference."

"Yes, sir, but you must teach, not dictate. You must teach society."

"To space-jaunte? Why? Why reach out to the stars and galaxies? What for?"

"Because you're alive, sir. You might as well ask: Why is life? Don't ask about it. Live it."

"Quite mad," Dagenham muttered.

"But fascinating," Y'ang-Yeovil murmured.

"There's got to be more to life than just living," Foyle said to the robot.

"Then find it for yourself, sir. Don't ask the world to stop moving because you have doubts."

"Why can't we all move forward together?"

"Because you're all different. You're not lemmings. Some must lead, and hope that the rest will follow."

"Who leads?"

"The men who must . . . driven men, compelled men."

"Freak men."

"You're all freaks, sir. But you always have been freaks. Life is a freak. That's its hope and glory."

"Thank you very much."

"My pleasure, sir."

"You've saved the day."

"Always a lovely day somewhere, sir," the robot beamed. Then it fizzed, jangled, and collapsed.

Foyle turned on the others. "That thing's right," he said, "and you're wrong. Who are we, any of us, to make a decision for the world? Let the world make its own decisions. Who are we to keep secrets from the world? Let the world know and decide for itself. Come to Old St. Pat's."

He jaunted; they followed. The square block was still

cordoned and by now an enormous crowd had gathered. So many of the rash and curious were jaunting into the smoking ruins that the police had set up a protective induction field to keep them out. Even so, urchins, curio seekers, and irresponsibles attempted to jaunte into the wreckage, only to be burned by the induction field and depart, squawking.

At a signal from Y'ang-Yeovil, the field was turned off. Foyle went through the hot rubble to the east wall of the cathedral which stood to a height of fifteen feet. He felt the smoking stones, pressed, and levered. There came a grinding grumble and a three-by-five-foot section jarred open and then stuck. Foyle gripped it and pulled. The section trembled; then the roasted hinges collapsed and the stone panel crumbled.

Two centuries before, when organized religion had been abolished and orthodox worshippers of all faiths had been driven underground, some devout souls had constructed this secret niche in Old St. Pat's and turned it into an altar. The gold of the crucifix still shone with the brilliance of eternal faith. At the foot of the cross rested a small black box of Inert Lead Isotope.

"Is this a sign?" Foyle panted. "Is this the answer I want?"

He snatched the heavy safe before any could seize it. He jaunted a hundred yards to the remnants of the cathedral steps facing Fifth Avenue. There he opened the safe in full view of the gaping crowds. A shout of consternation went up from the Intelligence crews who knew the truth of its contents.

"Foyle!" Dagenham cried.

"For God's sake, Foyle!" Y'ang-Yeovil shouted.

Foyle withdrew a slug of PyrE, the color of iodine crystals, the size of a cigarette . . . one pound of transplutonian isotopes in solid solution.

"PyrE!" he roared to the mob. "Take it! Keep it! It's your future. PyrE!" He hurled the slug into the crowd and roared over his shoulder: "SanFran. Russian Hill stage."

He jaunted St. Louis-Denver to San Francisco, arriving at the Russian Hill stage where it was four in the afternoon and the streets were bustling with late-shopper jaunters.

"PyrE!" Foyle bellowed. His devil face glowed blood red. He was an appalling sight. "PyrE. It's yours. Make them tell you what it is. Nome!" he called to his pursuit as it arrived, and jaunted.

It was lunch hour in Nome, and the lumberjacks jaunting down from the sawmills for their beefsteak and beer were startled by the tiger-faced man who hurled a one pound slug of iodine colored alloy into their midst and shouted in the gutter tongue: "PyrE! You hear me, man? You listen a me, you. Grab no guesses, you. Make 'em tell you about PyrE, is all!"

To Dagenham, Y'ang-Yeovil and others jaunting in after him, as always, seconds too late, he shouted: "Tokyo. Imperial stage!" He disappeared a split second before their shots reached him.

It was nine o'clock of a crisp, winey morning in Tokyo, and the morning rush hour crowd milling around the Imperial stage alongside the carp ponds was paralyzed by a tiger-faced Samurai who appeared and hurled a slug of curious metal and unforgettable admonitions at them.

Foyle continued to Bangkok where it was pouring rain, and Delhi where a monsoon raged . . . always pursued in his mad-dog course. In Baghdad it was three in the morning and the night-club crowd and pub crawlers who stayed a perpetual half hour ahead of closing time around the world, cheered him alcoholically. In Paris and again in London it was midnight and the mobs on the Champs Élysées and in Piccadilly Circus were galvanized by Foyle's appearance and passionate exhortation.

Having led his pursuers three-quarters of the way around the world in fifty minutes, Foyle permitted them to overtake him in London. He permitted them to knock him down, take the ILI safe from his arms, count the remaining slugs of PyrE, and slam the safe shut.

"There's enough left for a war. Plenty left for destruction . . . annihilation . . . if you dare." He was laughing and sobbing in hysterical triumph. "Millions for defense, but not one cent for survival."

"D'you realize what you've done, you damned killer?" Dagenham shouted.

"I know what I've done."

"Nine pounds of PyrE scattered around the world! One thought and we'll— How can we get it back without telling them the truth? For God's sake, Yeo, keep that crowd back. Don't let them hear this."

"Impossible."

"Then let's jaunte."

"No," Foyle roared. "Let them hear this. Let them hear everything."

"You're insane, man. You've handed a loaded gun to children."

"Stop treating them like children and they'll stop behaving like children. Who the hell are you to play monitor?"

"What are you talking about?"

"Stop treating them like children. Explain the loaded gun to them. Bring it all out into the open." Foyle laughed savagely. "I've ended the last star-chamber conference in the world. I've blown the last secret wide open. No more secrets from now on. . . . No more telling the children what's best for them to know. . . . Let 'em all grow up. It's about time."

"Christ, he *is* insane."

"Am I? I've handed life and death back to the people who do the living and dying. The common man's been whipped and led long enough by driven men like us. . . . Compulsive men . . . Tiger men who can't help lashing the world before them. We're all tigers, the three of us, but who the hell are we to make decisions for the world just because we're compulsive? Let the world make its own choice between life and death. Why should we be saddled with the responsibility?"

"We're not saddled," Y'ang-Yeovil said quietly. "We're driven. We're forced to seize the responsibility that the average man shirks."

"Then let him stop shirking it. Let him stop tossing his duty and guilt onto the shoulders of the first freak who comes along grabbing at it. Are we to be scapegoats for the world forever?"

"Damn you!" Dagenham raged, "Don't you realize that you

can't trust people? They don't know enough for their own good."

"Then let them learn or die. We're all in this together. Let's live together or die together."

"D'you want to die in their ignorance? You've got to figure out how we can get those slugs back without blowing everything wide open."

"No. I believe in them. I was one of them before I turned tiger. They can all turn uncommon if they're kicked awake like I was."

Foyle shook himself and abruptly jaunted to the bronze head of Eros, fifty feet above the counter of Piccadilly Circus. He perched precariously and bawled: "Listen a me, all you! Listen, man! Gonna sermonize, me. Dig this, you!"

He was answered with a roar.

"You pigs, you. You rut like pigs, is all. You got the most in you, and you use the least. You hear me, you? Got a million in you and spend pennies. Got a genius in you and think crazies. Got a heart in you and feel empties. All a you. Every you . . ."

He was jeered. He continued with the hysterical passion of the possessed.

"Take a war to make you spend. Take a jam to make you think. Take a challenge to make you great. Rest of the time you sit around lazy, you. Pigs, you! All right, God damn you! I challenge you, me. Die or live and be great. Blow yourselves to Christ gone or come and find me, Gully Foyle, and I make you men. I make you great. I give you the stars."

He disappeared.

∞

He jaunted up the geodesic lines of space-time to an Elsewhere and an Elsewhen. He arrived in chaos. He hung in a precarious para-Now for a moment and then tumbled back into chaos.

"It can be done," he thought. *"It must be done."*

He jaunted again, a burning spear flung from unknown into

unknown, and again he tumbled back into a chaos of para-space and para-time. He was lost in Nowhere.

"I believe," he thought. *"I have faith."*

He jaunted again and failed again.

"Faith in what?" he asked himself, adrift in limbo.

"Faith in faith," he answered himself. *"It isn't necessary to have something to believe in. It's only necessary to believe that somewhere there's something worthy of belief."*

He jaunted for the last time and the power of his willingness to believe transformed the para-Now of his random destination into a real . . .

∞

NOW: Rigel in Orion, burning blue-white, five hundred and forty light years from earth, ten thousand times more luminous than the sun, a cauldron of energy circled by thirty-seven massive planets . . . Foyle hung, freezing and suffocating in space, face to face with the incredible destiny in which he believed, but which was still inconceivable. He hung in space for a blinding moment, as helpless, as amazed, and yet as inevitable as the first gilled creature to come out of the sea and hang gulping on a primeval beach in the dawn-history of life on earth.

He space-jaunted, turning para-Now into . . .

∞

NOW: *Vega* in Lyra, an AO star twenty-six light years from earth, burning bluer than Rigel, planetless, but encircled by swarms of blazing comets whose gaseous tails scintillated across the blue-black firmament . . .

∞

And again he turned now into NOW: Canopus, yellow as the sun, gigantic, thunderous in the silent wastes of space at last invaded by a creature that once was gilled. The creature hung, gulping on the beach of the universe, nearer death than life, nearer the future than the past, ten leagues beyond the wide world's end. It wondered at the masses of dust, meteors, and motes that girdled Canopus in a broad, flat ring like the rings of Saturn and of the breadth of Saturn's orbit . . .

∞

NOW: Aldebaran in Taurus, a monstrous red star of a pair of stars whose sixteen planets wove high velocity ellipses around their gyrating parents. He was hurling himself through space-time with growing assurance . . .

∞

NOW: Antares, an M1 red giant, paired like Aldebaran, two hundred and fifty light years from earth, encircled by two hundred and fifty planetoids of the size of Mercury, of the climate of Eden . . .

∞

And lastly . . . NOW:
He was back aboard *Nomad*.

> *Gully Foyle is my name*
> *And Terra is my nation.*
> *Deep space is my dwelling place,*
> *The stars my destination.*

The girl, Moira, found him in his tool locker aboard *Nomad*, curled in a tight fetal ball, his face hollow, his eyes burning with divine revelation. Although the asteroid had long since been repaired and made airtight, Foyle still went through the motions of the perilous existence that had given birth to him years before.

But now he slept and meditated, digesting and encompassing the magnificence he had learned. He awoke from reverie to trance and drifted out of the locker, passing Moira with blind eyes, brushing past the awed girl who stepped aside and sank to her knees. He wandered through the empty passages and returned to the womb of the locker. He curled up again and was lost.

She touched him once; he made no move. She spoke the name that had been emblazoned on his face. He made no answer. She turned and fled to the interior of the asteroid, to the holy of holies in which Jóseph reigned.

"My husband has returned to us," Moira said.

"Your husband?"

"The god-man who almost destroyed us."

Jóseph's face darkened with anger.

"Where is he? Show me!"

"You will not hurt him?"

"All debts must be paid. Show me."

Jóseph followed her to the locker aboard *Nomad* and gazed intently at Foyle. The anger in his face was replaced by wonder. He touched Foyle and spoke to him; there was still no response.

"You cannot punish him," Moira said. "He is dying."

"No," Jóseph answered quietly. "He is dreaming. I, a priest, know these dreams. Presently he will awaken and read to us, his people, his thoughts."

"And then you will punish him."

"He has found it already in himself," Jóseph said.

He settled down outside the locker. The girl, Moira, ran up the twisted corridors and returned a few moments later with a silver basin of warm water and a silver tray of food. She bathed Foyle gently and then set the tray before him as an offering. Then she settled down alongside Jóseph . . . alongside the world . . . prepared to await the awakening.

ABOUT THE AUTHOR

Alfred Bester was born in 1913 in New York. He went to college at University of Pennsylvania and Columbia, studying the humanities and psychology. His first SF story, 'The Broken Axiom', was published in *Thrilling Wonder Stories* in 1939. Bester continued to write and publish stories till 1942, when he started writing for DC Comics, working on some of their best known characters such as Superman and Batman. After 4 years of this he moved on to scripting radio shows for serials like Charlie Chan and The Shadow. In 1950 he started writing SF short stories again and during the 1950s he produced two novels *The Demolished Man* (1953) and *The Stars My Destination* (1956), while working as a feature writer for *Holiday* magazine, where he remained until the magazine stopped publishing in the 1970s. At this point he returned to writing SF with two novels *Extro* (1975) and *Golem¹⁰⁰* (1980). Bester died in 1987 after a long illness. In his will he made out his house and literary estate to his bartender.